Counting on Hope

Counting on Hope

= SYLVIA OLSEN =

sononis
PRESS
WINLAW BRITISH COLUMBIA

Copyright © 2009 by Sylvia Olsen

LIBRARY AND ARCHIVES CANADA CATALOGUING IN PUBLICATION

Olsen, Sylvia, 1955-
   Counting on hope / Sylvia Olsen.

ISBN 978-1-55039-173-2

   1. Coast Salish Indians--Juvenile fiction. 2. British
Columbia--History--1849-1871--Juvenile fiction. I. Title.

PS8579.L728C68 2009   jC813'.6   C2009-904248-7

Sono Nis Press most gratefully acknowledges support for our publishing program provided by the Government of Canada through the Book Publishing Industry Development Program (BPIDP) and the Canada Council for the Arts, and by the Province of British Columbia through the British Columbia Arts Council and the Book Publishing Tax Credit, Ministry of Provincial Revenue.

Editing: Grenfell Featherstone and Dawn Loewen
Historical review: Kathryn Bridge
Proofreading: Karla Decker
Cover and interior design: Jim Brennan
Map: Eric Leinberger
Cover photo © Getty Images

Published by
SONO NIS PRESS
Box 160
Winlaw, BC V0G 2J0
1-800-370-5228
books@sononis.com
www.sononis.com

Distributed in the U.S. by
Orca Book Publishers
Box 468
Custer, WA 98240-0468
1-800-210-5277

Printed and bound in Canada by Houghton Boston Printers.

Printed on acid-free paper that is forest friendly (100% post-consumer recycled paper) and has been processed chlorine free.

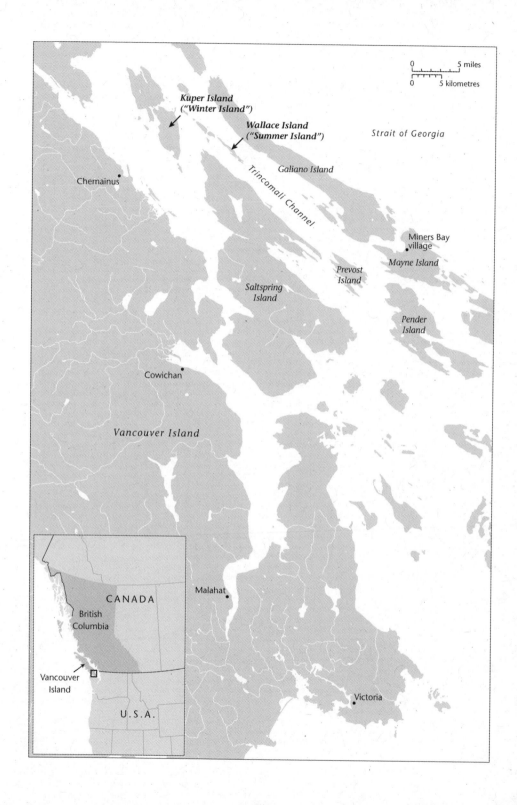

Kuper Island
("Winter Island")

Wallace Island
("Summer Island")

Strait of Georgia

Galiano Island

Trincomali Channel

Chemainus

Miners Bay
village

Mayne Island

Prevost
Island

Saltspring
Island

Pender
Island

Cowichan

Vancouver Island

CANADA

British
Columbia

Malahat

Vancouver
Island

U.S.A.

Victoria

0   5 miles

0   5 kilometres

England, 1858 🦗

My eighth birthday had been a wonderful day. Grandma Richardson had decided we should have a party. Now, a party was not something the Richardsons had very often. And the most exciting part of the party was that I was to be the guest of honour.

Grandma swept into the house, and, as she always did, took charge of the kitchen in spite of protests from Ma. From the moment she arrived, everyone did as Grandma ordered: crush the breadcrumbs, cut the onions, snip the parsley, while she made the stuffing and filled the goose. Charlotte, my sister, scrubbed the potatoes. Grandma salted and buttered them along with the turnips and beets. She roasted them in a pot with a big dollop of currant preserves. The house smelled delicious. When we sat at the table, Grandma sat at one end, I at the other, in Pa's chair of course; I was the birthday girl. Ma and Pa sat one on each side with the other children.

When the meal was laid out before us, Pa raised his glass to Grandma and said, "A banquet fit for a king."

"That means I have a gift for a very special young princess," Grandma said.

She reached under the table and pulled out a package she had been hiding. It was wrapped in white cotton and tied with a blue ribbon. With great pomp and ceremony, she presented the package to me. It was beautiful. Up until then I had never received a special gift—I had never been given anything wrapped and tied with a beautiful ribbon. Pa had made me miniature furniture in his wood shop, and Ma had knitted me beautiful stockings, but those gifts did not come with such an important presentation.

Everyone watched me as I slowly untied the bow and folded back the cotton. There, as if sleeping in a field of lilies, was a fine-looking doll. It had emerald buttons for eyes, yellow wool hair woven into long braids, a brightly checkered green dress and red yarn fashioned into lips with a most pleasant smile—a beautifully made doll.

Grandma said, "Hope, I wanted you to have something special. You have been a wonderful help to your ma since the birth of Baby Dot."

Pa said, "Hope has been a big help to me as well, and to Charlotte while she has been sick."

"A considerable responsibility for an eight-year-old," Grandma declared.

Ma smiled and said, "You have been a good girl, Hope. You must be very grateful to your grandma for such a generous gift."

"Thank you, Grandma. Thank you. I will call her Ruby," I said, "because of the colour of her lips."

"Marvellous," she gushed. "I think that is a beautiful name."

I felt a little embarrassed, not accustomed to being the centre of attention. And I could see that Charlotte, always the natural centre of attention, felt a little out of sorts.

It wasn't long after, when everyone had taken turns holding Ruby and expressing their fondness for her, that Charlotte burst into a fit of crying. Soon she was choking and coughing and complaining that she didn't have a doll as beautiful as mine. Which of course was true, for never had a doll as exceptional as Ruby resided in our home.

"Poor Charlotte, dear," Ma said. She rushed to her side and held her while Charlotte collapsed into her lap.

Grandma paid no mind whatsoever to Charlotte's outburst. She said, "It is Hope's birthday. God knows, Charlotte, you have been given enough. Now quit your crying."

Grandma's harsh words jolted Charlotte out of her fit, and Ma out of her pity. They both cast a ghastly shocked look at the old woman. They had not, and nor had I, ever heard anyone speak to Charlotte in such a manner. She was always the centre of attention because she was sick. It was a matter of fact—a well-established Richardson family habit, a habit that Grandma had interrupted for a few moments that day to make a special fuss over Ruby and me.

Another well-established Richardson habit was that when Charlotte didn't demand Ma and Pa's attention, Alec did—not because he was always sick like Charlotte, but because he was always misbehaving.

I was neither very good nor very bad; I was rarely sick. I was neither the eldest nor the youngest. And I wasn't the only boy, like Alec, so there was no reason for Pa or Ma to pay any special attention to me. But Grandma did.

From that day on, Ruby was my special companion. When I said goodbye to Grandma in England and wouldn't be consoled, Ruby was there. When I vomited so hard from seasickness that I thought I would die on the voyage across the Atlantic, Ruby comforted me. If there ever was a rag doll that could be a girl's best friend, then surely Ruby was that doll.

Lamalcha Village, Winter Island, 1859 🖛

The winter of my tenth year was cold.
    Snowdrifts piled higher than the door of our longhouse.
    Father made snow walls when he cut a pathway,
    but we didn't go out to play.
    The snow was too dusty and soft to make snowballs,
    and the wind was sharp
    and cut into our cheeks.

    During the day, I stayed inside.
    I prayed for the rains to come to melt the snow.
    Tsustea and I wrapped up in our blankets
    and huddled together near the fire.
    Everyone sat around, like bundles of hides.
    We murmured to each other
    and complained to the Creator
    that He should be more thoughtful of the creatures.
    At night, we slept together,
    side by side by side,
    and borrowed each other's heat.

    In the morning, I shivered.
    The air stabbed my nostrils,
    but Tsustea sat up and unwrapped her blanket.
    She draped it over her shoulders
    as if the spring had arrived.

"I am hot," she said. "My legs, my arms, my belly,
feel like they will melt."
"How can that be, Sister?" I said.
"It is bitterly cold.
Cover up—you will freeze to death."
She said, "My face,
it's on fire."

It took a few days for Tsustea's skin
to burst into blisters.
Sores covered her body with pain
from head to toe.

In a week, it wasn't just Tsustea.
Others
stripped off their blankets
and walked around the longhouse.
That's how we knew who would be next.

Then Tsustea lay in a pool of sweat,
delirious with fever.
I prayed with all my heart,
it should be me who is sick
instead of her.
"Great Spirit," I said,
as if I were making a deal with a human,
"I will die.
I will tie a giant rock around my ankle
and jump into the sea."
As if my actions would dry Tsustea's forehead,
even for a few moments,
or remove the horrible sores from her skin
for a day.

I didn't know what the Great Spirit

thought of my request, but I waited,
expecting.

One morning, after Tsustea
had tossed
and turned
and whimpered and cried all night,
warm air wafted through the longhouse,
as if it had been carried in on the wings
of a flock of geese.
I ran outside.
Icicles dripped,
and lumps of snow
dumped from the limbs of the cedars.
The sun was blinding and warm.
The winter was over.

I hurried to my sister to announce
that spring had arrived.
She smiled. "It surely has."
I cried, "Spring has arrived.
And you, Tsustea, will get well.
I know it. I know it."
And from the peaceful look on her face,
I knew she was pleased.
The nighttime wild hallucinations were gone from her mind.
She was clear-eyed,
so clear that I could gaze through her eyes,
down into a deep well,
and through a long tunnel,
and further still into her spirit.
I said, "Tsustea, I am so happy you are here with me again."

But I was shaken by her change of condition.
The fever had burned so long.

And then so suddenly,
it was gone.
"I will always be with you," she said,
and she sighed a sweet and lovely laugh.
I felt better to hear
the beautiful music of her voice.
"No matter what," she said
and closed her eyes.
I didn't like the way she said, *No matter what.*
But I didn't ask her what she meant.
I was not going to let anything
come between my sister and me,
not now she had returned.
That night Mother sent me to bed.
"No," I said, "I must not leave Tsustea's side.
Not now."
I lay down next to her.
I kissed my fingers and put them on her forehead.
It was cool,
and I fell asleep.
The next morning I touched her forehead again.
It was dry.
Her eyes were closed.
Her skin was cold.
The old women from the village came.
They took Tsustea out.
They got cedar boughs and scrubbed death out of our house.

Swiltu, my little sister,
tried to comfort me.
"I am here, Letia; I will be your friend."
She was kind, but she was no more
than a six-year-old little girl.

Little Brother and the other boys

collected shells and polished stones,
as gifts to ease my pain.

Big Brother and Kayah, a girl much older,
invited me into their conversations,
until then
off limits to me.

I was no use to them.
From that day, I would not be consoled.
When I thought of them taking Tsustea,
I felt they had taken a part of my flesh.
My arm.
My leg.
My hair.

Sunnydale, Wallace Island, Summer 1862 ৼ

Sunnydale, our new home on Wallace Island, was absolutely perfect. Ma and we children had survived the journey across Canada, and we couldn't have been happier...until the summer of 1862.

The trouble all started when we received our first visit from Mr. Haws and Old Man Albert. Alec and I were playing happily at the water's edge. I had a grand plan to build a sailing vessel that would circumnavigate the island. He tried his best to follow my instructions. Together we would tie logs and make a raft. I hadn't yet designed the sail or figured out how I would attach it in an upright position.

"Come on, Alec, try to wedge that branch under your end of the log. I'll see if I can get my end over this rock. Hold back. There now, push, like that...oh!" I jumped back as the log rolled down the rocks and into the water with a splash.

"Do you really think we can go all the way around the island on a raft, Hope?" Alec wiped the water off his cheeks.

"I don't see why not. But we will need at least two or three more logs. Quick! Pull that one back up on the shore before it floats away."

Alec stepped into the water and reached for the log.

"But Hope," he cried as the log bounced in the waves.

"Oh, Alec, try harder. It will be such an adventure. We will stay close to shore, of course. But imagine! We may see a bear...or the Indians."

I grabbed onto the log with Alec, and together we wedged the end of it into the pebbly seashore. Luck was on our side; the tide was going out. The log would be safely beached until we found some more.

Wet, exhausted and proud of our accomplishment, I sat down on the sand to survey the shore for another possible addition to our raft.

"Look," Alec shouted. "Hope, over there, near the point...a boat!"

I leapt up and ran a few paces along the shore, sheltering my eyes from the glare. Sure enough...rounding the point...a boat...bigger than Pa's...a scruffy sail.

My heart pounded. It wasn't often that anyone came to Sunnydale. In fact, in the two years since we had settled on Wallace Island, the only visitors I could remember were Ma's brother, Uncle Tom, from San Francisco...and the wonderful Mr. McDonald from a neighbouring island, who had come several times...and a few businessmen from Victoria for whom Pa made furniture.

"Alec." I beckoned with my hand that he should join me. "Let's welcome our guests."

We stood side by side.

The wind blew stiff and cool as it pushed the boat toward our shore.

"Who do you think they might be?" Alec said, clasping my hand.

"I don't know," I said, happy to feel my brother close beside me. Although I was two years older and, by disposition, much braver, Alec provided me with the support I needed when things got out of hand.

The boat's relentless approach was making me uneasy.

"It's not Mr. McDonald," Alec said. "It surely isn't Uncle Tom. And they don't look like businessmen from Victoria."

There was no doubt about that.

Our previous visitors had been stately-looking men with tall hats, straight backs and strong, wide shoulders. You could tell from a distance that their mission was honourable.

There was something about these two men in the boat that unsettled me.

I pulled Alec toward the path to the house and held on tightly to his hand. We could hear the grating of the clam and oyster shells under the hull of the boat as it drove ashore. The waves that followed the boat picked up the log we had beached and sent it back into the wake.

Out of the boat clambered two men. The first man was tall and lean, with stringy flesh on his neck and oversized hands and feet. He had eyes that were no more than thin grey slits. The other man was as short as the first man was tall, and as fat as the other was thin. He had a fringe of springy orange hair around his hat, and his neck flowed in continuous folds from his chin to his chest.

The tall man tied the boat to a log on the beach, and they headed up the shore.

"Well! Look what we have here," he said, rasping his words as if his throat were full of ash. "Does your father know you are greeting strangers on the beach, alone?"

"Little ones, you are," the short man said. "Well, Mr. Haws, it appears John has not heard of the danger here about."

He stuck out a grubby hand toward me. I cringed at the sight of his soiled, tattered sleeve and turned to avoid his greeting.

"Albert's my name, it is." He let out a wet warble of a laugh. "Old Man Albert's what they call me, it is. I'm a fine young man, you might say, to have a name like that."

He eyed me up and down and said, "And what may I call the pretty girl?"

When he spoke, it sounded as if there were marbles turning in his mouth, and the impolite noise made me feel queasy.

He didn't look at all young, and, as far as I was concerned, he wasn't the sort of man I would choose to address. But given the circumstances, and the fact that it appeared I had no choice, I replied in a squeaky voice, "Hope."

Beads of spit lodged on his moustache as he said, "Oh, and a pretty name that is."

"And the young feller?" He slapped Alec on the back. "Do you have a name, you?"

Alec crept behind me, peering out just enough to make himself heard as he said, "Alec."

"And where's your father?" Mr. Haws hissed.

Without waiting for a response, he walked briskly past us and up the path toward the house. Old Man Albert chuckled and followed.

"Who are they, Hope?" Alec asked. He stepped out from behind me.

"I don't know," I said. "But I am certainly about to find out."

We walked a safe distance behind.

The men's clothes looked as though they had once been worn by men of position: beaver hats, finely made coats and boots. Mr. Haws even had a red silk scarf in his coat pocket. But fine as the clothes had once been, they were now dirty and rumpled and ill fitted, given Mr. Haws's height and Old Man Albert's girth. And…there was something about the way the men smelled that reminded me of England.

Mr. Haws rapped on the door. Ma opened it unsuspectingly and gasped when she laid eyes on the men.

"Sorry to be a bother to you, ma'am," rasped Mr. Haws. "We are looking for John. Do you know his whereabouts?"

"No…I mean, yes," Ma stammered. "He is out the back…I mean he is in his work shed."

"You have two beautiful children, ma'am," Old Man Albert said. "They greeted us at the water's edge, they did."

"What were you doing at the seashore?" Ma said sharply when the men stepped off the doorstep. Then she laid her eyes on Alec's wet boots.

"Playing, Ma," I said. "Until the boat arrived carrying those men."

"In the water? With your boots on?" she said and plunked Alec down on the bench near the back door.

"Now take those off, and your socks with them. Hope, do I have to tell you again that you must watch your brother?"

"It was an accident, Ma," I said.

I stepped outside and peered behind the house. I wanted to keep the men in my sight. We had so few visitors at Sunnydale that even scruffy guests were exciting. In fact, it was the very undesirable nature of the men that stimulated my interest.

"You aren't going anywhere," Ma called over her shoulder to me. Her hands trembled as she helped Alec pull off his wet socks. "You have worried me quite enough today already."

I ran to the window and watched. Pa and the men stood outside the work shed. Pa had his head down while the men took turns speaking furiously. I strained to hear their conversation, but I couldn't catch a word through the glass.

At supper, Ma seated the men on one side of the table, with Alec, Charlotte, Baby Dot and me on the other side. I was in the unfortunate position of looking directly across at Old Man Albert.

"I think you have exaggerated the problem, Mr. Haws," Pa said, obviously taking up their earlier discussion.

The tall man's voice grated when he said, "Not at all. It is the talk of the town. Victoria is buzzing with concern."

"The Indians are rising up, they are," Old Man Albert said, his mouth still full of potatoes. "And it is not safe in these parts."

"I know there has been unrest for some time now," Pa said. "What do you expect? Do you think that the Indians should be pleased that strangers impose themselves in their territory?"

"It is the Queen's will that her new colony be populated with good citizens from the old country. How else will she protect this place from the unruly Americans?" Mr. Haws said.

The Queen of England, the Americans, the Indians, an uprising…the conversation confused me. It all sounded so complicated. But even in my confusion, I did understand two things: these rude busybodies had interrupted our peaceful life on my beloved Wallace Island, and I should think of something to do that would cut their visit short.

"But Sunnydale," I butted in. "It is safe here. Right, Pa? You made an agreement with the Indians that we should build our house and farm on their island."

"*Our* island," Ma snapped. "Hope, Wallace Island is *our* island. Granted to Pa by the Queen herself."

Lamalcha Village, Winter Island, 1859 ≋

Tsustea had become a part of my life
    long before I could remember.
    And although Grandmother
    had told her story to me a hundred times,
    I loved to hear it again.

    "It was a late spring," she said.
    "Winter hung on that year,
    with its icicles clawing into the ground.
    We were impatient for the sun to bring warmth.
    Everyone was tired of Winter Island
    and couldn't wait to eat fresh food.

    "But it was your arrival, Granddaughter,
    that was on everyone's mind.
    Your mother was already out to here…"

Grandmother linked her fingers and held her hands
way out in front.
She waddled and laughed
as she walked back and forth
pretending to be pregnant.

"Then," she continued,
"out of the blue, Tsustea's mother appeared on the shore.

Oh, she was a pitiful girl!
She wore a tattered blanket and a frayed hat.
She had a basket that carried only a comb
and a measly few shells.
She staggered up the bank from her canoe,
barely able to carry the weight of her own body.
Her arms hung like ropes.
Her legs were thin and gaunt.
Her belly was big with child.
No one knew where the young creature had come from,
for she hardly said a word.
I fed her a bowl of fish soup I had warming on the fire.
The bony, wide-eyed girl devoured the food.
She ate the last drop and then licked the bowl clean.
When her stomach was full, she told us
her People had died of the sickness.
Every one of them.
She was the only one left,
and her unborn baby.
The poor girl wasn't much more than a child herself.
She was ashamed to be a beggar,
destitute,
looking for a home.

"Father and Uncle Nanute said,
We will accept her.
She will have a place in our longhouse.
The young woman and her child will become as one of us.

"I agreed with my two sons.
Our visitor has no kin,
no mother,
no grandmother, I said.
We will adopt her, and she will become
one of our own children.

"Oh, that idea did not make your mother happy.
No. No. No,
she said. *Put the scrawny girl back in her canoe.*
Push her out into the channel to find another People.

"Your mother didn't like the way
Father and Uncle Nanute,
and the other men and women in the village,
gave the young girl so much attention."

Grandmother narrowed her eyes, all squinty,
wagged her head, one side to the other,
and spoke in a whispery voice.
"I don't think your mother wanted the competition," she said,
"for the girl was beautiful, even in her pitiful state.
And your mother,
who was considered to be
the finest woman in the territory,
wanted no distractions during her time with child."

Grandmother's eyes got wide,
for this part of the story excited her.
"Before your mother had time to send the girl away,
the skinny little foreigner gave birth to a baby girl.
She called the baby
Tsustea.
The name meant 'grace' and 'peace.'"

Grandmother smiled and was
satisfied that the story had turned out
the way the moons had planned.

"Each time the baby girl made a sound,
you leapt with joy in your mother's belly.

It didn't take long for your mother
to come to her senses.
The girl can stay,
she said, *and the baby Tsustea*.
You were born, Granddaughter, not many days later.
And you were a boisterous child.
But when your mother laid your board
beside Tsustea,
you became calm.
And that is the way the two of you became sisters."

Sunnydale, Wallace Island, Summer 1862

I didn't like the way the men talked about our island, or the way Ma became so engaged in their banter. The conversation at supper was very unpleasant. These men, who ate as if they had come for nothing more than a good meal, were disrupting our peaceful life on Wallace Island. And what business was it of theirs?

Wallace Island wasn't a very big island, but Pa had papers of ownership signed by the Queen's men for the whole thing. I had seen the papers myself. And, up until that moment, I had regarded our ownership as a right. I had taken great pride in the idea that my pa owned an entire island. I had dreamed of renaming it Richardson Island. Or John Island. Or even Hope Island. But I could not decide. None of the names seemed a large enough improvement on Wallace Island to warrant a change, and, in any case, they were each too common a name for the place of my dreams.

I only knew about Pa's agreement with the Indians from stories he'd told us. In 1859, a year before the rest of our family arrived, he said that he had travelled from Victoria, where he had been given the deed of ownership. When he arrived, he found an Indian settlement on the north end. It was their summer camp. With the help of an interpreter, Pa arranged with the Indians that Sunnydale would be built on the south end of the island, while the north end would be left for them.

It turned out to be a workable plan. As far as I knew, not so much as a minor quarrel between the Indians and Pa had ensued since then. There was only one part of the situation that I thought could be improved. One day, I hoped we might meet our neighbours and get to know them—

given there was no one else on the island. And I thought Pa should have inquired about children—maybe there would be playmates for Alec and me. As it was, Ma had made it plain that we would never play with the Indians.

"Hope is right, Eva," Pa said. "Sunnydale is safe. I have lived peaceably with the Indians for three years."

"John, you speak boldly. I don't think that the man they murdered would have been so bold," Mr. Haws said.

"Murdered!" Ma gasped.

"*Murdered*," the man whispered. "And an innocent man at that…just minding his own business on his humble farm."

"On an island such as this, it was," said Old Man Albert.

I bowed my head. I didn't like what the men were saying. And I didn't like the way they talked with their mouths full. They were troublemakers, that's all.

"John, a man was murdered!" Ma exclaimed.

"I heard Mr. Haws," Pa answered. "It was months ago, Eva. They are not bringing us anything new. They are coming to incite fear amongst the settlers."

"Wallace Island is dangerous. I have been telling you that since you brought us here." Ma covered the ghastly expression on her face with her hands.

"Ma, why do you listen to these men?" I asked her. I had to think of something to say that would change her mind about the men. I thought about what Ma's mother would think. "They are nothing but troublemakers, good-for-nothing rascals, that's what Gran would call them. And they smell, Ma, the men smell like rancid meat…like dog vomit."

"Hope!" Ma screeched, now defending men she would have otherwise despised. "Hope, how disrespectful; these men are our guests! John! Do something!"

"Hope," Pa said. He sounded angry, but he didn't look at me. He looked squarely at the men, which surprised me, because I thought Pa would be embarrassed by my insolence. "You will apologize for insulting our guests."

I said, "I am sorry for insulting you."

It was a lie. I was sorry that I would get sent off to bed, not for what I'd said to the men.

"Now off, young lady," Pa said, pointing to the stairs. "Get yourself to bed."

I'd expected my punishment and ran off without an argument. Insulting guests, no matter how distasteful they were, was a serious offence in our family, one I would not have normally committed. But I'd had to do something. And what else could a twelve-year-old girl do under the circumstances?

The next morning I dressed without disturbing my sister Charlotte. I listened at the top of the stairs. Ma was not making her normal complaints about the cramped house, or how she missed Gran.

"Mr. Haws says it is not safe here on Wallace Island, John," she said. "You must listen to him."

"Eva, the men are stirring up trouble."

"The *men* are not making the trouble. The *Indians* are the cause of the trouble."

When Ma said *Indians*, she spat the word out to make it sound mysterious and dangerous.

"Eva, you must not believe everything they say."

It was quiet for a short time. In my mind's eye, I could see Ma crossing her arms over her chest and sucking in her cheeks the way she always did when she was angry.

"John," she said. "When the men come back, you must listen to them. They will help us."

How could such objectionable men help our family?

"Eva, I have tolerated the men for long enough," Pa said. "They are nothing but whisky traders going from one village to another selling their poison to the Indians. And now it's unrest they are peddling and a good meal they are seeking."

"Fine men like them would never do such a thing," Ma said. "They are bringing us fair warning, John. We must take heed."

Fine men was not what I would have called Mr. Haws and Old Man Albert. I knew from my first glimpse of the men that I could not trust them. And normally Ma wouldn't call them fine men either. At any other time, she would not have liked them one bit, if only because of the way they smelled—as if they had washed their clothes but hadn't used soap or hot water.

"The Indians on Wallace Island are friendly, are they not, Pa?" I asked as I descended the stairs.

"Yes, darling," he said. "We have our agreement, and no reason to believe otherwise."

Ma harrumphed. "An agreement with the Indians is as good as one with the devil, John. They cannot be trusted."

"But Ma," I said. "Can we trust whisky traders?"

She snapped her eyes shut and turned away from me without a reply.

Lamalcha Camp, Summer Island, Spring 1859 ≋

We loaded up the canoes and left Winter Island,
    all our canoes together,
    ten or fifteen.
    On the way across the channel,
    Mother and the other women beat their drums
    and sang travelling songs.
    The People celebrated the passing into spring,
    but my heart was heavy.
    For although I wanted to leave winter behind,
    I did not want to leave Tsustea.

    All the summers before,
    we had spent stripping cedar, gathering grasses,
    picking berries, collecting eggs, pounding wool,
    together,
    on Summer Island.
    This summer I would be alone.

    Everyone was busy setting up camp.
    Father and Uncle were boarding our huts and smokehouses.
    Mother and the other women were soaking the floors
    and sweeping the sleeping benches.
    Grandmother brushed the lodges with cedar boughs.
    As she worked she prayed to the Creator
    that spring would bring the salmon,

and that the storms would cease.

"Letia," Mother said, "you take Swiltu.
She is old enough to help you dig clams for supper."
Swiltu was proud
and found the basket and digging picks herself.
The sun was high
when we headed down the forest path to the clam beds.
We sat on our heels and slid down the bank.
Swiltu tumbled head over feet into the long grass.
Crickets chirped.
Wind sounds floated high in the cedars.
Swiltu giggled, "Letia, look at me,"
as she untangled her arms and legs.

"Shhh." I put my hand up to her mouth and whispered,
"Can you hear the sound of men's voices?"
When she heard the sounds,
she righted herself
and hunched her bottom onto my lap.
We crouched behind the screen of grass.
The voices were deep and harsh
like grinding stone.
I peeked out and saw two bushy men,
the kind that Father had described:
                    "Hwunitum," I said.

[Hwunitum *is a Hul'qumi'num word broadly meaning "white people."
Hul'qumi'num is the language of the Lamalcha people who lived on Kuper
Island.*]

I was sure.
But Father's stories hadn't prepared me for the sight
of such strange creatures,
bound head to toe.

Swiltu stole a glance and buried her head in my chest.

One man was tall. The other fat.
And as surely as I had heard
Father's description of the
                    white skin,
I had never imagined
skin as white as the skin of
Round Man.
(For this was the name given him by Little Brother,
and Little Brother called his friend Long Man.)
Round Man's skin was
whiter than the whitest white,
as white as a boiled onion,
as a bleached clamshell.
I would have thought, from the colour of his skin,
that his blood could not be red,
except that his hair, which confused me,
was as orange as old salmon eggs.
It sprang out like a skirt under his hat.
Long Man looked as if one man had taken his arms
and another had taken his legs and pulled,
stretching him in both directions.
His fingers hung like strips of seaweed.
He had a ropy neck,
and a chin that formed a point at the end of his beard.

I put Swiltu off my lap.
"Come," I said, and took her hand.
"We must follow these men to see
what business they have with our People."
They hadn't pulled their boat up in front of our camp
or called out from the shallow water
asking permission to come ashore,
a common courtesy of visitors.

They had pulled up on the beach
a fair distance from the camp,
near the forest and the clam beds,
        like intruders.

They stole their way through the fallen cedars,
lugging boxes
into the woods, behind the sleeping lodges.
They grunted and snorted;
the boxes appeared heavy.
Sweat splashed off Round Man's brow, washing his face.
The contents of the boxes tinkled and clanked.

"Letia, I am afraid." Swiltu tugged on my hand.
"I don't like these men."
"Shush," I said, "don't let them hear us."

The men sat on their haunches,
searching the forest,
this way and that,
like wolves.
They were expecting someone.

"We are supposed to dig clams," Swiltu said.
"I know, and we will, but this is important,"
I said. "We must not move."
She wiggled and squirmed.
We were quiet for a long while before Uncle Penu,
Father's youngest brother, appeared.
He carried a bundle and dumped it on the ground in front of the men.
He untied the knot, laid the corners out flat.
He uncovered a pile of dried salmon,
lines and lines of it,
like Father would take to Victoria to trade.
Long Man picked up one piece at a time.

He passed it under his nose.
He eyeballed it—one side and then the other.
He grunted and nodded his head.
The men exchanged knowing looks,
grumbling,
nodding, frowning,
nodding, grunting, saying strange words.
Finally, it looked to me, after much head wagging,
as if they had come to an agreement.
They shoved the crates up to Uncle Penu's feet.
"Knaw," he sighed, the sound of approval.
He was as pleased as I had ever heard him sound.
He pulled out a bottle, put the top near his nose,
took a long whiff and placed it back in the crate.
He pulled out another and another.
"Knaw. Knaw."
He nodded.
The men nodded.
The nodding—one
and then the other—nodding;
I waited for it to stop.
"Their necks will get tired," Swiltu whispered.
Long Man retied the bundle of salmon
and heaved it over his shoulder.
Round Man grabbed Uncle Penu's hand
and moved it up and down.
He followed Long Man
back into the forest toward their boat,
the way they had come.

"We should tell Father," Swiltu said.
"Yes, of course," I whispered,
but I was afraid.
I had never known of such a thing:
that men should come to the camp in secret,

that trade should take place behind the lodges,
that a bundle of fish should bring two crates of bottles.
"Wait."

Uncle Penu took the crates,
one at a time, to his sleeping lodge.
He slept alone since his wife had died
of the sickness that killed Tsustea.
He leaned the boxes against the outside wall
and counted the bottles,
marking the house post:
for each bottle a slash.
He stepped back and looked at them
with a squinty eye, comparing them
bottle to bottle.
"Knaw," he said,
and then again, to express his satisfaction,
"Knaw."
He pulled out a bottle
and yanked the top off with his teeth.
POP.
He tipped it into his mouth,
sloshing amber liquid over his lips and chin,
soaking his chest.
"Tsharr!"
Choking and coughing.
"Tsharr!"
He tipped up the bottle again,
washing the contents over his face,
guzzling what found its way down his throat
until the last few drips fell from the bottle.
He wiped his face and chest.
He belched and licked the bottle
around and around,
tipped it up,

sucked air through his lips,
licked the top,
then threw it into the forest,
where it smashed like breaking clamshells.
He hugged the post, kissed the markings
and belched.
His actions confused me, the way he
embraced the post as if it were a woman.
Suddenly he stumbled back
and growled
and belched again. He thrashed at the air
as if he were punching an invisible creature.
"Tsharr!" he hollered fiercely.

"Letia, I am afraid," Swiltu cried.
What has become of Uncle?"

"I don't know," I said. "But you are right.
We must tell Father."

Sunnydale, Wallace Island, Late Summer 1862 ❧

For the following weeks I had only one thing on my mind: to continue constructing my sailing raft. My sense of adventure was not dampened whatsoever by the fearful announcements of the men. I wanted to forget all about them and their stories.

The men's visit had the opposite effect on Ma. She believed every word they said and was more nervous and agitated than ever. When she washed up, she clashed the dishes and cutlery. When she went outside, she slammed the door. Even when she knitted, her needles clicked together more loudly than normal. And the worst thing of all was that she never let us out of her sight.

If I didn't get out of the house and away from Ma's constant harping, I thought I would burst. It was a sunny, cool afternoon with dramatic thunderclouds building in the distance, so I packed my easel and watercolour paints as I had done many times before.

"I am going to the seashore," I said to Ma. I thought that if I returned to normal, maybe she would as well.

"Alone?" she asked.

"I am going to paint," I said. "Like I have done dozens of times before."

"No," she said. "Not by yourself, you're not."

Luckily for me, Pa had not yet finished his midday meal and was sopping up the last of his duck soup with a crust of bread.

He said, "Eva, the girl is twelve years old. She can take her paints to the seashore."

"No, John," Ma said, wringing a dishcloth until her knuckles turned white. "She cannot."

"Hold back one minute, Hope," Pa said. He filled his mouth while Ma and I stood watching and wondering what he had on his mind. Ma's fingers twisted and pulled. He chewed slowly and deliberately as if, by letting time pass, something would wash over all of us, and life would return to normal.

He swallowed. Then he said, "I will come with you, my girl. I have some reading to do."

This was not exactly what I had expected him to say. First of all, Pa was not in the habit of accompanying me to the beach. Especially in the afternoon! And to read a book? Surely he had work to do. Pa always had work to do.

When we got to the beach, he laid a blanket out and made himself comfortable, propped against a log. He opened his book without so much as a comment to me. He acted as if what he was doing were an everyday occurrence—as if father and daughter were in the habit of going to the seashore together in the afternoon.

I walked along the shore a short distance until I found a good spot. I jiggled the legs of the easel into the pebbly beach and sat on a stump in front of the paper. I eyed the lichen that crawled across the jagged rocks like a map of the world. I could make out England and Europe and the continent of Asia to the right. To the left the rocks were shiny like the Atlantic Ocean, and then there was the trailing mass of North America with a tiny island on the western shore—Vancouver Island. I put my nose as close as I could without crossing my eyes, but I couldn't see Wallace Island. I was sure there would be a tiny lichen island off the east coast of Vancouver Island, if only my eyes could focus enough.

I dipped my brush in the water and filled it with black and white, until I made granite grey. I swished the shape of the rocks. I had tried before. In my mind I could imagine the painting perfectly. But on the paper… well, on the paper I had not yet been able to capture the immensity of the cliffs or the creamy green of the lichen.

I put my brush down and stepped back to get a bird's-eye view.

Interesting…but not finished. Impossible! A painting shall never portray the magnificence of this place. Or how much I love Wallace Island.

"Hope," Pa called. "Pack up your things."

I turned to see Pa standing at the water's edge. The same dirty boat was heading for the shore.

"Good day, my good man," Mr. Haws hollered. The breeze and the pounding surf muffled the rest of his words so that I did not understand.

By the time the men climbed out of their boat, I stood next to Pa.

"I have no need of what you men bring to our islands," he said. He kept one hand firmly clasped to his book and the other to my fist.

"Mr. Richardson, you underestimate my good friend Mr. Haws, you do," Old Man Albert said. "He is a highly respected businessman."

"I have no need of his business or yours," Pa said. "The trouble you are spreading in these parts—the uprising of the Indians, the murders, the unrest, the distrust—is it not largely caused by the whisky you are peddling?"

"You are a hard man, John Richardson," Mr. Haws said. "But you are mistaken to place the blame on us. It is the Indians who cause the trouble in these parts. It is them you should fear."

Pa put his arm around me and turned me toward the house.

"It is good to see the pretty young girl is not alone this afternoon, it is," Old Man Albert said, a veiled accusation.

"You have come to Sunnydale uninvited," Pa said sharply. "But since a storm is brewing, you may join us for supper and the night, and then you will be on your way."

Pa and I walked ahead of the men past the sign that read *SUNNYDALE*. The sign was the first thing I'd seen when we arrived on Wallace Island. It was nailed to two cedar posts on the side of the broken shell path that led to the house. Pa had carved the letters into a plank and painted them green, a bright, cheery, promising green. The sight of the sign always made me puff up with pride. But now, with the men following closely behind us, the sign looked faded—in need of paint.

At the supper table, no one said very much at first. The only noise in the room was the clinking and scraping of knives and forks until Ma gracefully and precisely set her knife and fork next to her plate. She had a set way of using her cutlery, and even in a faraway place like Wallace Island she had manners fit for the Queen.

In England, Ma had been a beautiful woman with thick flaxen hair. Before Charlotte took ill, sometimes she took the comb out of her hair and left it loose over her shoulders and down to the small of her back.

Since coming to Wallace Island, Ma didn't play or smile as she had before. She tied her hair back tightly around her face, making her look stiff and uncomfortable. She had become rigid, as if her skin had shrunk. She looked as if she was putting up with each day because she had no other choice.

She dabbed her lips with her napkin and said, "It most certainly has been fine weather of late."

"Oh, but a change is coming," Mr. Haws said. "I can feel it in my bones."

"The seagulls know it for sure, they do," Old Man Albert said. "Squawking up a storm, they are. Hundreds of them. Circling the bay, they are."

"And isn't Victoria a fine town," Ma said, changing the subject.

"They are building a first-rate bank on Yates Street, they are. And the Dickson family are building a most superb house on the farm, they are. A fine farm, it is."

Mr. Haws described the cornices and porch spindles of grand and elegant homes that rich men were building on Government Street and Birdcage Walk.

I loved the way the street names sounded. I imagined beautiful homes with long and stately drives and fine coaches. There would be elegant women and well-dressed children coming and going. From what I had heard, and the little I had seen when we travelled through the city on our way to Wallace Island, Victoria was an excellent place indeed.

"Oh, John," Ma sighed. She had an eager look in her eye when the men talked about Victoria. "Someday we will build a grand house."

Pa stabbed his fork into his potatoes and turned it around to make a deep hole. Normally it would have been Pa speaking to the men during supper. Ma usually reserved her conversation for questions about food and tea, or instructions to us children about table manners.

That night was different. Pa had said all he wanted to say to the men. Once in a while he looked up as if he was going to add something, but then he cast his eyes back to his supper.

Ma said, as an afterthought, "But not on this godforsaken island."

When she served tea, she said, "You will join us in the sitting room, won't you? We are honoured by your company."

Pa swallowed hard. I thought he was going to tell Ma that the men would do nothing of the sort, that our hospitality extended no further, but he said nothing.

"It isn't often we have such fine guests," Ma said.

"Nor are we often able to enjoy such pleasant company," Mr. Haws said, ignoring Pa.

I couldn't believe Ma's charade. How could she pretend that these men were anything but whisky traders? Why didn't she know they visited Sunnydale for no other reason than to fill their bellies? Pa had revealed their identity, and their countenance verified it.

When the dishes had been washed, the pots scrubbed and the dish-cloths hung to dry, Ma said it was time for Alec and me to go straight to bed, which wasn't one bit fair. Baby Dot got to fall asleep in the sitting room next to the adults; and Charlotte, because she was the oldest, was allowed to stay up. In fact, she had already piled her knitting on her lap and was sitting near the fire. This was an injustice that I would not tolerate without an argument.

"But Ma," I said, "I will behave myself, I promise."

"Off you go," she said.

"But I would love to stay up," I begged.

If there was ever a time when I wanted to postpone my bedtime, it was that evening. How else could I know the business the men had with my family?

"I am old enough to stay up longer than Alec."

"Hope," she said, glaring at me. "Off to bed you go."

"What about Charlotte?" I persisted. "Why does she get to stay up? It's not fair."

Things were never fair when it came to Charlotte. Either she was older, or she was sickly; one way or another, Charlotte got special favours from Ma and Pa. She was allowed to stay up late because she was older and to sleep in longer because she was sickly. She got to teach me arithmetic because she was older and to miss school lessons altogether because she was sickly.

"I am old enough to sit with the adults for a spell," Charlotte said, holding her chin up self-importantly.

The greatest injustice of all, as far as I was concerned, was that Charlotte didn't even care about adult conversations. Staying up late to sit with the adults was entirely wasted on her. Charlotte never had anything to say, and, as far as I could tell, she didn't even listen to what was being said. The only reason she wanted to stay up was to claim the rights of the oldest. I was the one who was interested in what the adults were talking about.

But that night Ma was not going to change her mind, and I knew as much. To register my disapproval and disappointment, I stomped up the stairs as loudly as I could. I grabbed Ruby and stuffed her under my arm.

I poked my head on Alec's side of the attic and said disgustedly, "Goodnight, Brother."

I yanked the pillow and blankets off the bed and rearranged them so that my head was close to the top of the stairs. Ma might have been able to force me to go to bed, but I was not about to miss what would be said downstairs.

"Settlers are coming to this country and working hard to build farms, just as the Queen desires." Mr. Haws's rasping voice was just loud enough that I could hear every word. "Yet they are afraid for their lives. And why shouldn't they be? There has been another murder in these parts, John. And close by as well."

"And another good man, Elijah Woodsworth was his name, it was," Old Man Albert said clearly, and then he mumbled. "Stabbed...this country...for the British...it is."

His voice came and went. It was part whisper and part whistle, and every bit was difficult to understand. From what I could make out, it sounded as if there had been several violent altercations between the Indians and settlers in the past, and now there had been another murder since the men's last visit.

Elijah Woodsworth was a young Englishman who lived on a neighbouring island. From what Mr. Haws said, his wife and boy had found him face down in the dirt with a hatchet wound to the back of his head.

But that wasn't all that was said. Indians had killed cows belonging to settlers, leaving them dead in the fields. New fences had been destroyed, and horses set free. Someone heard an Indian say that if he came across one of the Queen's men, he would kill him on the spot.

"Settlers in and around Victoria are afraid the man will make good on his threats," Mr. Haws said.

"And there are more Indians," said Old Man Albert. "Many more who make the same threats, there are."

For a girl of twelve, especially one who had never been exposed to such atrocities, the men's announcements would have been distressing indeed, if I had believed them. But I could think only of Pa. He had said these men were nothing but whisky traders. Mr. Haws and Old Man Albert couldn't be trusted. And furthermore, what they said threatened our peaceful existence on Wallace Island, so I didn't want to believe a word of it.

But it was what Ma said that disturbed me the most. I couldn't hear everything she said: "Indians…dangerous…fear for our lives…murderers…our children, please, John." Her words made me shiver. I wanted to plug my ears.

It's not true what they are saying. The men are making it up. Please, Ma, don't believe them.

Wrapped in my blanket, I got out of bed and crouched at the top of the stairs.

Please, Pa. Say something. You must set it all straight.

Pretty soon, Alec crept over beside me—his feet and mine, side by side on the top stair.

"What are they talking about, Hope?" he whispered.

I didn't want to tell him what I had heard. But then again I needed him. Since we'd come to Wallace Island, it had been just the two of us—Alec and me—who were constant companions. Even though he was just a little boy, up until then I had not kept anything from him. Why would I? On Wallace Island I had no need for secrets. But now secrets were being kept from me, and I wanted to keep them from him.

When Alec heard the word *murder*, he started quivering.

"Hope," he said out loud. "It's just like the stories Ma told us about the Indians in America—the wars. The cavalry chases the wild Indians across the prairies on fast horses. Don't they, Hope? Do the Indians around here have fast ponies?"

"Shhh." I put my finger over his lips. "Ma will hear us and send us to bed."

I cupped one hand in front of his mouth and hugged him with my other arm. The last thing I wanted to think about was Indian wars.

"Old Man Albert said the Indians have guns," he mumbled through my hand.

"I don't want to talk about guns," I said.

At that moment I realized something: the conversation downstairs had the force to cause a rift between me and Alec...possibly between the whole Richardson family.

"If the Indians have guns, there will be a war, don't you think?"

"There will be no war, Alec."

Although I had never thought of such things before, I didn't think the Indians on Vancouver Island had fast ponies, and I'd never heard of a cavalry in Victoria. But how was I to know for sure?

Another thing I realized that night was that I didn't know very much about Victoria at all, or the other islands in the strait, or the Indians. Since we moved to Wallace Island I had never laid eyes on an Indian—even though in summer they lived no more than a twenty-minute walk from Sunnydale.

Pa was still being uncommonly quiet, while Ma, the one who was usually quiet, was asking the men questions, her voice becoming louder and louder as the evening wore on.

"John, say something," Ma blurted out in a shrill voice. "Why did you bring us to this place? We'll all be killed as surely as the sun will come up in the morning, and the guilt will be yours and yours alone."

She paused briefly and said, "You will take us back to England. Immediately."

I covered my ears and wished I had never heard her words. Before that night I had heard Ma complain about Wallace Island. I'd heard her cry over how much she missed Gran and England. But I'd never heard her say, *Take us back to England immediately*. Not in plain and simple words. Nor had I heard her lay the guilt of harm so distinctly at Pa's feet.

Charlotte, who up until then hadn't made a sound, burst into a loud flurry of cries and dashed up the stairs.

"I want to go home," she wept. "This is a horrible place."

We ended up in a tangled pile at the top of the stairs—Charlotte stumbling over Alec and me as we unwrapped ourselves from the blanket and scrambled back into our beds. My heart was charging like a wild horse.

Bewildered and afraid, I concentrated on the tender chorus of the tide, the crickets and the breeze coming from outside the window, blowing in the scents of Wallace Island.

Nothing could harm my beloved island.

I would protect Sunnydale with a deal. It was the only solution I could think of.

If Ma follows Charlotte up the stairs before I count to ten, then all will be well. And in the future, the unfortunate episode this evening will be considered nothing but a serious misunderstanding.

"One, two, three," I started to count quietly. Ma would come up the stairs behind Charlotte. I was certain of it. Charlotte was sobbing uncontrollably, and Ma never let her cry alone for fear of her choking.

"Four, five." I slowed the numbers down.

"Six," when I heard no sound of footsteps. "Seven."

Please, Ma, hurry.

I stopped counting altogether for a few moments, on the premise that I had to keep my brain quiet so I could hear if Ma was coming.

Nothing.

"Eight." Again I listened.

Finally I heard a faint sound of feet shuffling across the floor downstairs. Slowly I formed *nine* on my lips and paused again. I had to be sure the footsteps were Ma's. The bottom stair creaked and then the next.

"Nine. Ten," I said.

Ma sat on the edge of Charlotte's bed and stroked her fingers through Charlotte's hair.

"Calm down, sweetheart," Ma cooed. "We won't be in this awful place much longer."

Ma mounted the stairs before I reached ten. That means the men are lying. Their bad news is nothing but stories.

I stared at the outline of Ma's body hunched over the thrashing lump that was Charlotte. A familiar sight. I closed my eyes and hugged Ruby.

Nothing bad will happen. Not now. Not on Wallace Island. Not since I didn't reach ten before Ma followed Charlotte.

Ma sang quietly, "The Lord's my shepherd, I'll not want…"

Usually the sound of her voice made me sleepy, but that night I was wide awake. I had overheard Ma and Pa and the men say troublesome words. And although I had made a deal with myself that was conclusive, I was still worried. Ma's song could not erase her plans to move back to England. To leave Wallace Island. And Pa was doing nothing whatsoever, as far as I could tell, to stop her.

Please, Pa.

Lamalcha Camp, Summer Island, Spring 1859 🖝

In the same moon of the same spring
    as when Long Man and Round Man first arrived,
    Swiltu and I sat on our favourite rock.
    We looked out to the hills of Great Island.
    I liked to watch the sunlight make colour:
    grey, blue, green, yellow, orange…
    the shifts between the colours…
    the muted shades of two and three colours together.
    Not for more than a moment or two did one shade of colour remain.
    I thought of ways to achieve the glorious shades
    from the bark and roots of Grandmother's dyes.

    In the murky shadow of the Great Island a dot appeared.
    As it grew nearer, it became a square canoe
    with a sail like the one belonging to the whisky traders.
    I squinted and stretched to get the best look I could.
    The fine-looking sail bobbed in the rough water.
    There was one hat.
    Had one man returned without the other?
    With a hwulmuhw paddling behind?

[Hwulmuhw *is a Hul'qumi'num word meaning "people of the land." The two words,* hwunitum *and* hwulmuhw, *are used in reference to each other to identify the European newcomers and the original people in the territory.*]

It will be bad enough with one of them, I thought.
He will not be welcome if he comes to shore,
even if he has brought one of our hwulmuhw neighbours.
They will not be invited to our camp.

It was so because when Father and the others found out
about the deal Uncle Penu had struck with the men,
and when they saw Uncle staggering around,
belching up the belongings of his stomach,
barking rude and deplorable words to the women,
and strutting haughty and proud,
they were upset.
Well, they were more than upset.
Father said, "If these men sneak around like weasels,
to make deals under the cover of deceit,
then what can we do?"
Uncle Penu listened without looking at Father.
"You are a man, Brother," Father said.
"You will do what you will do,
but your whisky trading friends are not welcome in our camp.
They may not enter the way of a man."

As the boat drew closer, I saw it was smaller than Long Man's boat.
The man in the front was neither as tall as Long Man
nor as big as Round Man.
The boat touched bottom and wedged into the pebbles.
Swiltu and I jumped off our rock.
We ran up the bank.
"We have visitors," we hollered.
"There are two men waiting off the shore."
The People gathered near the weaving mats
to discuss the rights of the newcomer.
"One is a hwunitum," Uncle Nanute said.
(He was Grandmother's second-oldest son next to Father.)
"We have had enough of them."

"We don't know his request," Father said.
"May we enter?" the other man, a hwulmuhw, hollered.
"We come with good intentions."
The discussion went around and around amongst the People:
"Should we invite a hwunitum to our camp
or not?
But there are two men, one hwunitum and the other hwulmuhw.
What should we do?"
Finally the People decided that they
should invite the boat's passengers to pull up on the beach,
to inquire the purpose of the man's arrival,
and trust the hwulmuhw,
that he was right about his good intentions.
We walked to the shore and clustered around the two men.
The hwulmuhw said, "I am Wulistan.
I am from the Malahat People.
I come with this good hwunitum,
John Richardson.
He has been given the right, by the Queen of England,
to live with the Lamalcha on Summer Island."
Wulistan said something to the John Richardson man,
who held up a piece of paper and smiled.

Compared to Long Man and Round Man,
John Richardson was a fine-looking man.
His beard was almost black and neatly trimmed.
His skin wasn't as white as the other men's skin.
His eyes were blue, the colour of fresh water,
                                        clear blue.
They sparkled, and I thought
that maybe they had no colour at all
but were only reflecting the light from the ocean or the sky.
I had never seen eyes
                        so pale.
I couldn't stop looking at the Man.

Mother elbowed me and frowned.
"Letia, it is not our way to stare."
I lowered my head
and strained my eyes to the side until they hurt.
I pretended not to look, but tried hard to catch a glimpse.
Maybe, I thought, eyes so light would darken in the sun.
Or in the night,
would they be black?

Father and Uncle Nanute went straight to the Man's boat.
They rummaged through his bundles,
tossing his belongings onto the shore.
"There is no whisky," Father announced to the People.
"I can find none whatsoever.
Not a bottle of whisky anywhere."

Wulistan repeated what he had said earlier
and took the paper from the Man's hand
and waved it before Father.
"This paper is from the Queen.
It says the Man, John Richardson,
can build a house on Summer Island."
"Who is the Queen?" one of the People asked.
        "What is this paper?"
"Will his tribe come with him?"
"How can a paper talk to us?"
"How could one man come alone and build a house?"
Up until that day none of the People
had ever thought about such things.
What did the Queen of England have to do with our island?
How did a piece of paper make such a declaration,
that a man should build a house on Summer Island?
The People frowned and pressed their hands to their heads.
Father left the Man and Wulistan standing in the circle.
He searched the flat-bottomed boat again.

Satisfied,
he came back to the circle
and spoke to the blue-eyed man.
The Man spoke to Father.
I was amazed.
The People stood in awe.
"What is this foreign language that they share?"
For Father spoke in Chinook,
the language of trade in Victoria,
a language I had heard Father mention once before.
When they had finished speaking, Father said,
"The Man says he comes in peace.
He brings no harm to our People.
He has come from across the water.
His Queen says he can live with us."
The People mumbled,
        "His Queen,
                his Queen?
What is this Queen that tells the Man what he can do?"
After much discussion and wrangling around the circle,
Father said, "I believe the Man is a good man.
He has nowhere else to live.
He can use the south end of Summer Island,
between the cliffs and the ridge."

"I am not sure," Uncle Nanute said, wagging his head.
"Where is his tribe? There is no room there for a tribe.
Where will he live in the winter?"
Father asked the Man the questions from Uncle and the others,
back and forth,
back and forth.

Big Brother stepped up next to Father.
He was old enough by then to take part in the men's business,
and he would be, one day, the headman of the People.

His feet stood wide apart,
his hands clasped behind his back
and a grave look on his face.
He had been silent up until then.
"If the Man is to build a house on Summer Island," he said,
"he should bring gifts to the People,
to settle the arrangement."
Right away Father and Uncle Nanute agreed.

This was the point in the dealings
when the agreement was made.
"Yes,
yes,
yes," the People said.
Their heads bobbed in approval.
"Two crates of whisky!" Uncle Penu shouted,
and the crowd became silent.
"If the Man brings whisky," Grandmother said,
"I will chase him off the island myself."
She demonstrated her disapproval
by shooing and waving her hands about,
as if she were chasing a dog away from a new carcass.
Grandmother had a way of making her case understood
in no uncertain terms. She said,
"If the Man brings us blankets and cooking pots he can stay."

Mother disagreed.
"No."
She shook her head,
"No, no, no."
Over and over Mother said,
"No. No."
She was the only person that day
who wanted nothing whatsoever to do with
the hwunitum. She said,

"I do not want the Man to build a house on our island.
I do not want his gifts."
She walked around the circle,
taking everyone into her view.
"Why do you so quickly forget the stories
we have been told by visiting warriors?
There are violent and bloody battles
between the hwulmuhw and hwunitum in the south.
We know the stories are true."

The People looked puzzled.
It was not like Mother to scold.
Some nodded,
others shook their heads,
Father looked down to avoid Mother's eyes.
"Why don't you look up?" she said.
"Why don't you listen to me?"
Mother was the only one
who spoke harshly to the headman.
She trembled and was silent for a few breaths.
Then she said softly, "Night after night,
I have the same dream.
In my dream our summer smokehouses are lying in rubble.
Our winter supply of food has been tossed about in the dust.
Our burial sites are torn apart."
Silence covered the People.
The blue-eyed man stood without moving.
I don't think he knew the words Mother was saying,
but it looked to me as if he understood what she meant.
Grandmother,
who usually listened closely to dreams
and became especially concerned
over dreams that return night after night, said:
"Then we will be careful
and protect our smokehouses and burial sites."

Mother scowled.
She was not pleased with how Grandmother
so quickly dismissed her dream.
Grandmother said, "We must share our land with this poor man.
Where else will he go?"

Never before in my young life
had I seen my People
                    so bewildered.
I had never seen Grandmother dismiss a dream,
not a dream that augured such tragedy.
I had never seen Mother so angry
with Grandmother and Father and Uncle Nanute.
I didn't know what the changes in my People meant.
But I had a sense, in the bottom of my belly,
that my world was turning,
            but away from what or toward what,
                    I could not imagine.

After talking to him for some time,
Father came to an agreement with the Man.
The Man grasped Father's hand,
the same way Long Man and Round Man
had taken Uncle Penu's hand,
a gesture that I didn't trust.

Father had told me it was a simple hwunitum habit
that meant *good enough for now*.
I thought it was strange,
but if they had a gesture for *good enough for now*, then
it was good enough for now.

After that the Man set his sail and paddled to the north.
It was only a few days before he returned.
He laid his gifts out proudly before the People:

six blankets, two kettles,
two wide, flat-bottomed cooking pans
and three bundles of string.
Big Brother eyed the goods.
He nodded.
"Knaw, this is a good day.
The Man has shown respect for our hospitality."
Grandmother agreed.
Swiltu and I and Little Brother and the other boys
stood in a huddle and
watched the adults examine the goods.
They talked together and were pleased with the Man's generosity.
All except Mother, who sat on a log not far from the People,
and watched.

I kept my eyes on the blankets,
one corner lapped over the other.
I had never seen such a display.
They were different from our blankets.
They were brilliant,
with so many robust colours.
There were three red blankets,
one blue,
one green
and one white.
The sight of them made me think
they had a significance I didn't understand.
The Man's family might have been great chiefs,
and his women rich in wool and looms
and weaving tools
and dyes.
In the corner of each blanket
were straight bars of black,
each one the same,
suggesting a strange signature of the weaver,

or the totem of the Man's family.
The sharp black colour confused me.
It was the deepest burnt black I had ever seen.
How one could achieve such a colour,
I could not imagine.
I wanted to ask the Man how his blankets were made,
how the black dye had been cast so deeply,
but it would have been rude to ask,
even if I did know how to say words he would understand.

The Man pulled a bundle out of his tote and unwrapped it.
When we saw the contents,
all the children flocked around him.
He smiled and passed each of us a string of candy.
"Knaw," Little Brother said,
for he had received such a treat once before,
that Father had brought us.
"Knaw," the other little boys said.
"Knaw," Little Brother said again,
as he stripped the candy out of its packaging
and stuffed it in his mouth.
He chewed
and dribbled,
and candy dripped from his chin.
I thanked the Man, although I don't think he understood.
I sat on a mat with Swiltu.
I unwrapped the paper carefully and
exposed the candy,
hers and then mine.
It was the smooth and shiny colour of yellow cedar.
Together we licked the chewy rope and nibbled it
bit by bit.
I couldn't bear to put it down.
But I wanted it to last forever,
so I said, "That's enough,"

and took the candy out of Swiltu's hand.
"But—," she started.
"But nothing," I said.
I folded the paper over the chewed toffee,
end to end,
exactly as it had been to start.
"I will hide these under our sleeping mats," I said to Swiltu.
"As long as Little Brother doesn't find them," she said.

That afternoon Father took the Man
to the south end of the island.
A herd of us children followed them.
We watched Father show the Man
the territory he could use.
And later, when we returned to the camp,
Father told us that the Man planned to build a house,
and plant potato patches,
and hunt and fish and pick berries,
and that boundaries had been set.
Father had given the Man his instructions,
and the Man gave Father his word
and promised that the words that he had spoken could be trusted.

Mother was preparing supper.
She didn't say a word to Father
or to the rest of us
until the soup was cooked.
When her silence grew so heavy
she couldn't stand it, she said,
                    "This is not a good day.
You children listen to me.
You will not go near the hwunitum.
Your father has said the Man may live on our island,
and with that I can only disagree.
I cannot change your father's mind,

although I would if I could.
The hwunitum will build a house
and plant potatoes,
but you children will not go past the point.
You will not go near his berry patches.
You will not lay eyes
on the coming and going of the Man."

Father just nodded.
It didn't look to me as if he agreed with Mother.
It appeared more like he didn't want to have an argument.
All I could think about was how the Man
had given me candy.
I imagined
his weavers and the colour of their dye.
I thought about
his pale blue eyes and his friendly smile.
I tried to decide where such a Man came from.
What island had cast him out?

The morning dawned and I took Swiltu by the hand.
"Come on," I said. "We will go explore."
"Where?" she asked.
"To the clam beds," I said and went the other way.
"There are no clams here," she said.
We went along the shore to the south,
over the bank and into the forest.
We climbed on our hands and knees like sand crabs.
"You must be crafty," I told her,
"invisible."
"But where are we going?" she said.
"To see the Man," I replied.
"Mother will be angry," she worried.
"No," I said.
"She won't know where we've been,

because I won't tell her, and you won't tell her.
Don't forget,
we are invisible."

Not a stone moved when we crept through the forest.
We reached the place where Father told the Man,
You can build a fence.
We hollowed out a soft place in the bushes
and hid behind a great rock.
We spied on the Man as he felled trees and cut them into lengths.
Like two little mice,
we peered out from either side of the mound.
"What if he sees us?" Swiltu asked.
The Man stacked logs one on top of the other
and packed mud in the cracks.
I said, "We are invisible."

Sunnydale, Wallace Island, Late Summer 1862 ✺

In the morning I dressed quickly and ran downstairs two at a time. The men had gone. Ma and Pa sat alone at the kitchen table.

"If the government gave you this land, John, then it is ours," Ma said, without acknowledging my presence.

"The Indians were here first, Eva. We are their guests. We will share their island with gratefulness," Pa said slowly, as if he wanted to say it only once.

"*Our* island," she insisted and crossed her arms across her chest.

"The government says this is our island, Eva. So, yes, darling, it is rightfully ours. But the Indians don't agree. Why should they? The north end is their fishing camp," he said. "And probably has been for many generations."

"Because this country belongs to England. That's why," Ma said. Then she shut her eyes tightly. It was an odd habit of hers, one I didn't fully understand. But when she didn't want to hear any more, she shut her eyes to signal an end to the conversation.

Pa looked at me and shrugged his shoulders as if to say, *What's the use in talking? Ma will never understand.*

"Why can't we share the island?" I said. I stood between Ma and Pa. I got the feeling that I was standing in a trench between two armies.

"Exactly," Pa smiled. "That's exactly what I'm saying. We can share the island. And for a while at least, we can behave as if we are their guests."

Ma opened her eyes and glared at me without saying anything. She sighed a great harrumph and left the room, slamming the kitchen door behind her.

Soft, yellow sunbeams, not yet warm, lit up the kitchen. It was the time of day I usually liked best on Wallace Island. Mornings held promise that the day would be wonderful, but this morning there was no doubt it would be different.

Pa had no trouble sharing the land with the Indians. He couldn't clear off all the trees and farm the whole of Wallace Island anyway, even though the government had signed it all over to his name. There was plenty of land for everyone.

Sharing the island was an exciting thought. I would have visited the Indian camp if Ma had let me. But Ma had strict restrictions on how far away from the house we were allowed to go—and for now that meant not going anywhere near the Indians.

"Do you think there will be a war?" I asked Pa, thinking about what Alec had said the night before. "Like the wars in America?"

"No, there won't be a war," he said in a reassuring voice. Then he paused, as if to rethink what he had said. "We must ensure there isn't a war."

As far as I was concerned, it was a simple matter: the Indians had lived on Wallace Island first. I couldn't see why anyone would argue with that. As far as I knew, no one had paid them for the land, and they hadn't signed a deed to sell. So it seemed to me that sharing the island was the most sensible plan.

Charlotte, on the other hand, cried when Ma and Pa talked about the Indians. She wanted nothing whatsoever to do with them.

She said, "Why can't we just go back to England where no one worries about *Indians*?" She spat the word through her lips with the same contempt that Ma showed for our neighbours.

I stood silently beside Pa. I was sure both of us were thinking of ways to prevent a division in our family.

When Ma returned to the room, she said, "John, you must take us from this island immediately. If anything happens to us, John—if anything happens—I will lay the blame squarely at your feet."

She was angry. They were the same words she had said the night before, but now they were even more resolute.

"Eva, we will not leave," Pa said, firmly matching Ma's determination.

"This is our home. A few men from Victoria are causing a frenzy. They are nothing but whisky traders and cannot be trusted."

Ma pinched her lips tightly together, lowered her brows and said nothing.

"They are putting fear in your heart and for no reason. They are nothing but troublemakers. They have nothing better to do than sell whisky to the Indians and stories to the settlers. I have been warned about the trouble they cause. You know I talked to the Lamalcha before you arrived. We have shared their island for more than three years now. My dear, there are other families from the old country that have settled in this region in close proximity to the Indians. I hear they get along with their neighbours in a most agreeable manner. They trade butter for clams and clothing for a good day's work. There is no need for us to be afraid."

"*Our* island," she corrected him sharply. "And we can dig our own clams."

It was quiet again in the room. Ma's words hung in the air like bats dangling in the rafters. She stood on one side of the wood stove, and Pa stood on the other. Her lips were stretched like thin blue parchment over her teeth. Her eyes were dry and glassy, as if her eyelids might stick if she blinked. Although she might have been distressed just for the moment, there was permanence in the way she looked.

I sat at the table and watched a line being drawn down the centre of my family. Pa's forehead was creased in a deep V as he rubbed his hands together over the stove. He appeared to sense the line, but he did nothing to erase it.

"Wallace Island, Eva, belongs to God," was all he said.

I had never heard him put it that way, and while it didn't solve the problem, it did cause Ma to sit at the table and put her head in her hands. She did not close her eyes. I wished Pa's words had put an end to the conversation, but I knew there was more to come.

Lamalcha Camp, Summer Island, Summer 1859 🖎

Every afternoon Swiltu and I
    hid behind the rock and watched the Man
    working from sun up until sun down.
    From what I could tell, he must have been in a terrible hurry.
    Other hwunitum men came, once in a while,
    and helped him dig and cut trees and stack logs.
    But most of the time the Man worked alone.
    He dug a garden
    and built small sheds behind the house.
    He brought animals
    and fenced them into pens.
    We were invisible
    until one day Little Brother found our hiding place,
    for he had one of his own,
    not more than a stone's throw away.
    "Raccoon Man is a hard worker," he said.

I scolded him for calling the Man such a name.
    "He has a fine beard," I said,
    for I had come to like the Man.
    Even when he worked long hours,
    and for many days at a stretch,
    his beard was always neatly trimmed.
    Other than Father, the Man was the handsomest man I had ever seen.
    He stood head and shoulders taller than any man I knew.

His arms and legs
were like the limbs of an arbutus.
He reached higher and farther than I imagined was possible.
He sang while he worked.
Between the sound of wood sawing and mud sloshing,
I heard the sound of his voice,
a melody—like a woman singing.
He was a remarkable specimen,
and I marvelled at what sort of a human being he was.

Grandmother wanted to help the Man.
"Let me send Big Brother to our neighbour
with gifts of salmon and berries,"
she begged Father.
"I will set aside a bowl of duck stew and send it with the gifts."
"No, he is strong," Father said to his mother.
"His cheeks are not gaunt.
His work is not slowing from lack of food."
Uncle Nanute thought we should send Tsustea's mother to the Man.
"He needs a wife," he said.
"And Tsustea's mother is lonely."
"No, he has a family," Father said.
"They will come when his house is ready." ·
Big Brother wanted to help the Man
dig a water hole and haul logs for his home.
Again Father said, "No.
We will have nothing to do with the Man
unless he is hungry or hurt."

It wasn't Father's idea that everyone should avoid the Man.
We all knew that it was Mother
who convinced him that we should
keep our distance.
She had never forgiven Father
for allowing the Man to settle on our island.

"If it were up to me," she said,
"the Man would be sent back to where he came from.
If his people don't want him,
they probably have a perfectly good reason."
Father said to leave her alone to her opinion.
The People thought Mother was overly harsh.
But soon they forgot about the Man
and never paid one moment's notice to what he was doing.

Sunnydale, Wallace Island, Late Summer 1862 ❧

I squirmed in the chair. The only sound in the room was Ma and Pa breathing in and out so loudly they could hear each other, but neither one of them said a word.

Please, can't someone just say something and clear up the misunderstanding so that Sunnydale can be peaceful again?

It seemed to me as though it had been weeks since Ma and Pa had had a normal conversation. Everything they said to each other had become sharp and short, as if they didn't really want to say anything at all but were forced to. I was aching for something to be said, anything that would cut through the tension and make things good again.

I squirmed again and waited for one of them to speak. They stayed stubbornly silent for so long that I had to rush to the outhouse.

When I returned, the room was cozy and warm. The smell of bubbling oatmeal and the soft dampness in the air from the boiling kettle made it seem like every other morning. But Pa had disappeared, and Ma stood rigidly facing the sideboard with her hands on her hips.

"It's a beautiful morning, Ma," I said merrily. I thought if I acted cheerful, maybe Ma would become cheerful as well, maybe I could change the mood.

But other than a slight curl of her shoulder, Ma didn't move at all. I reached across her arm to pick up spoons to set on the table for breakfast. Maybe my being helpful would change her mood. Ma's icy fingers took my hand from the cutlery and let it drop with a crash to the counter.

"Would you like me to feed Baby Dot?" I asked. "Or refill the woodbox?"

I needed something to do, something that would make the morning feel normal. If no one else was going to do something, I was. I just didn't know what to do.

Ma jerked her chin from side to side.

"I'll empty the ashes from the stove into the outhouse," I said. I couldn't sit down and do nothing.

Charlotte was slouched over the table. She rested her head in her hands. Baby Dot sat on the floor at Ma's feet. She whined to be picked up.

What has happened to my family? It's breakfast time. Where's Pa? The oatmeal is cooked. Alec's not even out of bed. Has everyone forgotten him?

My mind raced from one thing to the next, and I began to panic. My stomach tightened as if I were waiting for my world to come to a complete end. Nothing made sense; nothing was the same; no one seemed to want to fix it except me. But what was I supposed to do? Before I had time to pick up the tin bucket for the ashes, Ma swept Baby Dot into her arms and charged out the door.

I stood paralyzed, trying to get my mind to think of something to do. All I could hear in my brain was a loud buzzing sound. Where it came from I didn't know, but it was so loud my head hurt. Suddenly an impulse struck me. I went to the base of the stairs.

"Get up, Richardsons!" I shouted. Only Alec was still in bed, but I yelled again, making myself sound as much like Pa as I could. "Get up, Richardsons! If you stay in bed any longer you'll start to grow roots."

A few moments later Alec stumbled down the stairs and sat next to Charlotte. I took bowls from the shelf and filled them with hot oatmeal.

"Where's Ma?" Alec asked, rubbing his eyes. "And Pa?"

"They are angry with each other," I said, sounding as in-control-of-the-situation as I could. "Pa went out earlier, and then a few minutes ago Ma took Baby Dot and left. I don't know where she went."

"What about our lessons?" Alec asked. He leaned into the sunrays streaming through the window.

"Here," I said, ignoring his question. I put a bowl of hot porridge in front of him.

I gave Charlotte a bowl and took one for myself. I sat across the table from the two of them, bowed my head and put out my hands. It took them a few moments to understand what I was doing, but finally Charlotte and Alec bowed their heads and grasped each other's hands and mine.

I prayed, "Thank you, God, for this food, for this house and for this family. Amen."

I didn't sound exactly like Pa, but it would do. And besides, I figured that it was better than no prayer at all. After I finished giving thanks, Alec and Charlotte set their hands on their laps and looked at each other, puzzled. Neither of them moved.

"Eat your porridge," I said, shoving the pitcher of cream toward them. "It's breakfast time, isn't it?"

Charlotte dutifully poured the cream into her bowl and spooned the cereal into her mouth. After a few mouthfuls, she began to wheeze. Then, as if the oatmeal had clogged her windpipe, she spewed the contents of her mouth onto the table. In a tizzy she pushed her bowl away and pounded her fist.

"Oh, Hope, I am so scared," she cried as she gasped for breath. "We must leave this godforsaken place and return home to England."

As if the words had used up every bit of strength she possessed, Charlotte curled over like an autumn leaf until her head was on the table. Her shoulders shook as she sobbed.

Alec paid no attention to her. He gobbled the last spoonful of oatmeal and passed his bowl to me for a second helping.

"If Ma's not here," he said, "I'm going to the seashore. Hurry up, Hope. Can I have some more oatmeal?"

Charlotte lifted her head. Her cold blue eyes seemed sturdy compared to her limp body. "You will not go to the seashore." Her voice was surprisingly severe. "And why do you think there will be no lessons today?"

" 'Cause Ma would be here setting up our books," he said, "and she's not even getting breakfast."

For Alec, it all seemed so straightforward. Things were different that morning, and he was always eager to get out of doing his lessons. He just decided he would find something else to do—as simple as that.

"She will return." Charlotte pulled herself up to a sitting position. "The day will proceed as usual."

In the absence of Ma, Charlotte did her best to control our little brother, although he didn't pay the slightest attention to her. Alec turned his back to Charlotte and looked at me. "Want to come with me?" he asked. "We can finish making our raft and sail it around the island."

"Don't talk with your mouth full," I snapped. All of a sudden sailing around the island seemed far-fetched. I was too busy thinking of ways to save Sunnydale to be dreaming about such frivolous games. "You will go nowhere, and I will not come with you."

I usually tried to be patient with Alec, although it was always a chore to get him to sit still. He wasn't a naughty boy, not really—although Ma thought so, especially when she made his lessons unnecessarily long and difficult. I found his stubborn refusal to do his lessons an admirable trait. Once he set his mind to something, he never gave up—a characteristic I thought would serve him well when he became an adult. But that morning his persistence annoyed me. I needed him to be quiet. Order. I needed order.

Can't everyone just do what they usually do?

A pain had been growing in the pit of my stomach since the early morning. I couldn't think of a time when our family did not sit together to eat breakfast. I had never been the one to say grace before breakfast, not once, and the more I thought about it, the more unusual it became. Would God be unhappy that Pa had left such an important task to a young girl? I had tried to make the prayer sound as much like Pa's as I could...but where was he?

I ate a few mouthfuls of porridge, forcing my throat to swallow what felt like huge lumps of paste. I cleared the dishes off the table, working around Charlotte, who was slumped over the table once again. I poured hot water from the kettle into the basin on the counter, and I washed and dried the dishes. By the time I had stacked the bowls in the cupboard, I began to think that breakfast had been quite normal after all...in spite of the fact that the morning was likely the most unusual of my life so far. The thought confused me as I folded the dishcloth and carried the basin of dirty dishwater to the door.

"Come on," I said. "Can someone help me?"

Alec scrambled to his feet and opened the door. I threw the water on the dry grass and put the basin on the back porch. I walked past the kitchen garden, noticing that the weather was warm for late summer. There were still root vegetables left in the ground, and gardening that needed to be done.

I crouched next to a row of carrots, pulled out a handful and wiped them on the grass. Munching on the vegetables, I inspected the roses, the few left unpicked now shrivelled, charcoal red and fringed in black. Within another few years, the bushes would mature and the flowers would be as beautiful as any in England. I saw that I needed to prune the bushes and string the renegade new stalks together to prevent them from breaking off.

In the spring Ma and I had planted the vegetables together. We had turned the soil and plotted where to plant the seeds. We'd mulched the roses and taken cuttings from the geraniums. Next to exploring and painting, gardening was my favourite thing to do, and Ma's as well.

Surely Ma won't leave the garden when the geraniums and hydrangeas are still in full bloom.

I found Ma on the maple stump by the shed. Baby Dot was sitting cross-legged near her feet, plucking petals from flowers. A gentle breeze rustled through the tips of the trees in the forest, and a faint sound of songbirds came from the distance.

It was a pleasant sight…like those I had seen on painted china plates used to serve cakes and pastries in the afternoon. Mother and child looked so serene, I did not want to disturb them. I stopped chewing the carrots and put the ones in my hand into my apron pocket.

Ma didn't look up when I approached. Her elbows were set on her knees, and her hands cupped over her face. She looked thin and fragile. Her narrow shoulders drooped lifelessly, and her arms were no more than spindles. From the cuffs of her dress, her hands and fingers protruded with unsightly knuckles—skin stretched over the bones.

"Ma?" I said quietly, so I didn't surprise her.

Baby Dot stopped plucking petals and looked at me.

"Ma?" I stepped closer and stretched out my hand to touch Ma's head.

"What are you doing?" I asked, although the question was meaningless. I could see as plain as day what she was doing. A better question would have been, *Why are you doing this?* But I knew better than to ask her such a thing.

Other than the slight rise and fall of Ma's breathing, she remained as unresponsive as a lump of stone.

I looked at Baby Dot. Her fine blond curls hung in her face. Her apron was stained and wrinkled, and her blue eyes looked tired and helpless.

She looks so pathetic for a Richardson child. What has happened to us?

I reached for my little sister's hand and said, "You must be hungry. There's warm porridge on the stove."

Baby Dot raised her arms for me to pick her up.

"You can walk," I said. I tucked her hair behind her ears and straightened out her dress and apron. "There you go, now. You are four years old. It's time for you to stop acting like a baby."

"Up, Hope," Baby Dot whimpered. "Pick me up."

I took her hand and pulled her toward the house.

How could my family have come to this? Even Baby Dot.

"It's time," I said under my breath, "for you to grow up, little sister. You are four years old and don't need to be carried."

We left Ma sitting in the same position as when I arrived.

"And hurry up, Dorothy," I said. "You don't need to be Baby Dot forever."

In the kitchen Pa sat at the table eating porridge as normally as could be. Opposite him, Charlotte stared at her fingers and fidgeted. Alec sat on the stair watching his father and sister—as if he expected something to happen.

I plunked Baby Dot on a chair, put oatmeal and cream in a bowl and placed it in front of her.

"Now eat," I said, handing her a spoon.

Obediently, and for the first time eating completely alone, Baby Dot dipped her spoon into her cereal and scooped porridge into her mouth, perfectly, as if she had been feeding herself for years.

"Don't just sit there," Pa said to Alec. "You have chores to do."

Alec didn't move. He stared at Pa. Pa stared back. It was as if something had been disconnected—the foot from the leg, the hand from the arm, the head from the neck. It seemed as though what to do next had to be thought out, each step of the way, as if it had never been done before. Things were just too out of the ordinary, and neither one of them knew what was to follow.

Pa snapped, "Go. I said go, Alec. Do your chores. There will be no lessons today."

"No lessons!" Alec shouted. "Are there really no lessons today?"

He leapt off the stairs and scooted out the door.

"But Pa," Charlotte wailed. She covered her mouth with her hand and jumped up. Charlotte was never someone who could tolerate a change in the routine, and she was now beside herself. I watched, expecting her to collapse into a fit of wheezing and coughing, which was her usual response to tension, but instead she swept uneventfully up the stairs. She left Pa and me watching Baby Dot spoon oatmeal neatly into her mouth.

Has my whole family lost control of their senses?

Ma was a lump of stone. Charlotte had dissolved like soap down the drain. Alec was going out to do chores and play instead of doing his lessons. Baby Dot sat at the table eating like a young lady. And Pa—I could hardly recognize him. He looked like a stranger, hunched over with a bewildered look on his face.

Does no one else but me see what is happening? Am I the only one who is trying to keep my family from breaking apart?

I pulled a chair back from the table and sat facing Pa.

"Pa," I said. I looked at him—eye to eye. "What is happening to our family?"

He shrugged his shoulders.

"At breakfast...? And Ma...?" I said. "It was breakfast time, and you and Ma weren't here with us. Your children ate alone. I was left to say grace."

I hadn't really thought about it before I spoke. But at that moment, the worst infraction that had been committed so far seemed to be the disruption in our family breakfast routine. That was the thing that had changed everything.

Pa shifted in his chair and pulled his fingers through his hair. I couldn't believe what he looked like. His eyelids were red and puffy. There were deep creases in his forehead I had never seen before. He looked smaller than usual, as if he had been stuck with a pin and air had seeped out of him.

He said, "Mr. Haws and Old Man Albert have gone to Cowichan. But they will return, probably within a week's time."

The very sound of the word *Cowichan* made me shiver. I had heard about that place before, and every time, it seemed as though something awful had happened there.

"Why?"

He clasped his hands together until his knuckles turned white. Finally he said with a frown, "Their business keeps them ever travelling." He paused and added, "And they bring the rumours from around these parts. The men say that there is going to be an Indian insurrection."

He looked at me as if to wonder whether a girl so young should take part in such an unsettling conversation. "Two settlers have been murdered in recent months, and people in Victoria think the Indians are going to continue to kill the settlers one at a time."

I wanted to ask him what an insurrection was, but I was afraid he would stop talking if I interrupted him. And besides, I was sure Pa needed me. So it was important that I appear as mature as possible.

"Mr. Haws and Old Man Albert say there is a village on Mayne Island, that it will be safer if we live near other settlers. There are others in Victoria who agree that we should leave Wallace Island. They say we are too isolated here. And they are convincing your Ma. She has asked Mr. Haws and Old Man Albert to help us."

Instantly a flood of hot blood rushed up my chest and neck and into my cheeks. It was as if my body was boiling inside with anger and panic. My eyes burned with salty tears, but I did not blink.

Send the men away, Pa. Tell them they will never be welcome on Wallace Island again. They will never eat another one of Ma's meals.

I screamed the words silently, all the while keeping my eyes straight ahead.

"I don't want to go," Pa said. "I love this house. I love this island."

He loves the house. He loves the island.

The words had a strange ring to them. I tried to remember other times

I had heard Pa use that word. But it was as extraordinary as everything else that had happened that morning. Never. I had never heard Pa say *love*.

When I thought about how much I loved Sunnydale, my eyes stung.

You can't cry, Hope. Not now. Pa needs you. But why is he talking about Mayne Island? How would that place make anyone happy?

"The Indians have never harmed us," I said. I tried as hard as I could to sound more mature than my twelve years. "And besides, you already talked to them."

"Yes, I did, and they are good people," Pa said. "But the settlers don't think the Indians can be trusted."

"Do you?"

"Do I?"

"Do you think the Indians can be trusted?"

Pa looked intently into my face. Then he said, "A man can be trusted to protect his family and take care of his people."

Trying to be a grown-up wasn't easy. I knew some things, but when Pa didn't talk straight and answer my questions directly, I didn't understand what he meant. I had a hunch that he was saying he agreed with the men: there truly was trouble coming; our family was in danger. But I wasn't sure.

Lamalcha Camp, Summer Island, Spring 1860 ≋

If they had approached Summer Island in the Man's normal manner,
    we all would have seen them
    in front of the camp.
    Instead, they came from the south,
    through the rapid currents.
    The spring day was almost exactly one year
    since he had started building his house.
    Little Brother spotted the Man's boat
    in spite of its strange approach,
    before it arrived on his shell beach.
    "The Man has arrived! The Man has arrived!"
    Little Brother hollered.
    He darted in and out of sleeping lodges
    and raced to the clam beds and carving shed.
    I heard his voice from here and there.
    I put my cedar broom down and ran outside,
    not because the Man had arrived
    (he had come and gone before),
    or because it was his first visit this year,
    but because there was such excitement in Little Brother's voice.
    "Why do you make such a commotion?" I called.
    "There are children in the boat," he hollered
    and darted past the lodge and on toward the south.
    I followed him to the point.

Children!

We had heard they were coming.
When his house is finished, Father had said,
he will bring his family.
It was the first thing we checked
when we arrived on Summer Island.
The Man had filled the gaps between the logs
and put on a roof.
It was a fine-looking house with windows and a door,
but the Man had gone,
and the house was empty
until now.

Children!

My heart took off, racing like a deer.

Others came running.
Pretty soon there was a crowd
huddled together at the point,
hiding behind the giant root of a beached maple
the best we could,
heads bobbing like ducks,
and necks stretching like geese,
        murmuring.
How strange we must look to the newcomers, I thought.
The boat skidded up onto the pebbles.
One by one,
the family disembarked.
The Man first,
and then a girl with hair as golden as the sun,
holding fast to her mother's hand.
The woman was wrapped so completely in clothing,
I was astounded she could manage to untangle herself

and step onto the shore.
Next a boy, the size of Little Brother,
and then the Man lifted a little girl,
barely bigger than a baby.
He placed her in the arms of her mother.
But it was the last child that caught my attention—

a girl, a little bigger than the first,
with hair the colour of dried grass.

She leapt out of the boat
and tossed her hands in the air.
She twirled
around and around in a glorious expression of joy.
Her dress was a whirlwind circling her legs.
She danced,
and from that moment
I could think of nothing else.

"You will not go near the hwunitum settlement,"
Mother said when we returned to the camp.
"You will abandon your hiding spot.
You will go no closer than the point."
Too far to catch even a glimpse of the girl.

So a strange arrangement
developed between the hwunitum and our People.
No more than a short walk separated us,
but Mother forbade us to go near them,
and Father enforced her rules.

"My love,"
I heard Father begin to tell Mother that night.
Her back was turned to him,
and her shoulder arched as if to say,

I don't want to hear.

"My love," he continued, "in neighbouring villages
hwunitum live side by side with hwulmuhw.
Hwulmuhw women take the newcomers
to be their husbands."
"No, never," Mother gasped.
She turned around; her eyes were wide.
"Promise me that our People
will never associate with the hwunitum," she begged.
"Other People can do what they want—at their own peril.
My dreams remind me night after night,
the newcomers bring us no good.
You must promise me."
She fell on her knees, imploring him,
"Promise me."
Father lifted her up and kissed her forehead.
            "I promise you."

So it was out of the question
that we should ever return to our hiding spot
to spy on the hwunitum.
And from what I could tell,
the Man had forbidden his children
to come near our camp as well.
A wall
might as well have been built
between us.
A line had been drawn.
            A line I could not cross.

Swiltu and I sat on a rock near the point
and waited.
"Letia," Father said when he saw us and came near,
"you are forbidden contact with the hwunitum.
You know that.

It is no use for you to dream and wait
for what will not be."
So from that day, I saw only the Man
when he sailed past our camp,
always when he was alone.

Apart from my dreams,
life returned to normal in the camp.
The hwunitum settlement caused no inconvenience at all,
except for the berry path.
I did not understand why Father had allowed the Man
to build his house and sheds directly on top of the path
that led through the forest to our finest berries.
It was an inconvenience that Father corrected,
once he realized his mistake.
He cut a new path to the berries
and a short arm to the path, so I could reach my bathing hole
without passing by the hwunitum settlement.

But Father's orders could not contain my dreams.
When I was awake and when I was asleep,
the girl with hair the colour of dried grass
lived in my mind:
the way she had thrown her hands up in joy
at the sight of the island,
how she had twirled
and danced up the path from the shell beach.

Sunnydale, Wallace Island, Late Summer 1862 ⁊

Until the whisky traders sailed into our little bay, life on Wallace Island
had been the same each day, each week. I loved it that way. On weekday
mornings, I would clear the breakfast dishes from the table. Once they
were washed and dried, Ma and I laid out our books—my books at one
end of the table, Alec's at the other and Charlotte's on the side. Gran had
said that if we were to advance in the world, we needed to be educated.
So she sent books from England—history, literature, Latin, arithmetic,
astronomy, health and writing.

"You must not just learn to read," she had said. "You must learn to
write. That way I will receive letters from each of you describing every
detail of your new country."

On Sundays we dressed in our best clothes, and after breakfast we
gathered in the sitting room. Pa stood near the wood stove while the rest
of us sat in our usual places. Pa said prayers, Ma sang hymns and everyone read from the Bible. Each of us read five verses at a time.

My favourite day of all was Saturday. There were no prayers or Bible
readings or lessons. Sometimes Ma packed bread and butter, hard-boiled
eggs and cookies. She spread a blanket on the beach or in the meadow.
Ma and Pa and all of us children played blind man's bluff, chuck-farthing
or hoops. Sometimes Pa set up croquet—my favourite game of all. I
had become the family champion, winning more games than Ma and
Charlotte put together. Even Pa trailed behind my score. But no one
could beat him at tossing the button into the hole—he never missed. If it
rained, we ate in the house and played checkers and charades.

But now it was Wednesday, and the family's normal routine had been turned upside down. Left with so much time on my hands, I didn't know what to do. I thought about taking my paints and easel to the seashore and trying again to capture the cliffs on paper. But I was frustrated by how my pictures had turned out. I thought about finding Alec and building our raft and sailing around the island, but the idea now seemed silly. I couldn't imagine steering such a cumbersome craft through the water, even if we did stick close to shore. Without lessons, or Sunday or Saturday activities, I could not think of anything whatsoever to do.

I walked up the path to the shed. I stopped at the maple stump where Ma had been earlier that morning. I sat down and leaned against the wall. The only sound was a peaceful whistle from the breeze in the highest tips of the giant fir trees. I closed my eyes and heard the forest noise like a choir of distant flutes.

I had dreamed many times of running through the trees to what was beyond—cliffs? Caves? Sandy beaches? It was all a mystery past Ma's strict boundaries around Sunnydale.

"The shed is as far as you go. And the front of the shed at that," she said whenever the subject came up.

Even when Pa asked Alec or me to gather kindling from his woodpile, Ma forbade us.

"John," she said. "The children are not to go beyond the front of the shed. You know that."

Until that day, I hadn't thought seriously of challenging Ma's boundaries. But in some indescribable way, as I sat there leaning against the shed, everything was beginning to feel different to me—as if a plot was being shaped. A plan was being put in place. I didn't know exactly what the plan was, but everyone seemed up to something. No one was talking about anything but trouble. And Wallace Island was in the middle of it all.

If we moved away from Wallace Island, I would never get the chance to explore the faraway places that Ma had forbidden. What if I never got to see the forest…the Indians…the bears…the beaches on the other side? What was the worst thing that could happen if I went beyond the shed?

I went to the side and peered around the back. The path continued— as if only briefly interrupted by the shed—into the forest. I took Ruby from my pocket and crept a few more steps to the corner, checking over my shoulder to make sure no one saw me. I put one foot carefully and quietly ahead of the other. A wall of cool air and shadow and darkness struck me, as if I had opened a window into the evening.

There were bears and cougars and other wild animals on the island—I knew that for sure. Pa had told me. They lived in the forest. Pa kept his gun above the door, always loaded and ready in case an animal came near the house. Only once had he shot a bear, but there were often droppings near the house and cougar tracks in the dirt near the chicken pen after it rained.

I had no gun, and it would have done me no good if I had. I had watched Pa clean and load it, but it was too heavy and cumbersome for a girl to use. Besides, Pa had said that if humans minded their own business, wild animals would keep their distance and not harm them.

As I crept into the forest, questions racked my brain. What if I came across a bear or a cougar unexpectedly? What if, by mistake, I wandered into a sleeping animal?

I set my jaw, clenched my fists and carried on. The path was wide and worn and cleared of growth and rubble. Pa had stacked chunks of wood in piles—enough for the winter. Past Pa's axe and wedge, which lay on a wooden shelf under a small lean-to, spiky green ferns sprang up where the path had once been smooth. A little farther on I picked up my skirt and climbed over sapling firs and old cedars that had been beaten down by storms.

As hard as I tried, I couldn't get Ma's warnings out of my head: *The forest is a dangerous place. The forest is no place for the children. The Indians may be lying in wait for them.*

I thought about the bear Pa had skinned. Its paws were bigger than Pa's hands. I held on tight to Ruby.

After I had walked a fair distance, the forest began to feel peaceful. The damp reddish brown of the bark on the cedars, the light green of the lichen that hung like beards from some of the branches, the brighter green of the ferns, so many shades of green. With each step I became a little more courageous…a little more curious…a little more relaxed. I kept an eye open for bears and wildcats.

The path was deep and smooth even though there were some ferns and fallen cedars in its way. Indians, from constant coming and going, must have hollowed it out long before my family had moved to the island. The farther I walked, the more sure of my deduction I became. Who else could have worn such a deep and wide trail? The Indians, I decided, must have lived and worked exactly where the house, workshop and chicken pen had been built. The path proved it. It all made sense. I closed my eyes and imagined hunters, in search of game, walking along in the very steps I was taking.

Suddenly I remembered something Pa had said to the whisky traders. *Settlers are building farms on their hunting grounds...*

A lump formed in my throat. I swallowed hard. What if there were Indians hiding in the forest waiting for trespassers?

Up ahead the path bent sharply around an enormous cedar tree. Its gnarled roots were flattened and worn as they snaked and heaved through the compacted dirt. Could there be hunters hiding behind?

Trembling, I crept around the tree's gigantic trunk, leaning against it when I arrived on the other side.

I could hear the sound of trickling water and, if I craned my neck, see a stream.

A young deer with a downy, dappled coat stood at the edge of the water, its feet braced awkwardly on the stones. It stretched its neck toward the water and sucked a long cool drink through its teeth. I slunk back into a knot of salal and, without making a sound, I crouched down and hid myself in the bushes.

Even though they ate the new beans and peas in the garden, I loved the deer that visited Sunnydale. But this deer in the forest was unsettling. It made me think of the Indian hunters. Were they nearby? Did they still come to this place? I was a trespasser, just as Pa had said.

My legs ached from the uncomfortable cramped position I was sitting in, but I didn't dare move or take my eyes off the animal. It nosed the water making a snuffling sound and then moved on. Slowly it made its way upstream and then stopped once again to drink. I pulled a branch away from my face to get a better view.

There, not more than a few strides away from the fawn, a young girl was bathing in a shallow pool in the stream. A rush of hot blood flooded my body. I had been caught—an intruder—an interloper in the girl's private affair. Feeling guilty for looking, I squished my eyes tightly closed. But even on the back of my eyelids I could see the curve of her golden skin glistening in the filtered forest sun.

I held my breath. My heart raced.

Could she see me?

I opened one eye just wide enough to steal a glimpse of the girl. She filled her cupped hands with water and poured it over her head. The water formed beads as it passed over her shiny black braided hair and smooth shoulders.

I was alone in the forest with an Indian girl—it was a thought I could hardly believe. Yet here I was, not in a dream or my wild imagination. I could almost reach out and touch her.

I held Ruby close, but I was afraid that if I moved, the moment would end. For an instant I thought about how it would feel to take off my clothes and bathe freely like the girl in the pool. I opened my eyes completely and stole a longer look. Then I snapped them tightly shut once again. I thought God might not approve of my spying. Surely it was an evil thing to see another's nakedness. Ma would be beside herself if she could see me now.

I kept my eyes closed and tried hard to erase the girl's image from my mind. By the time I opened them again, she was wearing a woven skirt that looked as if it was made out of grass. Her long black braids covered her naked back. She was beautiful.

She picked up a basket and stepped lightly, with no shoes on her feet, through the underbrush. She turned in the other direction from Sunnydale and headed up along the path. When she was far enough away that I was sure she couldn't see me, I stood up, stretched my stiff legs and back, and as carefully as I could so I did not disturb the undergrowth, I tiptoed through the bushes back onto the path and followed the girl.

I stayed close enough behind to catch glimpses of movement through the trees and far enough away to be sure I was not discovered. After a short time, I saw her stop in an opening in the forest. Dodging stealthily from behind one tree and another, I closed the distance between us until she was fully in my view. In the crevice of a large tree, I hid safely and watched. The girl was picking berries.

I had an idea. Quickly and quietly I slipped out of my hiding spot and crept down the path. When I was sure I was out of sight, I gathered my skirt in one hand and raced through the forest. I jumped over fallen trees and wove in and out around the ferns, past Pa's woodpile, past the shed, past the chicken pen and into the house. I snatched the berry basket, which was hanging on the kitchen wall near the stairs, and sped off back up the path.

"Where are you going?" Alec shouted as I approached the chicken shed.

"To pick berries," I hollered without slowing down.

"Wait. I'm coming."

"No."

I didn't usually say no to Alec, especially when it came to helping me pick berries. But this time I couldn't have him tagging along. The Indian girl was my secret.

"Hope?" he called. "Why not?"

I couldn't say that I was going into the forest. We weren't allowed in the forest. And I couldn't think of anything else to say, so I said, "Come on, then. But hurry up."

He burst into a sprint and caught up to me near the shed.

"Why are you going up here for berries?" he said. "They're on the other side of the house near the animals."

"Shhh," I said.

I checked over my shoulder to make sure Ma and Pa were nowhere in sight and then dragged him around the corner.

"Alec, quickly, behind here," I said.

"Hope, Ma says we must not go into the woods."

Alec knew the penalty for breaking Ma's rules: a good hard licking, and he got plenty of lickings.

"Ma's not here," I said, clutching his hand and dragging him behind the shed.

"But only Pa comes into the forest to cut wood and hunt. Ma says if we…" He squeezed hard on my hand. His jaw fell slack as he looked around.

"Hope. The path. Look. It goes all the way into the forest."

"Yes," I said. "I think it leads to a berry patch. Don't you?"

"I don't think so," he said. "And even if it does, berry season is over."

"But the berries near the house ripen so early. There may be late berries somewhere."

The last ripe berries on the patches close to the house had been picked weeks earlier. The only ones left were green and would not ripen even if the weather stayed hot and dry. But I had seen the Indian girl picking ripe berries. Late berries. I was sure of it.

"We'll find some up here," I said, picturing the girl's smooth, copper-coloured skin and beautiful, silky black braids. "I know we will."

"Hope, it is damp and eerie in the forest," Alec said. "Do you think we should go back? I don't see any berries here."

"Oh, Alec," I said. "You are such a scaredy-cat. This is an exciting adventure, don't you think?"

"No, Hope. It's too dark and shadowy," he said. He had been keeping up with me as I walked quickly along the path, but now he began to look about. "The trees are so tall."

"…and beautiful. There are so many shades of green."

I slowed down when we came near the opening in the woods.

"Look, Alec," I whispered, pointing at dozens of juicy, ripe purple berries. "Just like I said. Late berries."

"We shouldn't be here," he said, glancing back and forth. "There might be bears, Hope. Big bears like the one Pa shot."

"Pa said if we leave them alone, they will leave us alone."

"Ma will be angry. We are not to go beyond the shed. You know that."

Alec wasn't usually concerned about getting in trouble or what Ma or Pa would say. He was the kind of boy who was driven by impulse: act first, think later. This trait got him in trouble more often than all the rest of us children put together. But the boundaries around Sunnydale had become a different matter. Even Alec had begun to believe that danger lurked outside.

"Ma will be happy if we bring her berries for a pie," I said, knowing that Ma would not likely be in the mood to bake a pie or anything else.

"We must not tell her that we got them in the forest."

"Of course not."

"Do you think there are wild animals nearby?" he asked when he caught my eyes flitting around the bushes and giant rocks in the clearing.

"I don't think so."

Some of the berries were already mushy from recent rains, but many were still plump and purple. It didn't take me long to cover the bottom of the basket.

"Mmmm, these are good," Alec said. He picked a few berries and tossed them in his mouth. In a few minutes, he forgot to be afraid.

"If you wouldn't eat so many, Ma would have enough for a pie." I laughed at the stains around his lips. "The way you pick berries, we'll never have enough."

The shrubs beyond my left shoulder shuddered and then fell still. My hands continued to pick berries, while I kept my eyes on the prickly stalks. The leaves shook and settled; sometimes only a leaf or two shuddered and then stilled again. It wasn't long before I saw the girl's foot, then her shoulder. Suddenly what I had thought was an exciting adventure had become a terrifying situation.

What was I doing in the forest so far away from Sunnydale? In a place so strictly forbidden? With an Indian! And I'd brought my little brother.

I didn't move. I couldn't have even if I had wanted to. My body froze with fear, but my mind was racing like a wild horse. Never in my life had I been so bold. Never had I broken Ma's rules so thoroughly.

If there was one Indian, there could be more. What would Pa say if he knew where I was?

The girl stepped out from behind the thicket, and, for a fleeting second, our eyes met. But as quickly as we had looked at each other, we looked away. We continued to loosen berries and drop them into our baskets.

Alec was facing the other way and too busy eating berries to see the girl. It wasn't until he dropped a berry on the ground and bent over to pick it up that he turned around.

"Ah!" he exclaimed. His mouth went slack at the sight of her. A mixture of fear and amazement swept over his face. At ten, he was old enough to want to look and to know that he shouldn't. When his eyes finally found me, he gave me a look as if to say, *What do I do?* An unchewed berry fell from his mouth.

I scowled and motioned to him with my chin that he should not stare. His hands hung limply by his sides while he gazed at the shrubs, as if he had forgotten how to pick a berry.

Overhead the forest birds were silent. The only sound in the berry patch was a lazy hum of dozing creatures.

I emptied one branch and moved to the next, a little closer to the girl. The girl emptied a branch and moved to the next, a little closer to me. After a while we were so close to each other that if we'd reached out our arms we could have touched with the tips of our fingers.

Other than what her short woven skirt covered, everything was exposed to the air—her belly, her legs, her arms, her shoulders. I tried not to look, but she didn't try to cover herself. In fact, she paid no attention to her nakedness.

She appeared to watch me with equal fascination—her eyes on my dress and bonnet and apron, my legs, my boots. Only when our eyes met did we look away.

She must be thinking it is warm, too warm to be wearing a bonnet and dress and apron and undergarments and stockings and boots.

I could take off my dress, I thought, and then shivered.

Stop it, Hope.

It was too sinful and too cold to think of such things. I tried to push the thoughts out of my mind, but I couldn't think about anything else. The girl looked as light as air. I imagined her running fleet-footed and nimble through the forest…not bogged down with a cumbersome dress and apron that got twisted in the bushes whenever she played in the woods…not bothered by a hem that drooped in the water whenever she dug clams.

Before long we had inched our way close enough to each other that we were standing shoulder to shoulder, picking berries from the same bush. I turned my head, and we were eye to eye. This time neither one of us looked away.

I gazed with amazement into the girl's black eyes. It wasn't so much the look of her eyes that made me shudder; it was how intensely she stared. Never before had eyes so dark been fixed so exactly on me for such a long time, and all the while I did not see her blink. Then her eyes softened and her lips turned up in the creases. I smiled in return. She picked a berry and tossed it into her mouth. I did the same.

"Mmmm," I said.

"Ahhh," she said.

She picked another berry and put it in her basket.

I found one and put it in my basket.

"Ahhh," the girl said.

"Ahhh."

"Mmmm."

"Mmmm."

I pointed to myself and said, "Hope."

The girl looked confused.

I did it again. "Hope."

She pointed her finger at me. "Huuuupe?"

"Yes, yes, Hope," I said excitedly.

"Huuuupe," the girl said again. She pressed her finger against my cheek.

She patted her chest and said, "Letia."

"Lah teee ahhh?" I said.

"Letia." She patted her head and chest. "Letia. Letia."

"Lah teee ahhh!"

She took my hands and lifted them into the air. She kicked her feet in a dancing motion and laughed. "Huuuupe. Huuuupe!"

"Lah teee ahhh. Lah teee ahhh," I said. We moved in a circle, lifting our knees and laughing aloud.

Alec watched in astonishment. Nothing in his short life had prepared him for what to do in such circumstances. Usually he was full of confidence, planning ways to make mischief, but he stood rigidly without saying a word.

When Letia stopped dancing, she picked up her basket and motioned with her shoulder for me to follow her. She skipped through the clearing to where it joined the path.

"Come on," I said to Alec. "Let's go."

We ran along the path in follow-the-leader style, Letia in front, me next and Alec trailing. When she reached a fork in the path that pointed in the opposite direction from Sunnydale, she slowed down and tossed her head as if to say, *Follow me this way.*

I would have followed her without hesitation if I could have. I would have gone with her all the way to the Indian camp and farther if I had been alone. But on account of Alec, I stopped and shook my head.

"Goodbye," I said, and pointed to my brother. "I am sorry. I must go home and take him with me. He is only a little boy."

I knew she did not understand my words exactly, but she knew what I meant. And I think she knew the most important part—that I wanted to be her friend.

I threw my hands into the air the way I'd seen her do earlier.

"Letia!" I said.

She raised her hands and said, "Hope!"

Lamalcha Camp, Summer Island, Late Summer 1862 ≋

When the berries ripened, I was excited.
    The rains had lasted long into the summer.
    The blossoms had been plentiful.
    This year there would be a good harvest of plump, juicy fruit.
    For years before, I had picked berries with Tsustea;
    we raced to see who would fill her basket first.
    Her fingers were faster than mine,
    but with my determination
    I could find berries she overlooked.

    This year Swiltu was old enough to go with me.
    Mother said, "Take your sister,"
    and usually I did,
    but I pleaded that this time I should go on my own.
    For I wanted to bathe alone
    and pick berries in the quiet,
    without Swiltu's constant chatter.
    I took my basket,
    left Swiltu pouting
    and headed into the forest.
    I followed the path
    that led to my bathing hole;
    the water was cool.
    And then to the rock clearing,
    where the sun shone brightly into the heart of the island.

The air was thick with the late summer heat.
The trill of the thrushes
and the wheezy song of the warblers
wafted in the soft breeze high in the trees.
I hummed a gathering song
and let the lull of summer
and the sweet scent of ripe berries
            melt away my thoughts of Tsustea.

I looked under a tangle of twigs,
a favourite place for berries to hide,
and stopped…
I heard footsteps
from one,
no,
two sets of feet.
I crept behind a clump of bushes
and breathed deep into the bottom of my stomach.
They weren't the footsteps of my People.
They were heavy,
not with weight or size,
but with small stomping strides.
There were voices.
I peeked from my hiding place
and saw the Man's little son,
his tousled mop of curly yellow hair
and his terribly bad manners.
As fast as he picked a berry,
he tossed it in his mouth
            and gobbled it up.
I watched and was amazed by his disrespect
and imagined how Grandmother would scold him:
One berry, she would say, *or two in your mouth.*
The rest in your basket.

I loosened a berry
and dropped it into my basket.
I sensed the other hwunitum close by.
Keeping the boy in sight,
I took small steps,
little by little around the bushes,
until she was there:
the girl from my dreams,
the girl with hair the colour of dried grass,
the girl who'd danced and twirled
at the sight of Summer Island.

We were together. Finally
face to face.
She looked away, but she didn't move.
I stepped a little closer
to where she was picking.
Her fingers were thin and pale,
with long white fingernails
and fine and delicate hands.
Before long we were picking berries
shoulder to shoulder.
She didn't move away. I think,
but I am not sure,
that she moved closer to me
        …a little.

I didn't want to stare at her.
Mother had taught me—it was not the way of our People,
to look closely in the eyes of another.
But I couldn't help myself.
She was so beautiful
and I looked
and looked.

She looked deeply into my eyes.
And then away.
I didn't want to scare her
or alarm her,
or ignore her,
to appear too eager
…or not eager enough.
How was I to approach a hwunitum girl?

I looked away
and kept my eyes on the berries,
only stealing a glance after that
out of the corner of my eye.
She was much more beautiful next to me than far away.
Under her hat, her hair shimmered in the light.
Her skin was as smooth, as white,
as stones tumbled by the tide.
Her body was covered in layers of clothes,
like the dresses I had dreamed of,
the ones Father had described.
Dresses I had once imagined
floating
in the sky, up close
appeared to tie her down.
The thought of wrapping layers of cloth
around my middle,
      tightly—ugh.

The girl lifted her head,
her hat fell back
and I looked again into her face.
Her eyes were bluer than the Man's.
She spoke like a chirping bird. I said,
"Welcome,"
although I knew I had no right

to welcome her to our berry patch.
She chirped again, and I said,
"Your hat is very beautiful,"
although the strings under her chin
looked very uncomfortable.

We picked berries
until the ripe berries were gone.
I told her my name.
"Letia," I said. And she told me her name,
"Hope."
Hope,
Hope, the word got stuck behind my teeth.

Grandmother was excited
when I got back to the camp
and told her about the girl.
"Young girls need friends," she said.
"Now your heart will not long for Tsustea."
But don't tell your mother or father
about the girl and boy."
"I will not say a word," I said,
and I vowed not to tell anyone,
not even Swiltu
or Little Brother. Grandmother said,
"Your mother will be furious
that the hwunitum children
were picking our late berries."
Of course she was right.
Berry patches were strictly protected.
It was a grave offence
to pick from another family's patch.
I was happy that I had not told even Grandmother
about the way the little boy had devoured berries,
without even putting them in the basket.

She would have found no excuse for that.
"It was the girl's eyes," I said.
"I will never forget them.
They were a blue, so light...so clear."

If I had been bolder,
and if the girl had not looked so embarrassed,
I could have looked into her eyes
and seen through them into her heart.
Grandmother and I wondered
whether blue eyes saw things the same as brown eyes.
"Say, for instance," I said,
"do her blue eyes see the golden colour of the sun,
and the deep purple colour of berries
the same way our black eyes do?"

"Or say, for instance," Grandmother said,
"are her eyes able,
because they are so light,
to see in the dark?"
"Does she see things upside down?" I asked.
"Or back to front?" Grandmother laughed.
"Or light, dark
and dark, light?"

Neither one of us had any answers,
only questions.
And how could we ever know for sure?
But,
I continued to think,
  for as long as I live,
      I will wonder how the world looks through blue eyes.
There had to be, I was sure of it,
at least a small discrepancy
between the imaginations of

blue eyes
and those of black eyes.

But in my excitement,
I was unable to keep my vow of secrecy.
I told Little Brother.
The moment I saw him, I told him
about the little boy's bad manners:
"He gobbled the berries like this," I said.
I made scooping and shoving motions into my mouth.
He laughed and promised not to tell.
"The story of the gobbling boy is safe with me."
He pinched his lips closed.
I knew I had made a mistake
as soon as I had spoken.
Of course, Little Brother,
being the way he was,
a little jabber mouth,
couldn't resist telling Father and Uncle Nanute.
Around the fire that night
the People spoke about the berry gobbler,
and I learned that some things
a girl must keep to herself.
At first the People laughed,
but before long they began to argue. Big Brother said,
"We must defend our berry patches
from the hwunitum,
          or we will starve!"
The People became aroused.
          "We will starve!"
they cried.
They remembered a few years earlier,
when we had been hungry.
"The hwunitum will take
our clams and oysters and ducks and deer."

Finally Grandmother said,
"From the sound of you I would think
a tribe of warriors has invaded our territory
and stolen all our goods.
These are only children
picking a few berries, and what is more,
Letia needs a friend."
After Grandmother spoke,
the People settled down.
"The berry gobbler is just a little boy," they murmured.
"I will speak to the Man," said Father.
"...and ask to be repaid," Big Brother added.
"Let it rest," Father advised.
Even Mother agreed with Grandmother.
"Children need to have friends," she said.
"But Letia is not allowed
to go to the hwunitum settlement."
It wasn't long before the other women agreed:
"The hwunitum children
are no threat to our People."

The argument was over.

Sunnydale, Wallace Island, Late Summer 1862 🕭

Alec and I didn't say anything to each other until we reached the shed.

"Hope, you're in trouble," he said.

I peeked around the side to make sure no one was in view. I pulled him by his arm to the front. I flopped onto the stump, and Alec fell, spread-eagled, onto the grass near my feet.

"What do you mean, I'm in trouble?" I asked.

"Ma will be angry at you for going into the forest."

"She won't know."

"How come she won't know?"

"Because I won't tell her, and I am very sure you won't tell her either."

I had no guarantee that Alec wouldn't tell. It wasn't that he would say something just to get me into trouble. He wasn't like that. The problem with Alec was that whatever he saw, he couldn't resist making into a story—and telling everyone.

"Alec, you must listen to me," I said seriously, peering into his eyes. "You can't tell Ma or Pa or Charlotte. You can't even tell Baby Dot or the cat that we went into the forest. You can't even hint a word of our adventure to the chickens."

"Yes, Hope."

"Or the goat."

"I know. I know. I can't say a word."

"You'd be in for a scolding too."

"Yes, Hope. Ma would give me a licking for sure. And you as well."

"I know that, Alec. But the most important thing of all, the thing you

97

must remember..." I scowled the most serious scowl I could.

"What is it?" he asked, wide-eyed.

"You cannot say a word about the Indian girl. Not one word."

"She was wearing no clothes."

"Yes, she was. She wore a skirt."

"A skirt?"

I understood why Alec was confused. The short woven garment Letia wore around her waist was not like any skirt he had seen before, or I had seen before, for that matter.

"Yes, Alec. She wore a very short skirt. But never mind about that, you can't say a word about her."

"What about the berries? What will we say about them?"

"Alec, leave it to me. I will tell Ma they came from under the leaves in the berry patch near the house."

"All right."

"You will say nothing at all. That's our plan. All right, Alec?"

"All right."

"Promise?"

"I promise."

"Double promise?"

"Double promise."

"Triple promise?"

"Triple promise."

"It's a sin against the laws of God and the entire universe to break a triple promise."

"I know."

I wasn't sure a triple promise was enough. Alec had made such promises in the past, and as far as I could remember he had lived up to his word in each case. But it had never been so important. If Ma discovered we had been in the forest and had picked berries with an Indian girl she would...well...I could not imagine what she would do. All I knew was that my life would become unbearable.

I pulled Ruby out of my pocket.

If Alec doesn't tell Ma before supper is over, then Letia will be my friend forever.

"Why was the girl in our forest?" Alec asked.

"She was picking berries."

His little boy face had disappeared. He was overcome with a mature look of concentration.

"Who says that they're our woods?" I said.

"The whole island is ours. Ma says so. Pa allows the Indians to camp on the north end in the summer."

"But the path, Alec...can't you tell? It's been walked on for years and years, and by many, many people. What do you think that means?"

Although Alec was only ten, I thought he was smarter than most boys his age. And if ever I'd wanted that to be so, it was right then.

"That Pa wasn't the first person to use it?" he said uncertainly.

"Exactly, and what do you think that means?"

"That the Indians used the path first?"

"Exactly."

He closed his eyes and scrunched up his forehead as if he didn't want to think the thoughts that were pounding in his brain.

"The Indians probably think the island belongs to them, and they are just letting us live at Sunnydale Farm," I said.

He rolled over, pinned his elbows into the grass and cradled his chin in his hands.

"Do you think we are safe?"

"Pa talked to them and made an agreement," I said.

"Does Pa trust the Indians?" he asked.

"Pa said you can trust a man to protect his family and take care of his people."

Alec didn't move. Sunlight streamed across his curly blond hair, lighting his crystal blue eyes.

"I don't understand," he said.

"I think...," I began, not knowing exactly how to say what I was thinking. "If we are not a threat—if the Indians don't think we are going to take what belongs to them and if they don't think we'll hurt them—then they will stick to their word."

"So we *can* trust them?"

"You know what, Alec?"

All of a sudden the word *trust* became a very complicated idea.

"I think what Pa meant is that all men are the same, whether they are Indians or not. A man will protect his family first—that's the important thing. Just like Pa would protect us and our house and farm. The Indians are just like that."

"We won't hurt them," Alec said with a relieved and satisfied look. "We're not taking anything that belongs to them. Right?"

At that moment the turn in our conversation worried me—especially now that I had seen the well-beaten path…and how it appeared that our house and shed were plunked right in the middle of it…and after meeting Letia in the berry patch. I wasn't at all sure that we *hadn't* taken anything that belonged to the Indians.

"Are we, Hope?"

"Yes…I mean no, Alec. We won't be a threat or take what is theirs—unless they agree. Pa will make sure of that."

But Pa wasn't the problem. It was men like Mr. Haws and Old Man Albert. They were the ones instigating the trouble. They were the ones spreading stories and stirring up fear in everyone.

"I just wish Mr. Haws and Old Man Albert would stay in Victoria where they belong. They should keep their busy bodies out of our business," I said, trying not to sound worried. I just wanted the conversation to be over.

"But Ma said the men—"

"Alec," I interrupted. "There's only one thing you have to worry about concerning Ma."

I stood up and gave him a hand. He almost pulled me over as he yanked himself upright.

"And that is…" I steadied myself just in time before spilling the berries. "…if you tell her one word about the forest, the berries or the Indian girl, I will personally murder you."

"I promise, Hope," he said in an annoyed voice. "I already triple promised."

"Come on, then," I said. "Let's help Ma make a pie."

I hurried down the path, trying to get the troubling thoughts out of my mind.

Can the Indians be trusted to keep the agreement they made with Pa about Sunnydale? What if they think their families aren't safe? What if they think other settlers are going to take what is not rightfully theirs? What if they don't understand that Pa is different? Why, oh, why can't I stop my mind from thinking so much?

"Hurry up, Alec."

I slowed down to match his pace.

"We're not going to have to move away from Wallace, are we?" he asked.

"No, not if Pa has anything to do about it."

He took a few more berries and shoved them into his mouth. "Good," he said. "Because I love Sunnydale."

"And you love berries. There are only a few left. Ma will have to mix them with apples if she is to make a pie."

I watched my short, billowy shadow as I walked toward the house. I imagined Letia's shadow, long and lean, with only the outline of her skirt and the curves of her body.

My problem was building. I loved Wallace Island. But never did I fear losing it as much as I did now that I had the prospect of a friend.

Ma was plucking feathers from a duck when we approached the house.

"Look, Ma, we have berries for a pie," I said.

"Where did you get them?" she asked. "Our bushes are stripped."

"Under the leaves," Alec offered. "There were some late berries left to ripen. We had to look hard for them, and there's only a few."

I tossed him a stern look as if to say, *Remember the triple promise.*

Ma looked at his stained hands and the purple smudges on his chin. Her mood changed a little. "It looks like there were a few more than this." She smiled.

It was the first time I had seen her real smile in a long time. For an instant Ma's expression was light and cheerful. Her fine lips outlined her perfectly formed teeth and made her appear as young and beautiful as when she was in England. She looked like the woman in the cameo she wore, a woman with an elegantly straight back, slender waist and gracefully long neck. Pa used to tease her and say that her long neck was proof of her good breeding, for only women from the true aristocracy bore their heads with such elegance. Pa would tickle her neck, and she would giggle.

On the rare occasions when Pa had tried to make her laugh in recent weeks, she had pushed his hand away.

"John," she would say, "please don't." There was a growing agreement between the two of them—to keep their distance.

Now, Ma closed her mouth and her smile disappeared. She took the basket and set it aside.

"As long as you didn't go past the shed," she added. It was as if she knew we had not told the whole truth, but for some reason had decided to accept our story.

"Of course not, Ma," Alec said, exaggerating his effort to seem innocent.

Ma tossed the gangly naked duck into the stew pot and wiped her hands on her apron.

We ate supper quietly—the duck, potatoes, carrots, and custard with stewed berries. Alec, especially, hardly said a word.

Letia will be my friend forever.

Lamalcha Camp, Summer Island, Summer 1862 ≡

Even from the beginning,
    that summer had been different from the summers before.
    I couldn't decide exactly what made it so different.
    The People seemed busier than usual,
    especially Father,
    for he had set himself an enormous task:
    to build the biggest canoe the People had seen
    since the time of my great-grandfather.
    "This canoe," Father said,
    "will be as grand as the canoes
    the Lamalcha paddled
    when our People were the threat of the coast."
    So he chinked and shaved and cut and transformed
    a giant cedar tree.
    Big Brother helped. And Little Brother
    …a little.

    Mother was also busy that summer.
    During the winter, she had prepared enough
    mountain goat wool, dog hair, stinging nettle and cleansing earth
    to weave a new blanket,
    a large blanket that would be a sleeping mat.
    Her loom was set up near the lodge,
    where she sat,
    her fingers twisting and knotting the wool

under and over,
back and forth.
The blanket had to be ready
for the cold weather.

Everyone was not just busy that summer; the People
were unusually impatient with each other
                        and complained more.
"The rain," they said,
"will never leave."
"The rain is like the whisky traders," they said.
"It leaves and then,
before you know it,
there it is again."

I think Long Man and Round Man
were the cause of much of the disruption in our camp.
For their visits had become frequent,
and the complaints had increased.
Uncle Penu was the only person
who was happy to see them.
He had come to love their whisky,
and after each visit he drank more
and became noisier than the time before.

When we heard the traders' voices,
Swiltu and I ducked into the lodge,
out of their way,
and waited until Uncle Penu hollered goodbye.
I was sure the men were gone
when the bottles clinked
as he picked them,
one by one,
out of the crate and marked the wall.
"This is a great day!" he cried.

The top popped off a bottle,
and I heard him guzzle and choke and slobber.
And then another top popped.

We crept outside the lodge and watched
Uncle Penu stamp his feet
and beat his chest and holler:
"I am a great man! A great trader!"
We kept out of his way,
crouched near the door of the lodge.
He staggered around the camp
from lodge to lodge
and from tree to tree.
The People ignored him
as if he were invisible.
"Tsharr," Grandmother said when she found us.
"Stay away from him, Granddaughters.
He is not one of the People
when he is drowned in that poison.
He is a stranger."
She led Swiltu and me to the mats and huddled with us.
"The monster will possess him for a while
and then pass through him.
Penu will return," she said.

But he didn't stop.
He didn't collapse and sleep as he usually did.
He charged from one tree to the next,
foaming at his mouth
and growling like an angry bear.
Suddenly he bolted,
as if transformed into a warrior,
and attacked the lines he had hung with fish and seal meat.
He stabbed and battered
the goods he was preparing to trade

for the next crate of whisky.
He sent it flying in all directions
onto the dusty ground.
And after he had wrecked all of his belongings,
and cursed the People and the Creator,
finally, in the midst of the destruction,
he dropped into a heap near the firepit
and fell into a noisy sleep.
Father and Uncle Nanute
pushed him out of the way of the embers
to save him from burning himself.
They left his meat to rot.
"He has taught himself a lesson," Father said.
          He wagged his head in disgust.

Another thing that was different that summer:
our camp had many visitors.
Not just the whisky traders;
neighbouring hunters came more often than before
to consult with Father
about the business of the territory.
They came with more urgency than usual
and all bearing the same news:
"Hwunitum are showing up everywhere," they said,
"building houses, planting fields
and erecting barns wherever they choose.
Their cows roam throughout the territory
destroying our camas and potato fields.
Our People are hungry.
          Hwunitum are like bees, coming in swarms."

The dusky grey of one late afternoon
had already muted the bright summer day.
The fire was hot.
Mother and Grandmother had roasted seal for supper,

and mushrooms and onions.
I stared into the flames
and wished for the food to be ready.

"Tell me your name and where you are from!"
Father hollered, jolting me out of my stupor.
"We are Tzeztuscan and Comitum.
We are from Cowichan," the men hollered back.
"We come in peace."
The two men sat in their canoe
and held their paddles high, waiting for Father's reply.
"You are welcome in my camp," Father said,
"for I know your father and your grandfather.
Pull your canoe up on the shore.
Come and eat with my People."

I swept the benches
and tidied the ashes around the fire.
And when the men sat down,
I served them the food Mother had cooked.
I brought them water to drink.
The men thanked me and said to Father,
"Your daughter will make a good wife.
We have fine sons in Cowichan."
Father frowned and said,
"I will make a hard deal,
for she is accomplished like her mother."
"And we can see," the men said,
"that she is not only accomplished,
but beautiful like her mother as well."
My cheeks grew hot and I cringed.
I was embarrassed to hear
my beauty spoken out loud.
But the People laughed.
After he had eaten,

one of the men grinned and rubbed his belly.
"Lamalcha women are known for their beauty
and because they are good cooks."
He belched. "Knaw," he said.
"That was a fine meal, fine woman."
Mother blushed.

A serious mood settled over the People.
We sat in a circle, watching the men,
waiting to hear their news.
"We have come bearing a troublesome report," one man said.
His forehead was creased;
sweat trickled down his brow.
The other man, Comitum, put his head in his hands.
"A hwunitum was killed near our village.
He was trespassing in this family's territory,"
Tzeztuscan said, pointing his hands at his companion.
"The man cut a stand of firs
until not one was standing next to the other.
He had no respect for hwulmuhw laws.
And what is worse,
he had brought big dumb animals. Oh, they are so dumb.
They don't know their front end from their back end.
A band of warriors could descend on them,
and they would not move.
These stupid beasts are left to roam free
as if the land belongs to them.
If the hwunitum are not on our land,
their animals are.
We have put up with this insult in our territory
and not raised our hands to the man."
The other man said,
"But our young men became enraged,
and the hwunitum was killed.
Now the Queen's men in Victoria are angry."

The People began to murmur.

"Who is this Queen we keep hearing about?"

Comitum carried on,

"Her warriors are searching high and low

for the man who killed the hwunitum.

They call him a murderer.

We are afraid that the Queen's men

will take anyone to be the culprit.

These newcomers don't know one hwulmuhw from another.

They will punish whomever they find."

Not one eye of the People moved off the men.

"They will look near and far."

Big Brother said, "But trespassers must be punished.

You must protect your territory."

I was beginning to understand

why the summer had been so different from any before.

The world was changing...

everything.

Of course, Big Brother spoke sensibly

about the laws of our People.

How could our laws be broken without reprisal?

What would become of us?

Our territory?

The men said that in every hwulmuhw village

throughout the islands,

People were gathering around their fires

talking about resistance.

The hwulmuhw were saying that the hwunitum roam too freely.

They must be controlled.

Boundaries should be set around them,

to keep them in certain places,

so they do not think they can go everywhere.

Wherever they choose,

they build houses and then bring their families.
We must stop them or soon there will be
   more hwunitum
     than hwulmuhw
     in our territory.

The People became agitated.
That night they argued:
   "Who are the Queen's men, anyway?"
   "Why did we allow the Man and his family
   to live here on our island?"
"We must join the resistance and fight back."
I listened to the adults,
and I thought about the girl with hair the colour of dried grass.
I thought about the berries.
I only wished to see Hope again.
How could she be a threat?
How could they talk about sending the hwunitum
to a place to control them?
Would they fence them in the way the Man did his animals?
The Man and his family had caused no ill to our People.

I had heard adults talk about frightening things before:
warriors from the north,
plagues...
but this time it was different.
   Something was coming over the mountains
   or across the channel,
I could feel it.
Something was about to change my life forever.
Whatever it was had begun to unsettle my stomach.

Sunnydale, Wallace Island, Autumn 1862 🦎

"Would you like me to help with supper?" I asked. Without our routine, for days I'd had nothing but time on my hands.

"No," Ma said. "Take some bread and preserves. You and Alec go to the seashore. I'm busy preparing for guests."

I knew who the guests would be. I wanted to shout, *Ma, they aren't guests—they are thieves. They come here only to eat our food on their way to sell their whisky to the Indians. The only thing they give us is trouble.*

But I didn't say anything. I cut two wedges of bread, covered them with berry preserves, wrapped them in a cloth and put them in a basket. I opened the door and stepped out into the sunshine. The autumn was all copper and amber and gold. The smell of baked leaves and dried grass hung in the air, filtered through my skin and seeped into my blood.

"Come on," I called to Alec. "Let's go."

He got up lackadaisically from the step and slowly followed me past the front of the house, through the meadow and over the grassy knoll.

"But what about dinner?" he asked. "Don't we need to have dinner?"

"I have dinner in this basket," I said.

We climbed over the craggy rocks onto the pebbly shore. I sat down on a beached tree and leaned back against its smooth, twisted gnarl of roots. I breathed in the seaweedy scent of the tide going out. Soon it would reveal burbling clams and oysters.

Hmmm, I should go home to get a spade and bucket. Alec and I could dig clams and help Ma make stew.

But I was tired, and Ma hadn't seemed to want help.

I watched the waves surge onto the shore and retreat, and I listened to the pebbles rumble against each other. I scuffed my feet into the tiny rocks, and I shivered at the tinkling sound and feeling under my soles.

"Here," I said. I reached into the basket and pulled out the bread. "It's a picnic for you and me."

Alec stuffed the bread into his mouth.

"Do we get to play this afternoon?" Crumbs sprayed onto his chest when he spoke.

"Don't talk with your mouth full."

Hungry as I was, I could only nibble on the bread.

When I closed my eyes, even to blink, I saw Letia—her copper-coloured legs, her glistening black hair. Ever since meeting her in the forest, I could not get her image out of my mind. She was, without a doubt, the most beautiful girl I had ever seen. I remembered the way her white teeth flashed against her deep-coloured skin and full rosy lips, and the way her dark eyes lit up like candles when she laughed.

Alec went down to the water's edge.

I pulled out Ma's vanity mirror I had hidden in my pocket. I looked in the glass and smiled. My lips were tight and thin, not rosy red but a purplish colour. My teeth were small. Each one was straight, but against my pale lips they looked more yellow than white—a much deeper tone than the colour of my skin. I put my face right up to the mirror and stared into my eyes. They were bluer than I had imagined and pale, very pale, like Pa's. I squinted, and they turned into thin slits hardly large enough to see. My eyes were not striking and black like Letia's eyes, but upon close scrutiny, I liked the way they looked. They were soft and knowing and, I thought, hinted at a person with intelligence and strength. I thought a poet might say they were like *deep pools of still water*. I liked how that sounded.

"What are you doing?" Alec hollered. He was digging gullies in the pebbles and filling them with snakes of seaweed.

I secreted the mirror back into my pocket.

"Watching you," I said.

I put the bread back into the basket and cradled Ruby in my arms.

I wish Mr. Haws and Old Man Albert would sink in their boat. I hope I never lay eyes on them again.

I knew it was evil to think such thoughts, but I couldn't help it.

I watched the waves ripple over the stones and listened to them pull back and jingle like a million glass beads. Apart from the gentle swell and retreat of the tide, the water was calm and the sunlight danced like ballerinas on ice. Wallace Island was as close to heaven on earth as I could imagine. And now that I had a friend, the island would be even better than before. I closed my eyes and watched Letia on the back of my eyelids.

Swoosh, swoosh, swoosh.

I woke to the sound of a raven's wings displacing the air as it swooped down to the beach and soared back into the sky. I straightened my back and stretched my cramped shoulders.

"Alec," I said, looking around and expecting to see him digging holes and filling his bucket with sand and pebbles.

"Alec?"

I scrambled to my feet, sensing that he was not close by.

"Alec! Alec! Where are you?"

Until Baby Dot was born, Alec never left Ma's side. But since then it had been my job to take care of him. And to Ma's sense of justice, it was my fault whenever he got into any trouble, or, God forbid, got lost. A quick twinge of fear crawled up my back.

"Alec!"

I ran to the south where the bay was carved out of high, jagged cliffs. But what would he be doing near the rock face? There was nowhere for him to go. The rocks were much too craggy and steep for him to climb. I turned and headed north along the bay toward the maple. The large maple tree was halfway between the path to Sunnydale and the point. Its limbs reached over the beach with golden plumes, like a giant umbrella. It was the farthest place on the seashore where Ma allowed us to play. It was the closest I had ever been to the Indian camp, which was located somewhere on the other side of the point. Second only to the cliffs, the maple tree was my favourite place to paint. I had a series of spectacular paintings of the tree—in full green leaf in the summer, golden in the autumn, brown and bare in the winter and budding chartreuse in the spring. It was much easier and more satisfying to render than the cliffs and lichen.

"Alec!"

I darted in and out and around the driftwood. Maybe he had also fallen asleep and was hidden behind a stump or log. Dread welled up in my chest.

"Alec, answer me. Wake up!" I hollered.

Should I run home to see if he is there?

But it wasn't like Alec to return to the house, not when he was allowed to play at the seashore. And, if he wasn't at the house, and I went to check, Ma would be angry with me for not watching him closely enough.

No. It is not time yet to alert anyone that he is missing.

The raven, perched on a branch of a scraggy arbutus tree near the point, swivelled its head from side to side and warbled as if it were searching. It couldn't see Alec either—I could tell—at least not on the Sunnydale side of the point.

I had no reason to look around the driftwood any further; Alec wasn't there. I reached the maple, stopped and peered around the giant trunk.

I had often thought about going past the tree, all the way to the point and the Indian camp beyond. I had dreamed about it, but I'd never had the courage. Ma's boundaries were strictly enforced. Alec had never gone past the tree either, but he had been sent to his room just for saying he wanted to. Ma had convinced all of us, except Pa, of course, that the maple tree was where safety ended and danger began. So just thinking about stepping on the *other side* gave me tremors of fear.

But I was in a predicament, and my problem was more immediate and potentially more important than Ma's boundary rules. Alec was missing, and I had to find him.

I pulled Ruby out of my pocket.

If the seagull lands before I reach the other side of the point, I will find Alec safely.

I hugged Ruby for courage and stepped out from behind the maple. Without stopping, I walked toward the end of the point. From Pa's description, just on the other side and a little farther on would be the Indian camp.

Pa isn't afraid of the Indians. Why should I be afraid?

Besides needing to find Alec, I was curious. I wanted to see the Indian camp up close. But at the same time the sound of Ma's warnings echoed in my brain and muddled my thinking. *The Indians can't be trusted.* What if they had stolen Alec? What if they were watching me at this very moment and waiting to steal me?

A knot formed in my stomach, and it felt as if it were being pulled tight from either end.

Lamalcha Camp, Summer Island, Late Summer 1862 ≋

Father laid out the goods
   upon returning
   from one of his trading expeditions.
   We ogled.
   What a fine exchange he had made.
   Mother was pleased with the scissors.
   She struggled with her fingers and thumb,
   awkward at first,
   in one hand and then the other,
   until with choppy motions
   she snipped the twisted ends off a handful of dried grass.
   He brought Grandmother
   a length of purple fabric,
   Swiltu a ribbon,
   and Little Brother
   a bucket.

Never before had he neglected to bring me a gift.
Had he forgotten me?
He had one thing on his mind:
his new knife.
Big Brother and Uncle Nanute crowded around him.
"Let us look. Let us look," they pleaded.

He allowed them to stroke the handle:

it was made of the finest bone
inlaid with abalone.
Father held the blade to the sun,
blinding us with great flashes of light.
We all sat like crows lined up on a branch
and watched him shave a piece of cedar,
sending fine soft yellow curls onto the ground.
The men were envious
and thought of ways to get a knife like Father's.

Early the next morning,
I sat with Swiltu on a stump.
We watched Father's knife graze the wood,
slick,
accurate, sharper than any other knife.
Soon the wing of an eagle began to appear.
It would sit proudly on the bow of his new canoe.
The sun released the baking scents of late summer.

I forgot, for a time,
thoughts of things to come,
        things I could not control.
It was a pleasant thing
to watch a thick block of cedar
become a handsome bird.
No one spoke.
I liked it that way, and besides,
as I had instructed Swiltu,
if we talked too much
he would ask us if there wasn't
something we should be doing to help Mother.
Or he would tell us to go and play.
Before midday, he stood up,
slapped his hands together
and stretched his fingers.

Cracking one knuckle at a time,
he looked at me
as if he was about to tell me
something important
or troublesome.
I waited.
From the look on his face,
I thought his lesson would be harsh:
that he had it in his mind to correct me,
        to forbid my new friendship.
Was that why he had not brought me a gift from Victoria?

I was uneasy as he walked away,
silent.
Before I jumped down from the stump,
he came back
with a piece of red trade blanket tied with string.
"This is for you, Letia," he said.
He put the bundle
into the palm of my hand
and sat beside Swiltu and watched.
The two of them
…their eyes fastened on the gift in my hand.

I untied the string
and folded back the fine red cloth.
"Oh, Father," I gasped.
There, lying exposed,
his old carving knife.
He closed my fingers around the bone handle.
They slipped easily into the grooves
that had been burrowed by his grip.
"You will make beautiful things with this knife," he said.
Then I knew he had not forgotten me.
He had honoured me with the best gift of all.

He gave me a thin column of cedar the size of my arm
between my wrist and elbow.
I was clumsy at first,
but after a few nicks on my fingers,
my movements became steady.
I trimmed the column, as Father would have, until it was
smooth
and round,
without a flaw.
I stroked the wood,
but I could not decide what figure I should carve.

One morning I woke up from a dream.
Still on my mind was the perfect dream image of a doll,
the likeness of Tsustea;
it had long braids and a sweet and gentle smile.
The way I remembered her.
Exactly, I thought.
I will carve the image exactly.

Tsustea's appearance never left my mind
until the piece of cedar became her likeness.
Grandmother gave me dye from boiled bark
to colour Tsustea's hair dark
and her lips red.
I looked at my dream creation
and thought about Tsustea:
the quiet that came in the morning
when her eyes would not open,
when they took her from me
and swept her spirit out of the longhouse
        …leaving me alone.

I smiled, and I told the doll
that now I felt no need to cry.

Walking to the Lamalcha Camp, Autumn 1862 ❧

I knew Pa visited the Indians from time to time.

Ma never said a word about it, but it was obvious. Sometimes he brought home fresh fish for supper when he hadn't gone fishing, and deer when he hadn't been hunting. Another thing I had noticed was that when Pa went to Victoria alone, he paddled northward past the Indian camp. But on the few occasions when the whole family was with him, he bucked the tides and took an alternative route. For Ma's sake, I was sure.

She had said, "If you were to force me to lay eyes on them, I wouldn't be able to sleep at night."

Pa had tried to change her mind. He told us about Indians in other places who helped the settlers, traded with them and worked on their farms—their children even played together.

"Not on Wallace Island," Ma said with curt decisiveness. She had no tolerance even for hearing about the Indians. Ma thought of them as something entirely different from herself…as if they didn't share the same kind of flesh and blood.

She tried to explain herself once, when Pa attempted to have a reasonable discussion about our neighbours.

"Eva," he said. "There are so few of us on this island…doesn't it make sense to you that we should get to know each other? Maybe we could help each other out?"

"Does an eagle need to get to know a deer, John? Or a raccoon? Does it need to get to know a goat?"

Pa had looked at her and then looked at me as if to say, *Sometimes there's no point, Hope, trying to talk sense.*

I walked steadily toward the point. This time I *had* to break Ma's rules. What else could I do? I had to find Alec, and there was one more place I had to look before I told anyone that he was missing.

When I got to the end of the point, I waited for a bit.

The raven sat like a sentinel, its head turned toward the Indian camp; the seagull swooped in circles toward the shore and then high into the sky.

I looked back toward Sunnydale, hoping with one last glance that I would see Alec.

For a few minutes, I listened to my own breathing.

It wasn't my usual habit to take such a long time and have so much difficulty making what otherwise would have been a simple decision. But my mind kept flipping back and forth, first afraid and then curious.

Alec is missing. Ma will never forgive me if I return home without him.

When I looked at the problem straight on, there was only one thing to do. There was really no decision to make at all. Being afraid or curious wasn't important. I had no choice but to continue.

I took one step and then another. The point was wide, and for a short time the Indian camp continued to be out of sight. The seagull plunged and soared over the channel.

If the seagull lands…

It circled again, pitched toward the island and then wheeled back up.

I held my breath and took one, two, three, four shortened steps, making sure not to lose sight of the bird.

Please, seagull. Please stop flying and come to rest.

Lamalcha Camp, Summer Island, Autumn 1862 ≋

The days passed slowly in the camp.
    Each day I thought about Hope,
    excited and burdened
    by the images playing
    on the back of my eyelids:
    of Hope and me playing on the beach,
    running through the forest,
    bathing in the stream,
    steaming clams and oysters.
    I wished the images were true
    and wondered if I would ever see her again.
    I turned the words over in my mind,
    the words I would teach her:
    hello,
    friend,
    thank you,
    songbirds;
    and the words I wanted to know:
    dress,
    boots,
    play,
    dance
    …words that she could teach me.
    My thoughts drifted to Victoria.
    I would go there, like Father.

I would see for myself
all the wonderful things he spoke about.
But as each day passed,
so did my chances of seeing Hope again.

There was work to be done,
grass and reeds
to be gathered and sorted
for the winter.
"Letia," Grandmother said,
"Father will make one more trading expedition to Victoria
soon after we return to Winter Island
before the winter weather sets in.
There are baskets to make,
each one of us, for winter supplies."
But my fingers were stiff and stubborn.
They refused to pick up the grass.
Usually I could see a basket
in my mind's eye,
the colour and knots
coming together to make a design.
But that day
I could not think of a thing.
So while the women were weaving,
I snuck off to watch Father
put the finishing touches on the canoe.
He slid his knife gracefully
across the wood in long steady lines,
trimming every bump and imperfection,
until the surface of his canoe
was as smooth as the skin of a baby.

"What is that?" Father said.
It was the women.
Their voices rose above their normal din.

Pitched with excitement,
voices said, "Look, look!"
I ran from the stump to see.
The women pointed.
I followed their fingers with my eyes to the little boy.
In the midst of Little Brother and the other boys
was the yellow-headed boy.
"And over there," Tsustea's mother said.
She motioned with her chin.
"It's a girl.
She's hiding and thinks we don't see her behind the logs."
They chuckled at the sight of the girl
thinking she was invisible.
"But she is just afraid," I said.
"We must not frighten her."
I sat next to Grandmother.
"Can I go and greet her?" I asked.
"No," she said,
"your friend must find her own courage to join us,
like the little boy."
Hope stayed in her hiding spot,
and I watched, hoping she would come.
But it wasn't long
before she ran to her brother,
took his hand and raced toward the point.

Lamalcha Camp, Wallace Island, Autumn 1862 ❧

I walked a little farther up the mound of pebbles, shells and logs that covered the point and blocked my view. One, two more steps, and I was standing in full view of the Indian camp. Surprised by how close it appeared, I crouched down to hide myself behind a log and leaned back on my heels.

When I looked up from my hiding spot, there it was. The seagull. Perched on the tip of a stunted fir tree.

If the seagull lands before I reach the other side of the point...

Although I was unsure when exactly the seagull had landed, with respect to when exactly I'd reached the other side of the point, I was relieved and partially certain that I would accomplish my task.

I will find Alec safely.

It was hard to be completely confident, hunkered down in such an unfamiliar location. And on top of that...a place so completely prohibited and potentially dangerous. Alec's safety was now as important as my own, and I wasn't sure either of us would get home safe and sound.

When I caught my breath and settled my nerves, I peered out from behind the log. A wide bay with a rim of smooth sand scooped into the pebbled seashore like a giant horseshoe. Golden autumn oaks and maples ballooned over the banks. Crudely hewn wooden sheds stood side by side facing the sea. They had no paint or stone or bricks and no tiles on the roofs. They looked as if they had been built quickly and could be dismantled easily.

Men were hanging what looked like fish on clotheslines. Women sat nearby surrounded by mounds of reeds and grass. From what I could see they were weaving.

Overturned canoes were lined up along the beach; some looked big enough for one person, while others were so large they could carry a whole family and supplies as well. I could see no sign of Letia or any children other than three or four little boys squatted in a huddle near the water's edge, playing in the sand.

Suddenly, in the midst of the boys, up popped a heap of blond hair. *Alec!*

I was both relieved that I had found him and afraid to get up and retrieve him. If I hollered loud enough for him to hear, the Indians in the camp would hear me as well. He was busily playing with the other boys, oblivious to my predicament and no help at all.

I had to do something, so I bunched my dress into my lap and crawled, crablike, to a beached tree stump a little closer to where Alec was playing. I waited a few minutes, ten minutes, safely hidden and kept my eyes on the Indian boys. None of them seemed to pay any particular attention to the little blond boy. They spoke to each other in a mumble mixed with an unusual clicking sound. They passed seaweed and stones and beach wood back and forth to Alec. He seemed to miss nothing for lack of knowing their language.

I would have stayed and watched the boys' industry, but the sun was getting low over the western mountains. In a little while Ma would be worried and send Pa to look for us. I had to get Alec, and we had to get home.

"Alec," I said, straightening my knees. The words got stuck in my throat and came out hardly louder than a whisper.

No one moved.

"Alec," I called again, and then crouched down quickly to hide.

My voice was louder than the first time, but Alec didn't look up— none of the boys so much as turned their heads. I peered around the log and looked toward the camp. One of the women looked up and pointed to my hiding place. I retreated farther out of sight. I held my breath. I had been seen. I had to act quickly.

I judged the distance between the camp and the boys, and between the boys and my location. I decided that if I moved quickly, I could race to the boys and grab Alec, and the two of us could outrun the women back to the point. We would have enough of a head start that no one could catch us, even if they could run twice as fast as we could. I imagined the whole scenario and was sure we were in no danger of being caught.

But I didn't move. I couldn't. Ma's warnings of danger buzzed around in my head like bumblebees. My legs were stiff and heavy like beached logs.

What if there were men lurking about nearby? What if they were waiting behind the very logs that surrounded me? I wondered if they were watching me at that very minute. And Alec. To steal us. Or worse.

To my surprise, Letia appeared in the doorway of one of the sheds… with a little girl. They sat next to the women, who were by then craning their necks, searching the seashore in my direction.

I waited another two minutes…five minutes…hoping Letia would come and join me. But then, out of the blue, Alec stood up and stretched his arms over his head. It was my chance. I sprang to my feet and shouted, "Alec, come here right now."

"Hope?" he called.

"Over here, come!" I hollered and swung my arms wildly in the air.

He picked up his bucket and started toward me. I ran to meet him, grabbed his hand and dragged him along the shore.

"Hope," he protested.

"Just hurry," I said.

We raced to the point, leapt over the mound of logs and sand, and didn't stop running until we reached the maple. Alec let go of my hand and collapsed on the ground.

"Hope," he gasped. "That was a long run."

I leaned against the tree and wrapped my arms around myself as sharp pains stabbed into my sides.

I said, "Your boots! They're wet. Look at them."

Then I stopped—I couldn't scold him. He was safe.

All I could think about was how much I wanted to take off my boots, my stockings, my bonnet and apron…and run back to Letia. I would tie my dress in a knot and splash through the water with my new friend.

Alec's chin drooped against his chest as he prepared for a good telling off.

"I was so worried about you, Alec," I said softly. I brushed the sand off his trousers. "Why did you go past the maple tree?"

"I heard something, and I followed the noise. It was the ravens squawking. I followed them to where the boys were playing, and I joined them." His face was bright with anticipation. "Can we go back tomorrow?"

The day's events rushed through my head. And with the men coming for supper, I knew it wasn't over yet.

"I don't know," I said.

How could I possibly know what tomorrow would bring?

Lamalcha Camp, Summer Island, Summer 1862 ≋

The things that concerned me most that summer
    were the habits of Acheewan.
    He was a great man in Lamalcha territory.
    He lived nearby,
    although no one knew for sure
    precisely where his home was located.
    The whisky traders called him a warrior,
    but to us he was a headman.
    Not a headman like Father
    with a family and a village.
    Acheewan was the headman
    in charge of protecting the territory from invaders.
    He had magical skills and powers
    that only spirit beings understood.
    When he was trapped or cornered
    by a warring tribe,
    he became invisible—
    only to reappear in safety later
    to mock his pursuers.

Grandmother said Acheewan
    had lived not just one lifetime
    like a human being.
    She could not remember his birth—
    no one could—

or the name of his mother.
He came from generations ago, she said.
Since before Grandfather
and Great-Grandfather,
he had been in charge of removing foreigners
from Lamalcha territory
when their canoes came to shore
with no-good intentions.

Grandmother said Acheewan was the reason
the Lamalcha were feared throughout the coast.
And he was the reason we lived safely on our islands.

At first, looking upon him, he appeared angry
because across his forehead and between his eyes
was a deep purple scar,
proof of a man's attempt
to cut his head into two pieces.

Acheewan was my favourite visitor.
He was the greatest storyteller in the territory.
When he came to our island,
the evenings were set aside for his stories.
We sat without a word while he told us
how he waited for the Haida and the Bella Coola
when they came with five or ten canoes together
heading south to Victoria.
"They were hungry, those northern hordes," he said,
"not for food but for excitement.
They came for our women, because our women
are the most beautiful women on the coast
and hard workers as well.
Our women make the Lamalcha the envy of every man."
He paid special attention to Mother when he said such things,
for there wasn't a woman among us more beautiful.

Our eyes bulged and jaws gaped with amazement
when he swung his arms wildly
and pitched his voice with excitement.
Each time he told a story,
it got longer and bigger
and bigger and longer.
We cooked a feast in his honour
when he arrived,
and the men filled his canoe with food and provisions
when he left.

But the summer of my thirteenth year
                    Acheewan's visits were different.
He scowled when he told his stories,
not anymore of the Haida and Bella Coola.
"It is the hwunitum that threaten our territory,"
he said more seriously than before
                    and not with nearly as much pride.

One day, when Acheewan's canoe came to shore,
Swiltu and I rushed to meet him,
excited.
I remembered the greetings he once had for me:
a bonk on the head, a dance, a laugh.
Father and Uncle Nanute overtook us on the shore.
"Letia," Father said, "leave us alone.
We have to attend to business."
Acheewan didn't so much
as toss his hand at me or look my way.
He followed Father up the bank
to where they stood behind the lodge,
elbow to elbow.
Grandmother and Mother and a few of the other women
stood with the men,

their backs to us.
"Take Swiltu," Mother said to me.
            "This is not a place for children."
A chill shot up my spine.
Never before had I been excluded
from Acheewan's visits.

His intentions were no doubt important
and not in a good way.
The adults had grave looks on their faces
and shook their heads furiously.
He had come to express a disagreement with the People.
What could that mean?

Grandmother said that when a man's stomach is full
he is happy,
so in the evening,
when the adults finished their business,
I served Acheewan stew and roasted clams,
tried to persuade him to eat.
He took only a few bites,
and without looking,
he turned his back on the food,
mumbling something under his breath
I could not understand.
We sat in the circle.
I waited anxiously for him to speak.
Flames darted into the night sky,
            snapped noisily
                    and exploded.

"My People!"
He leapt to his feet and spoke with a loud voice.
"We have a more dangerous enemy
than the Haida and Bella Coola.

The hwunitum have come to our land
in numbers we cannot count.
They stay.
They take what they want.
They do not know the laws of our People,
for they think our land is their land."
He paced around the circle,
fiercely driving his spear into the ground and
then lifting it over his head.
His voice boomed,
"We must drive them away,"
and then he shrank
like a raccoon skulking into a den.
There were no stars and no moon in the sky that night.
I did not take my eyes off his form.
Around and around he skulked,
cast by the light of the fire
and then into the blackness,
grinding holes in the sand with his footsteps.

That night I did not sleep.
Would the Queen's men think
Acheewan had killed the Cowichan hwunitum?
If the men in Victoria took Acheewan and accused him of murder,
what would become of us?
Did he plan to kill all the hwunitum
who travelled through the territory?
What about Hope and her family?

      Did Acheewan plan to kill them?

Sunnydale, Wallace Island, Autumn 1862 ❧

It was almost suppertime when we got back to the house. I could smell bubbling hot apple pie before I swung open the door.

"Ummm, yummm," I said. "Something smells delicious."

Ma was sitting at the table cutting vegetables.

"It's a beautiful day," I said, my blood still rushing from the excitement of losing and then finding Alec. "Alec and I have been playing at the seashore. The water is unseasonably warm."

"Yes," Ma said, without expression or acknowledgement of our current burst of energy or our earlier absence.

"Can I help?" I asked.

"No," she said shortly, her lips pinched thin, and then added, "Thank you, dear. I am almost finished." I stepped closer to her. She passed me a carrot. "You must be hungry. Supper will be ready soon."

I took the carrot and headed upstairs. I might as well have been invisible. Ma, who had once been diligent in her control over every one of our activities, had become uninterested. It was as if her mind was so fully consumed with worry about our safety, in her fear she abandoned us altogether.

I took Ruby from my pocket and flopped on my bed. I pulled out a favourite book, which I had stored under my pillow. I crawled under the blanket beside my doll and began to read:

Little Martin was a great favourite in the Indian village...

The next thing I heard was the hammering sound of a man laughing, *har, har, har,* rousing me from sleep.

I started to read again:

Little Martin was a great favourite in the Indian village. The Indian who saved his life was particularly fond of him...

"Har, har, har."

The sound of Old Man Albert's laugh gave me goosebumps. I tried to ignore his loud outbursts.

Little Martin was a great favourite in the Indian village...

"Hope, Alec," Ma called. "It's suppertime."

I closed the book and held my breath. Suddenly I was overcome by an awful thought. It was a feeling that I'd had before, but one that I had successfully pushed away without letting it form a clear idea in my mind. But when the awful sound of Old Man Albert imposed itself on me, I could no longer avoid the thought: the fate of my family was being decided without me. I had no say in what would become of Wallace Island, Sunnydale, the Richardsons. I didn't have a say in what was going to become of me, or even Ruby. Fuelled by Ma's panic, the future of our family was being determined by the likes of Old Man Albert and Mr. Haws. The thought left me feeling queasy.

Little Martin was a great favourite in the Indian village. The Indian who saved his life was particularly fond of him...

Tears welled in my eyes until the words became so blurry I couldn't read.

"Hope." Ma's voice sounded the way people talk when there is a party—full of airs and graces. Not at all the way it had earlier—dismissive and removed. "Supper is ready, dear."

I held my book up to my face and waited for Charlotte to call. Suppertime followed a very distinctive pattern in our family—Ma called Alec and me once, and then a few minutes later she called again. After another wait of three, not more than five minutes, if we didn't show up at the table, Charlotte called a last time and warned us that Ma was getting impatient. Ma and Charlotte were very precise about supper. Once it was ready, they expected everyone to appear instantly.

If I read the paragraph completely before Charlotte calls my name, then the decision has not already been made. There is still time for me to persuade Pa to stay on Wallace Island.

I read as fast as I could.

Little Martin was a great favourite in the Indian village. The Indian who saved his life was particularly fond of him, and he was loath to let Martin's pa take him away.

I heard Charlotte's voice downstairs.

But the trapper had saved the life of the Indian's boy, and he could not refuse…

Before I had time to finish the sentence—*to restore the white boy to his pa*—Alec called from the bottom of the stairs.

"Hope, Ma is getting angry. It's supper, and she's already called twice."

His words were exactly as Charlotte's would have been.

If I read the paragraph completely before Charlotte calls…

I thought hard. Now what? I didn't get through the paragraph. And it was Alec, not Charlotte. But he'd said the same words as she would have. Exactly. So it was almost Charlotte.

I sat on the side of my bed and pointed my toes toward the stairs. The sound of cutlery and chairs came from the kitchen. I picked up my book and read the rest of the paragraph, just to be sure.

"Come on, Hope. Supper is ready," Alec called with the same annoyed tone as Charlotte would have used.

"Coming."

I stood on the landing and waited.

I think I can be sure. Charlotte has still not called, and I have surely finished the paragraph.

I took one step, and with much deliberation, another and another. I was in no hurry to see the men or hear what they had to say.

Ma met me at the bottom of the stairs. All signs of her earlier distress had disappeared from her face.

If I could have anticipated Ma's moods, I would have felt more settled. And Pa's as well, for I could not foresee his disposition any better than Ma's. In fact there was nothing about my family that I could depend upon, nothing that made sense to me anymore.

At the table, Ma sat at one end with Baby Dot. She wore a new lace collar and had a pert and unusually curious look on her face. She eagerly asked the men questions about a ship that had arrived from England full of young women. A hundred or so had come to the new country to be wives for single men in the territory, for there were far too many male settlers compared with the number of women.

"And imagine," Ma said with a coy look at Old Man Albert. "You might have gotten one yourself."

"Only a day late, I was," he gurgled. "They took the women, dozens of them, to the marine barracks. Single men from miles around, those eligible to take a wife, came and looked the women up and down. Some as young as sixteen."

I found it an unpleasant thing to hear him tell such a story.

"The men only had to point to a girl, like that." He directed his stumpy finger at Charlotte. "And she was his, as easy as that. From there, he took her home to marry. A man of God was there, he was, to bless the union."

What pitiable girls! I imagined them holding onto each other...men of all ages and sizes examining them...like goats at the market...*oh, what a fine neck she has...and strong*...until each man found a girl who would tickle his fancy. I shivered to think that some of the poor girls were only four years older than I was. How lucky for them that Old Man Albert was a day late!

"Oh, how grand: that the once unfortunate girls will now be hon-oured to live in Victoria." Ma accentuated her voice with as distinguished and pretentious an English tone as she could muster. "Not like the prison we are forced to tolerate here on the island. Just think, Charlotte, you will soon have a house and a husband in Victoria. And when you do, I will be a regular guest."

At that moment, the conversation turned sharply from the frivolity of Ma's gossip to the business of gossip that had brought the men to the island.

"Oh, my dear lady," Old Man Albert whined. "This is not just a prison. It is worse than that, it is. You are right, my most gracious hostess, it will be God's blessing when your precious family leaves this desperately dan-gerous place. I must tell you, conditions are getting worse, they are."

Old Man Albert tried to speak with sophistication, like a man who had been educated, but lumps of potatoes sprayed from his mouth back onto his plate and the table. He wasn't a bright man, but he knew enough to recognize Ma's high breeding, and enough to know that he should try to put on the best manners he could muster. But his attempts at high speech were slovenly and grotesque.

An angry rush of mottled red skin coloured Pa's neck and behind his ears. His lips quivered as if he were about to speak, but he held his tongue.

"There was one murder before Christmas, the two on nearby islands in the last few months, and now we have heard there was one more near Cowichan, John. That makes four murders in less than a year." Mr. Haws counted his fingers, pulling each one on his left hand up with those on his right, and then held up his palm as if to say *stop*.

Before Pa had a chance to reply, the men began describing terrible confrontations south of the border. Wagon trains were brutally attacked. Unruly Indians appeared in the dead of night and carried away innocent women and children. Settlers died at the hands of the Indians and were left strewn in the fields with their scalps mercilessly sliced from their heads.

"The Indians ride fast ponies," Alec said. His eyes bulged with excitement. "Uncle Tom told us about the ponies."

"Yes, very fast ponies," Mr. Haws said. "But not as fast as the cavalry."

"The women and children…," Old Man Albert said with the gripping anticipation of a chilling ghost story. He closed one eye and squinted out of the other, first at Charlotte, then at me and then Alec.

"What about the women and children?" Charlotte whimpered.

Old Man Albert put his fork down and straightened his rounded shoulders the best he could. "They steal and kill the women and children, they do," he said. A hush fell over the family. "And more."

No one dared to ask what he meant by *more*. Finally Pa interrupted the horrible conversation.

"Albert, there are children at the table. And furthermore, there is no need for such fearsome talk here in this country." He spoke impatiently. "The United States has blood on its hands in regard to the Indians. Hopefully, sanity will prevail in this country and fear mongers like you will be quieted by reason. We are not a warlike people."

"John," Ma said with exasperation. "How can you be so sure? You don't know these people. They can't be trusted. It's not us; it's them who are a warlike people."

"They will protect what belongs to them, Eva," Pa said. "Any man would do the same, no matter who he is. If we treat them with respect, they will treat us with respect. They are not wanton murderers. We need our governor to come to more agreements with them about the land."

In my book, *The Trapper*, the Indians were friendly to the white boy. They looked after him well until his pa returned.

Old Man Albert opened his mouth, full of food, and was about to speak, but Pa wasn't finished.

"I am not a slow-minded man," Pa said. "I hear what you men are saying. What we need to do, Albert, is talk to the Indians. Just as the governor did with the Indians at Victoria and Nanaimo, he must come to an agreement with the Cowichan about what land we may live on safely, and what land they want to retain for themselves. The governor promised to do so, but has not yet kept his word. It is no wonder they are angry."

"Pshaw," Ma exclaimed. "Don't talk such nonsense, John. What do you mean, the land they want to retain? What do you mean, an agreement? I am surprised at you. This is all our land, rightfully granted by the Queen of England."

"Eva is right," Mr. Haws interjected. "The government gave you a pre-emption for this land. The Indians must be dealt with. There's no more to be said."

Pa ignored Mr. Haws and shot an angry look toward Ma. "Trust me, Eva," he said with disdain. "What I am saying is far from nonsense."

Old Man Albert cleared his throat and said, "You may have a point, John, but we are here to tell you that no one is going to have that discussion with the Indians of this territory. You and your family are in danger, you are, unless you move off this island, as we have discussed, and find safety where there are other settlers dwelling."

Old Man Albert's words, although seemingly less harsh than those of Mr. Haws, gouged my belly.

Move off this island?

I hated the way it sounded. And it had been said before. The plans were already being made…without me.

Lamalcha Camp, Wallace Island, Autumn 1862 🖎

When Mother finally finished weaving her blanket,
   she called us together.
   We gathered around her loom.
   Father, the men, the women and children,
   the whole camp stood facing her loom.
   It had been specially built
   to accommodate the size of her new blanket.
   It was a matter of great importance and pride for our People
   to have a blanket of this size and worth,
   and a blanket weaver of this skill.
   The People looked on in awe.
   The thing about the blanket
   was that we had all seen it,
   every day,
   as Mother sat in front of her loom
   weaving row after row.
   But it was the thought of completion
   that struck the People:
   that she had started and finished such an enormous blanket
   in just one summer.

"Oh, what a beautiful blanket..."
"You are the most talented weaver in our village..."
She was bashful.
It was not becoming for a woman

to boast of her accomplishments.
But Father knew, as did everyone else, that
Mother was a woman of vast worth.
Men and women came to her
to hear the history of the People.
She could recite the names of the ancestors
to ten and twenty generations.
She knew the tangled web of sons and daughters,
marriages, deaths and second and third marriages.
She could unwind the story back and back and back...
to a time when giant People
stepped from island to island across to the mainland.
If there was a dispute
whether a girl and boy should marry,
the parents came to Mother.
She told their family stories backwards
to see if the two young people were related.
Her father had taught her these things
when she was a little girl.
"You have a special gift of memory," he told her.
"Your mind is like a deep cave.
It holds onto everything you hear."
Memory and history were not Mother's only gifts.
She was skilled in womanly arts.
Her hands were as deft at weaving
as those of any woman on the islands.
She dreamed of beautiful designs,
and as her fingers twisted the wool,
fine-looking combinations of colour and pattern emerged.

Grandmother and I stood on either side of her loom.
We held the corners of the blanket
while Mother pulled out the dowels.
The giant sleeping mat fell heavily into our arms,
almost knocking me over.

Mother and Father helped us lay the blanket down
on the clean grass under a tree.
The People lifted the edges with their fingers
and expressed their amazement at what they saw.
After a while Mother quieted them down
to make an announcement:
"This blanket is a new sleeping mat for my daughter Letia," she said.
"May her rest be always peaceful.
May she learn the art of weaving, as I have,
and as my mother and her mother did before me."
Even though Grandmother had already told me of Mother's secret,
for Grandmother and I shared everything,
I was as surprised and delighted
as if I had not known.
It was surely the most beautiful blanket in the world,
and as highly valued as any of our People's possessions.
The centre panel was white, a very bright white,
made with the finest goat wool and dog hair,
bleached for many days in the hot sun.
The borders had lines of red and yellow and brown,
designs fashioned after arrows and waves and leaves and flowers.
The People formed a circle around the weaving.
Mother led me to the blanket,
where I sat
as if petals had opened
to reveal me at the centre.
Father and Uncle Nanute drummed.
Grandmother sang about the beauty and wealth of women.
She thanked Mother for being such a good wife for her son
and teased her about her beauty.
"My son has been blessed with a swan
with a long, slender and elegant neck," she said.
The People laughed.
That day I was the richest and luckiest girl in the world.

Sunnydale, Wallace Island, Autumn 1862 ❧

Pa stood up from his chair.

"There is a nip in the air," he said. He turned away from the table. "Eva, we'll take our pie in the sitting room."

The men followed him. The rest of us trailed behind. Charlotte and Ma served pie and fresh cream.

"The water is darkening, and the tides shifting," Pa said. "The seagulls are determined to let us know the weather is taking a turn for the worse."

No one said a word.

"The Indians are preparing to return to their winter village on Kuper Island. They will be gone before another month is over," Pa said.

"Can we watch them? Can we go to their camp and help them?" Alec asked, immediately perked up by the thought of playing with the little boys.

I shot a look in Alec's direction that meant, *Be careful what you say.*

"What an absurd idea," Ma snapped. "Why would you say such a thing?"

Luckily, Alec caught my eye and decided not to say any more.

After a prickly silence, Old Man Albert coughed up a gurgling lump from his throat and spat into his handkerchief.

"Have you thought about the lovely village on Mayne Island?" he asked. "There are five families there. They've recently built a church, and they have a teacher for the children. They hold school lessons in the new building, they do. The Saanetch Indians have a summer camp nearby, but the settlers feel quite safe in their numbers. I have talked to Samuel

Cooper, and he is looking forward to your move. The children will make a welcome addition to their village, they will."

Ma picked up her knitting and, without looking at him, she asked, "How will we move our belongings?"

"We have a boat ready. It's available whenever you are, it is," he replied.

"And where did you say that we will live?"

Suddenly things became clearer. Ma was making the plans, the men and Ma—not Pa. Did these despicable whisky traders stick their noses in everybody's business for the sake of a few meals?

"The Cooper family has room for you temporarily, until the barn is converted."

"How many other children are there on Mayne Island, did you say?"

"Eight."

Was this Ma's way of telling us that the plans had already been made?

One man had donated a barn to be converted into a house; another had room for our family while the conversion took place; others had offered to form a building crew—all that was left for Pa to do was buy the land. And apparently the men had arranged that as well. If Old Man Albert was to be believed, our family could be moved immediately and resettled in a matter of a few months or so.

My fingers and toes began to tingle. A numb, prickly feeling moved up my arms and legs until my whole body felt as if it no longer belonged to me. Could this be true? Who'd come up with the idea of moving to Mayne Island? Were there plans that had been settled? Had everyone been informed but me? Was I the only one who was alarmed?

I wanted to scream: *What about Pa? Isn't anyone going to listen to him?*

"Mr. Cooper is a good man," Pa said.

Mr. Haws said, "A wonderful man."

Suddenly it sounded to me as if Pa was siding with the men—that he was part of their plans. If he had really wanted to stay on Wallace Island, he would not have allowed the plans to advance unchecked. I knew that Pa didn't like the men any more than I did, yet his protest was so feeble. If I'd had my way, the men would have been banished from Sunnydale as soon as they first arrived. The whole dreadful plan would have been laid to rest, and my family would not be contemplating relocating to Mayne Island, or any other island.

After the men and Ma discussed for a few more minutes the details of moving to a village, Pa leaned forward in his chair.

"Eva," he said firmly, pointing his finger at her. "We will consider these things together. Later. Alone. I am perfectly capable of taking care of my family. I don't need Mr. Haws and Old Man Albert making plans for us."

Pa's words fell on the room like sleet. The chilly hush that followed was broken only by the clicking of knitting needles and the fleshy sound of Old Man Albert's wheezing.

I was working on a pair of blue socks, trying to turn the heel, but my fingers had become too numb to move. I put the needles down and rubbed my hands.

Pa needs my help.

It was obvious to me that he was about to do something he didn't want to do.

Ma and the men had persuaded him to leave his beloved Sunnydale. I couldn't sit idly by and watch his dream slip away because of a scary tale told by whisky traders.

Mr. Haws broke the silence. "What you are forgetting, John, is that the Indians can't be trusted. You never know what danger you may be in."

I hadn't intended to speak. I hadn't planned what to say or imagined that I could, even with careful thought and articulation, change Ma's mind and reverse the desperate state of affairs. But, without warning, my mouth opened and words spewed out.

"You can trust a man to protect his family and take care of his people," I blurted. All eyes turned in my direction.

"We don't need to run away from the Indians. They are people like we are, and this was their home first. Why wouldn't they be angry with us for taking their land? Why don't the men from Victoria talk to them? Like Pa did. And besides, what business is it of yours what we do on our island?" I fastened my eyes on Old Man Albert. "Why don't you leave us alone?"

Ma remained slack-jawed until my impertinence was more than she could bear. "Hold your tongue, child," she said through lips that barely moved.

Old Man Albert shook his head. "Tsk, tsk," he said. "If only life were as simple as the mind of a child, if only."

Pa looked at me. His eyes were tired.

"And it is, Albert," he said. "It is as profound as the mind of a child as well. If only, Hope...if only." His chin dropped to his chest, and his shoulders slumped forward, as if he had run a long race and lost.

Pa had given up! He had conceded to the men and Ma. He hadn't lost the race; he had let them win. I could not bear to see him so defeated. Sunnydale would soon be gone forever—his dreams, all that he had worked for...my dreams...gone. I was watching it happen right before my eyes. I threw my knitting into the basket and dashed across the room and up the stairs. I flung myself onto the bed.

One minute, two minutes, I waited and listened.

If Charlotte mounts the stairs before I count to ten, then Pa will change his mind. If Charlotte mounts the stairs...

"One, two, three," I started slowly. "Four, five."

I paused and listened. "Six."

I heard Alec say, "Goodnight."

"Seven...eight..."

Charlotte's footsteps? "Nine."

I stopped counting to listen. The bottom stair creaked. "Ten."

I was sure. The quiet padding of Charlotte's feet was undeniable.

I got out of bed and slipped into my nightdress.

I hadn't reached ten before Charlotte mounted the stairs. There was still time for Pa to change the direction of the conversation downstairs.

When I wake up in the morning, it will be life as usual at Sunnydale.

Lamalcha Camp, Summer Island, Autumn 1862 ≋

It was a breezy morning
    a few days after I received my blanket.
    I was playing a game of imagination
    with Little Brother on the shore.
    We danced and sang a Persuasion Song,
    convincing the salmon in the channel
    that they should follow us
    into our imaginary river and to our lake,
    where we would climb on their backs
    and ride the great fish back out to the deep sea
    to meet the ocean monsters.

    Acheewan paddled up to the shore.
    Little Brother and I stopped our game
    and watched him lift his canoe,
    using one hand, as if it were as light as a twig.
    He dropped it hard near the bulrushes.
    We were ready to follow.
    We expected him to climb the bank in search of Father.
    Instead, he plunked himself down beside his beached canoe.
    He bent his knees around his ears
    and buried his face in his hands.
    Little Brother and I kept our eyes on him.
    He didn't move.
    His chest was still;

not one breath went in or came out.
We crept closer
so we wouldn't miss a thing,
so close we met a wall of cold air
and went no closer.
He looked more like carved stone
than a man of flesh and blood.
If he had not been such a great man,
we would have approached him
and poked him with our fingers
to see if he was alive or dead.

But Acheewan was a mighty man,
and we were only children.
So we snuck up the bank to find Father.
We explained that it had been at least half the morning
since Acheewan had arrived.
"From that time," we said,
both Little Brother and I,
talking at the same time out of excitement,
"he has not taken one breath."
Before long, Father joined Acheewan on the beach,
with the two of us following closely behind.
The two men sat side by side.
Grandmother brought them each a bowl of duck soup,
and they talked quietly.

At the fire that night, Acheewan didn't sit down.
He stood off to the side of the circle.
He looked sharply from one person to another,
then off to the trees,
the sky,
his eyes flitting wildly like the flames.
He was searching,
but it didn't seem to me that he could see.

Father ignored his strange behaviour
and welcomed him.
"Acheewan," Father said,
"has come with a message for our People."

Acheewan strutted around in a circle behind us,
lifting his knees to his chest with each step.
I didn't turn my head
or even dare take a breath when he came near.
A cold draft of air washed over me
each time he passed,
just as it had when he was sitting at the beach.
He snorted and growled like an angry bear.
The People were as silent and still as flies in the night.
Even the sparks from the fire
burst with no more than a murmur into the night sky.
Suddenly, into the silence,
he erupted into a thunderous roar.
The ferocious sound of hordes of wild animals
came from his belly.
He squatted,
then leapt into the air,
both feet reaching higher than the head of a man.
Like an ungainly bird attempting to fly,
he took to the sky.
I shivered…
for we were in the presence of the spirits of the ancestors
who had entered him.
Father walked a short distance behind him,
to guide his earthly body safely around the fire.

Suddenly, as quickly as his outburst had begun,
it stopped.
He breathed a few terrible, mournful gasps.
In the shadow of the fire,

I saw him squish his eyes tightly shut and
then open them wide.
He twisted his lips and nose.
He made one last contorted expression;
then his countenance was calm
and his voice
as soft as a mother murmuring to her baby.

"Hwunitum are descending on our land like flocks of vultures.
With them have come diseases our People cannot endure.
They bring their dung and strong drink.
They spoil our land and our bodies.
And now there are only a few of us left.
We have allowed ourselves to be deluded by pots and pans.
We must stop their insolence,
                    and our delusions.
Our dead, who are still warm,
are here tonight with us.
I have heard the recently departed speak.
They say that while the hwunitum have not yet taken the bodies
of those of us who are still alive,
                    yet we are giving them our minds and our spirits.
We are empty vessels walking blind and dead.
The recently departed see our folly clearly
from the other side. They say,
Do not be enchanted by their trinkets.
Listen to your ancestors
before it is too late for you as well.
This is what they have said to me tonight."

Then he sat down,
and no one said a word.
The People bowed their heads. Then, one by one,
each person got up from the fire
and went off to bed.

I followed Grandmother,
but I could not sleep.
I sat up wide-eyed and quaking
and saw the faces of the dead
                    and felt their chilly fingers pointing.

The next morning Mother got up early.
She filled a cooking pot with fresh water
and put it on the fire to boil.
She went out into the forest
and collected healing medicines.
When I woke,
steam was rising out of the pot
and filling the air with the herbs' sweet fragrance.
Mother swept the ground
where Acheewan had passed
with freshly cut cedar branches,
swish,
swish,
to send the ancestors away peacefully.

A few days after Acheewan's visit,
the whisky traders returned.
After completing their mission of trade
with Uncle Penu,
they brought news for Father. They said,
"Acheewan has been accused of killing hwunitum.
Men in Victoria are searching for him.
They say he is a dangerous man on a killing rampage."
The whisky traders warned the People,
"Don't be seen with this man."
Father led them back to their boat
and dismissed them coldly:
"We do not need you coming to our camp stirring up trouble."
He told the men nothing of Acheewan's whereabouts.

Sunnydale, Wallace Island, Autumn 1862

Days went by; the men didn't return to the island. Yet life was anything but usual. Ma and Pa didn't tell me that our family was moving, not in so many words; in fact no one said much to anyone about anything. But I knew. We all knew.

Ma went about cleaning everything—the cutlery, the china, the blankets, the windows. Pa spent from early morning until evening in his workshop, lining up his tools as if counting them over and over again. Charlotte helped Ma hang the wash on the clothesline and polish the silverware. Alec was pleased enough to skip his lessons, although he spent most of his time walking aimlessly, wondering what to do. Preoccupied with their own unspoken missions, Ma and Pa seemed to forget to charge Alec with even his most rudimentary chores.

I wanted to do something, anything, that would change everything, but nothing I did made any difference. No one listened to me.

"Ma," I said. "With time, this tension will pass. The Indians will accept the settlers. We will be safe."

She dipped her cloth into the sodium and scrubbed a silver spoon.

"You don't understand, Hope," she sighed.

I did understand this much: Ma wouldn't change her mind.

During the day I was free to do as I pleased. After some time passed, my curiosity about Letia overcame me, and I began exploring the forest each day at the same time as before. I waited near the stream where Letia had bathed. I made Alec triple promise that he would not tell a soul, not even if his life depended on it. I walked to the berry patch, although there was not one ripe berry left.

I had no success until the fourth day. I knew from the minute I passed Pa's woodpile that the day would be different. I raced through the shafts of sunlight in the forest, nimbly jumping the moss green forms of old windfalls and dodging the snaking salal. My heart was light. I felt the presence of my friend in the trees. I passed the unsullied calm of the bathing hole with only a sideways glance. She was not there.

I stopped when I reached the opening in the forest where the branches of the berry shrubs mounded over the giant granite outcropping.

"Huuuupe!" Letia called.

She was sitting on the grass with her back against a rock, as if she had been waiting.

"Lah tee ahh!"

She got up. She took both my hands in hers and held them high in the air. Together we turned in a circle, our eyes catching brief glimpses of each other. After a few turns, we stopped dancing. With one hand she led me deep into the heart of the forest. I was alone with Letia.

I shivered in ripples of cool, damp air. I strained to see in the shadowy darkness where only thin streams of sunlight reached the ground. We walked quietly for twenty minutes or so—linked by our fingers—until, like a curtain pulled back, the forest opened onto a meadow and the eastern shore of the island. Letia guided me to a soft blanket of mossy grass. We sat side by side, hip to hip, our legs lined up in a row like four branches, and we watched the ravens swoop and holler.

It was a dramatic performance indeed. The birds teamed up like a gang of hooligans, squawking an awful racket as they chased a lone eagle, pecking at the poor victim's tail feathers.

We laughed, Letia and I, at the audacity of the black birds, and at the utter hopelessness of the eagle. Although it looked to me that with its mighty wingspan and majestic soaring flight the eagle could have, in one swoop, defended itself and driven away the inferior birds, it did not do so.

As the afternoon progressed, the wind stiffened. I shivered and my teeth chattered so vigorously that Letia motioned for us to return. I was clothed from head to toe, yet I was covered with goosebumps. Letia's bare legs and arms and belly were smooth. She had no need to rub her skin or wrap her arms around herself to keep warm. It made me wonder if clothes succeeded in their duty to keep the body warm. It seemed to me that the habit of covering might cause a dependency. If I wore only a short skirt, would my body become accustomed to the cold in time to prevent me from freezing to death?

We walked side by side, hand in hand, through the forest to the fork in the path. We stopped.

"Goodbye," I said.

"Goodbye," Letia said perfectly. She picked up my other hand and squeezed them both tightly.

"Huuuupe," she said.

"Lah tee ahh," I said.

Our friendship was sealed. I had no doubt that Letia felt the same.

That evening I rushed through my chores anticipating solitude, aching to recall every moment of our hours together.

I said, "I'm tired."

And I retired quickly up the stairs, slipped into my nightdress and slid into bed. I pulled Ruby next to me and closed my eyes, waiting to dream of Letia.

I am looking for her in the dark green quiet of the forest; then she is beside me at the mossy edge of the still green pool. We swim together. We dive under the surface...

"I'll be right up," Ma called to Charlotte, interrupting my glorious dream.

Charlotte trudged up the stairs and dressed for bed. Ma followed a few minutes later. She wrapped the blankets around Charlotte and sat beside her.

"But Ma," Charlotte whined. "I thought we were leaving this god-forsaken place. You promised, Ma. You promised."

"I know I did, darling," Ma said. "But the timing isn't up to me."

"You said Pa had agreed. We have already prepared."

"He has. But the day has not been set. The good people at Mayne Island are waiting for us...yet Pa stubbornly delays our departure."

"Please, Ma. Get him to hurry. Another day will be too many. I cannot bear the wait."

I lay perfectly still, feigning sleep. Pa had agreed. In my absence, in my fixation on finding Letia, not only had my fate been sealed, but the preparations had been made without me. I had, I suppose, without a word, struck an agreement with my mother and sister: they left me alone, and I did the same to them. And now, with a jolt, I was thrust back to the horrid truth.

"We must be patient, Charlotte. My nagging only made him dig his heels in deeper. I have not said a word to him in days."

The plans had been made, there was no doubt about it, but Pa had been reluctant to make our fate known, to announce the move to Mayne Island. I wasn't sure whether to be grateful or resentful for my weeks of ignorant bliss.

Charlotte sobbed.

I didn't sleep until the early morning. I was annoyed and exhausted by thoughts so relentless I could not stop their flow. I was vexed by the belief that if only I tried hard enough, I could think of a way to convince Pa to put a stop to the giant mistake he was about to make.

Lamalcha Camp, Summer Island, Autumn 1862 ≋

Before that summer, I had looked forward to visitors.
They marked the best times on Summer Island,
especially Acheewan and Uncle Moosma.
We'd watch the channel and wait for the black dots
to turn into sails and canoes,
then guess the identity of the stick men
before they became visible.
But in the summer I met Hope,
one visitor after the other
had brought news of trouble.
It was as if everything foretold a catastrophe:
Whisky traders.
Murders.
Hwunitum descending on Lamalcha territory.
Acheewan.
A storm was surely boiling around our gentle little island.
Something monstrous
was twisting and turning behind the mountains.
I didn't know how the disaster would happen or when,
but the heaviness of it
wrapped itself around my shoulders
and weighed me down.
At the bottom of it
were the hwunitum,
and that meant Hope and her father.

Oh! I wished it weren't so.

I sat on a log and gazed over the horizon,
thinking about Hope
and how I might plan to see her.
I had gone to the berry patch
every other day or so
and found nothing.
If only I could talk to her,
tell her the trouble brewing
and make a plan to keep her safe.

Swiltu sat next to me,
        fidgeting.
"Let's go, Letia," she said,
"and find Little Brother,"
who was not little at all
compared to her,
but was named *Little* in comparison to Big Brother,
and the name just stuck.
"You go," I said.
"I will stay for a while
and watch the sun turn the mountains red."
She frowned and leapt off the log.
She scurried up the bank.

As Grandmother said,
        "Nothing stays the same."
I watched the sky changing colour
and wanted to slow it down.
I wished it would take its time,
for the world was changing too fast for me.
I did not know where it was going.
All I wanted was the calm I used to feel
before fear had disrupted

our peaceful island.

I saw the black spot on the horizon.
I followed it as it grew
and came closer and closer.
I knew it was Uncle Moosma,
Mother's brother, from Chemainus,
our neighbours to the south.
"Uncle! Uncle!" I called
and ran to greet him at the water's edge
—for he required no formal welcome and permission
to come ashore.
"Letia, my little butterfly," he said.
He picked me up
and twirled me around and around
until I was giggling and my head was spinning,
my eyeballs loose in their sockets.
But instead of putting me down and laughing
while I staggered like a short-legged bird,
he set me hard on the ground and asked,
"Where is your father?"
The tone of his voice surprised me.
Before I had time to answer,
he stomped directly up the bank
past Mother and the other women.
I staggered behind him trying to regain my balance,
curious why he appeared so severe.

He found Father packing dried fish.
"It was not in protection of our islands
that the hwunitum have been killed," he said,
without so much as a greeting.
He raked his fingers through his hair
and shifted from foot to foot
as if he were standing on hot coals.

"It was for their guns and boots.
Acheewan did not kill the hwunitum.
The culprits are two young warriors from my village
who, like your brother Penu,
have befriended the whisky traders.
The young men have only just learned
the discipline of the warrior spirit,
yet they fill themselves with strong drink
until they are mindless and stupid."

I was relieved
when he said Acheewan
did not kill the hwunitum.
Surely if he had not committed the murder,
the men in Victoria could not accuse him.
Someone would tell them the truth.
Acheewan would be safe.
But my mind could not forget
            the rumblings of the spirits.
They were not pleased.
And I knew that if a warrior
used his spirit power to do wrong
instead of right,
he would bring a curse to the People.
It felt to me
            that a curse was brewing.

Father slumped forward.
He knew well the effects of whisky.
He'd often tried to persuade Uncle Penu
to pour the poison onto the rocks,
to send the foul traders away.
He'd warned Uncle Penu
that the whisky would one day take his mind
and never give it back.

"You will be left a madman," Father said.
Uncle Penu laughed and chided Father when he spoke this way.
"Then I will be a happy madman," he said.

Father shook his head slowly from side to side
at what Uncle Moosma had to say.
Never before had I seen his face look so glum.
"We must stop the whisky traders." Uncle's voice was stern.
"And our young men…
they will lead us into a war
for no cause other than their own folly!"
I could see
from the troubled look on Father's face
that there was no simple solution to this problem.

Uncle Moosma pulled on a few long hairs on his chin.
He lowered his brows
and peered out of slits in his eyelids.
"The hwunitum will use their own law, not ours."
His voice was rising.
"Once hwunitum law rules our territory,
as it does in Victoria, we will have no say
over our People or our land
or our way of life.
We will be their slaves in our own home."

"No, Brother."
Father spoke politely but in disagreement.
"Our People will find a way
to live in peace with the hwunitum.
They are our brothers as well."

Uncle Moosma was blunt:
"I think not."
Then he softened a bit.

"We will see, we will see.
I hope you are right,
but I fear you are not.
We will see, we will see."

That was all he said.
He did not call Father *Brother*
or hug him around his shoulders
or slap his back as he usually did.
I thought he went away angry,
but I wasn't sure,
because he turned quickly and made for his canoe.

That night I put my sleeping mat and blankets
as close to the warm embers of the fire as I could.
I lay awake for a long time.
The stars were bright.
Cold air bristled around my nostrils,
as if winter would set in early.
I rolled up in my blanket
to keep the chill from stealing its way to my body.
As if in a cocoon, I lay perfectly still
and gazed into the sky,
illuminated by layers and layers of stars
from one end of it to the other.
Suddenly the sky exploded,
flashes of light burst in every direction.
Stars zoomed across the night world
and plunged to the ground
to my left and right,
so close
I thought I would be lit on fire.
Thunder rumbled behind the mountains,
        closer and closer until the earth shuddered.
I squeezed my eyes tightly shut.

Shards of lightning lit my eyelids.
If these are the spirits, I thought,
then I will not move.

I remembered what Grandmother had said about such times
when the firmament speaks.
"Don't be afraid.
Be still and listen.
You will know what the spirits have to say."

So I stayed motionless,
until splatters of rain began to beat on my face
and trickle down my neck.
I wriggled free
and dragged my sleeping mat into the lodge
and set it down close to Mother and Father.
My heart pounded.
I snuggled close to Mother.
The ancestors are warning me,
I thought and listened hard.
I wanted to know what they had on their minds,
but I couldn't understand a word they were saying.

Sunnydale, Wallace Island, Autumn 1862 ❧

In the morning Pa was not in the house. I looked for him everywhere. I checked the animals, the workshop, the meadow. Without hesitating, I went behind the shed to the woodpile. He wasn't there—he was nowhere. His gun rested in its place on the gun rack above the door; his fishing gear stood in its place in the workshop; his axe and wedge were side by side on a chopping block. Where was he?

I hurried past the house, through the meadow and over the rocks to where the path met the pebbly seashore. I looked left and right. There was no sign of him. I ran toward the cliffs a short distance. He wasn't sitting on the rocky crag that had become his favourite perch from which to watch the tides.

Other than the white curly tips of the waves, the ocean was murky grey. The sky and the granite outcroppings shared the same dim colour. A stiff wind blew off the water and spits of rain cut into my cheeks. I raced to the maple tree and passed it without slowing down until I reached the point. Exhausted, I leaned over and gripped my sides.

There was only one place he could be. I gulped in a few deep breaths, stood up and took off again. I ran along the seashore to the Indian camp. There was no time to be afraid. I had to find Pa.

If Pa had made up his mind, if it was a sure thing that we were to leave Wallace Island, if we were moving to Mayne Island as Ma said, then why had he not told me? Could it be because he had not yet made up his mind? Was there still a small chance that Pa wavered? That the final decision had not been made? Then I had to find him. And quickly. I would convince him that an error had been made. The Indians were not to be feared. I was sure. I had a friend.

I stopped near a shallow bank in front of the camp, more than a little amazed by my confidence. But before I had time to consider my circumstances, an old woman appeared from behind the shacks. She motioned to me with her chin. I paused, unsure of what her gesture meant. She waved insistently until I scrambled up the hill. She took my hand and led me toward the shacks. Her hand was bony thin and felt like tanned leather. She smelled like greasy smoke. She walked quickly for someone so old—so quickly that I had to hurry to keep up with her.

Behind the first shack, in a place stacked with hides and bones, a group of women huddled together. Letia was with them. She had a little girl by her side. A few paces beyond the women, Pa and three Indian men were speaking to each other, their faces grimly set, as if the expressions were carved in stone. The Indian men's hair was long and bushy as if it hadn't been cut or combed for weeks, maybe months. Two of the men had bare chests and legs and were wearing only short woven skirts. The other, who was biggest, was draped in a thick white blanket bordered with a fine-looking red, yellow and brown geometric design. All three men stood shorter than Pa but were broader in the shoulders. They had thick muscled legs and wide feet that looked as though they had never worn shoes.

The old woman pulled me into the huddle of women next to Letia. She dropped my hand. I stood shoulder to shoulder with Letia, facing the men. Watching. Listening. I wanted to stare at Letia, but I could only steal a glance sideways. Large white shells hung from her ears, and she was wrapped in a red blanket. I watched from the corner of my eye for her to look at me. She did, a glimpse and a smile.

Pa stood, his back to the women, facing the three men. He and the man in the large blanket spoke in a language I had never heard before. (I came to know later that it was a trade language called Chinook, and that it was used in business between Indians and people from the old country.)

The man nodded to Pa. Then he spoke to the other men in the language I had heard the boys using a few days before, a jumble of the unusual clicking, snapping and deep guttural sounds. There were long pauses, during which the men tightened their lips and wrinkled their noses.

"Knaw," the old woman said in a low voice, nodding her head. It was a soft and friendly sound.

Another woman frowned and said, "Tsharr." She pointed hard at the men with a crooked finger. "Tsharr. Tsharr."

The old woman made a gesture at the other woman with her shoulder. I took it to mean disagreement. She made a loud clicking sound that attracted the attention of the man with the blanket. He spoke to Pa, causing him to turn around and see me.

"What are you doing here?" he asked with surprise, but no anger, in his voice. His forehead was creased in a deep V as if he was very tired.

I said, "I am sorry, Pa." He put his hand out to me. I took it and said, "I had to find you."

He pulled me toward him.

He said, "Hope, daughter," and turned me so that I faced the man wearing the blanket. "Okustee. Daughter."

The man came close. He frowned. "Okustee," he said. "Knaw."

With sharp eyes he looked at me from my head to my feet as if I were a sheep or goat at the market.

"Knaw," the other men nodded. "Knaw, knaw," they said, nodding and looking at each other.

"OOOww, okustee." The blanket-covered man stroked his chin. He made a clicking sound that the other men repeated. "Glckkk. Okustee. Daaauughterrr. Knaw."

The old woman came near and looked closely into my face. "Knaw," she said. "Glckkk. Okustee. Daaauughterrr."

Murmurs spread through the crowd. "Knaw." "Tsharr." From their expressions and emphasis, I took these to be sounds of agreement and disagreement.

I stayed rigidly still without taking more than a sip of air until their investigations ended. The blanketed man rolled back on his heels as if surveying a landscape.

Suddenly he broke into a wide, toothy grin and then laughed. One by one the men and women began to smile and laugh noisily.

"Knaw," the men said, slapping the sides of their legs. "Daaauughterrr, okustee, Huuuupe. Knaw. Knaw."

The women clapped. Even the one who had frowned slapped her legs, laughing heartily.

Letia laughed as well. "Daaauughterrr, okustee," she said. "Huuuupe."

The man in the blanket tapped the top of my head and tickled his finger under my chin. Pa laughed. He hugged my shoulders. I was now sure the Indians could be trusted—certain that Pa would understand what a serious error he had been about to commit.

It wasn't long before the commotion quieted. The crowd returned to watchfulness. The blanketed man stretched his palms upward and waved his arms. The other men followed, then the women and Pa. Last, I lifted up my palms like the others and made the strange motion to the heavens. Of course, I did not know the meaning of the gestures I was making.

A hushed chorus of *Knaw* came from the crowd as Pa took my hand and led me toward the seashore. We walked past the shacks and lines of fish, down the bank and through the reeds.

When our feet met the pebbles, I turned to look at the camp. Letia stood in front of the shed. She clung to the old woman with one hand and the little girl with the other.

"Goodbye," I called to her.

"Goodbye," she called back.

Pa walked in deep contemplation. When we reached the point, he said, "I told the Indians that we are leaving the island."

A ringing sound clanged in my ears.

"I said we wouldn't be coming back."

"No, Pa!"

My eyes filled with tears.

"No. No. No, Pa. You are making a mistake."

I had never corrected Pa so vigorously before, without apology. But I had no other choice. I had ignored the subject for too long. I had to say something.

"Hope, it is the right thing to do. Our family will relocate to Mayne Island. We will begin to pack immediately," Pa said. His voice was stern and determined.

"But you don't want to go. I know you don't. This is our place. You built it with your own hands," I said. Hot tears streamed down my cheeks. I wept without control.

"Hope," he said. He passed me his handkerchief.

I ignored his offer. I snuffled and wiped my eyes with my sleeve.

"I'm fine," I said, trembling. I took a deep sobbing breath.

"You can't let those brutish men tell us what to do. Wallace Island is the finest place on earth, Pa, you know it is. And besides, these Indians can be trusted. I am sure of it."

"It's not these Indians who cause us to leave the island, Hope. It's Ma." Pa looked me directly in the eyes. "She has laid down an ultimatum: if I don't relocate our family to Mayne Island, she will return to England and take you children with her. She has given me no other choice. I don't like leaving the island, but I couldn't endure losing you. Eva is afraid, child. And it isn't right that she be afraid."

"But it's the men who have convinced Ma."

"Yes, and mightily convinced she is."

"Then we must tell her that there is no cause for alarm."

"But there is cause, Hope."

"No, Pa, there's not. I saw the Indians. I looked in their eyes. They are kindly men. And Letia, the young girl: she is my friend."

"Your friend?" Pa asked, looking perplexed.

"Yes, my friend. I met her in the forest picking berries."

"The forest?"

"She is kind and beautiful, Pa. She is…"

He squeezed my hand, and I said no more about her.

"You may be right, my girl. These Indians won't hurt us. But there are others. And they are angry. I believe they have good cause to be angry. They have no reason to believe that we are friendly, because there are others like us who aren't. How should they know we want to live peaceably? Shall I tell each one of them that we have no interest in their territory besides our humble needs at Sunnydale? They have heard of the wars in the United States, and they are afraid."

"Yes, Pa, you should tell them. Tell all of them, just as you have spoken to our neighbours. They *will* listen…as these good people have listened."

He took in a deep breath and let out a long and troubled sigh.

"Oh, that it were that simple," he said.

"Then what, Pa? What is not as simple as it appears?"

"There is a man named Acheewan," he began reluctantly. "He is the chief warrior in this territory. He is angry that people from England and Europe are trespassing on his people's land. He has been heard to say that he does not like the newcomers and that he will kill people whom he finds intruding. He believes, Hope, that we are his enemy. There are other Indians who agree with him. Government officials are planning to teach the Indians a lesson. What they will do I cannot say, but these are dangerous times."

I had heard Ma and the men say the times were dangerous. But when Pa said it, it sounded frightening. Suddenly everything was clear. Sunnydale Farm was lost. Forever. Pa was not going to fight.

"The garden? Who will tend the hyacinth bulbs you promised would bloom in the spring? And the geraniums. They are still blossoming. Who will enjoy them?"

My mind sprang from one thing to another. "And the carrots and beets and potatoes that have yet to be dug? The roses, they won't mature for another few years. We've yet to see them in their fullest bloom."

Pa didn't respond.

"I haven't finished my new watercolour of the cliffs...and the raven, Pa. I am painting the raven."

It is all without sense. Futile. What do my watercolours have to do with anything?

"Pa, please do something."

We collapsed on a log, my head on his lap.

Lamalcha Camp, Summer Island, Autumn 1862 🖎

I collected the grasses and rushes
    that had been cut but not yet woven.
    I laid them carefully in piles on the weaving mats,
    each blade of grass on top of another,
    even and flat,
    each colour with its colour,
    each variety in its own bundle.
    I tied them together into neat and tidy sheaves
    with pieces of new string
    I had cut with Father's carving knife.
    I stacked the unused sheaves,
    ready to be packed in the canoe
    with the other summer supplies,
    set to return to Winter Island.
    I smiled at my work.
    The order of the grasses,
    lined up, every one in its place,
    each covering the events of the night before.
    I thought, *It is a good day.*
    I will pay attention to my tasks,
    and the ancestors will be pleased.

    I was surprised to see the Man appear,
    as if out of nowhere.
    There had been no announcement of his arrival.

With great determination,
he walked up the bank to Father,
who was tying nets.
His voice was serious.
Its sound drew Big Brother and Uncle Nanute.
Soon Grandmother and Mother
and the other women came into a circle
to hear what was going on.
"What are they saying?"
I asked Grandmother when I joined the crowd.
She hunched her shoulders.
"If it isn't one visitor, it's another," she said.
"Tsharr."
She wagged her head and sighed.
"And from the look of his face,
he brings us no good news.
But then who does?" she said,
sounding disgusted and walking away.
Even though I could not understand their words,
I didn't want to listen either.

"Grandmother is right. Enough," I thought
and turned to walk away
when there, to my surprise, Hope appeared
holding Grandmother's hand.
My friend!
My heart leapt like a salmon sunning himself in the bay.
I edged my way behind the other women
until I stood close to Hope.
I was so close that I could feel her heat,
as if she had been running.
I moved a little closer
until the fabric of her dress rubbed against my arm.
For a while we stood without moving,
Hope and I, together,

and I wondered if the ancestors wanted us to be friends.
Was that what they had been saying?
But when Hope and her father were gone,
the People waited for Father to speak,
and I knew the ancestors were not concerned
with Hope and me.

"The hwunitum will leave our island," he said.
"They will not return."
Father sounded disappointed.
"They are afraid."
Some of the People cheered
as if it were a good thing
to be rid of the hwunitum.
Father hung his head while the People gloated.
Then he raised his hands.
"Listen," he said loudly to get their attention.
"You have cheered in joy
because the hwunitum will leave our island,
but this good man and his family
are not our problem.
Today we have no cause to rejoice.
This man is not the only one who is afraid.
Fear has washed over you as well. Like the autumn mist,
fear has clouded our vision
and dampened our spirits.
We have lived in peace with these people
for three seasons,
yet now we are all afraid."

That was all Father said.
He looked as if he wanted to say more,
        but he was defeated.
Fear had come to grip the People,
and Father did not know how to fight it.

Even Mother did not look pleased.
She knew that even with Hope's family gone,
nothing would change.

I burst away from the People.
This could not be what the ancestors wanted.
I ran into the forest without stopping, past the big tree,
over debris left from the winter storm
and beyond the Man's tree-cutting stumps.
I didn't slow down until I reached the Man's shed.
I collapsed against the wooden slats
and breathed in a giant whiff of the cedar.
It smelled the same as the cedar of our lodges.
The wood made my skin itch
like the wood on our winter houses.
Tears ran down my cheeks.
I crept silently around the corner of the shed
and peered toward the Man's house,
past the animal sheds and the gardens.
The settlement was quiet.
Then in the window
I made out the form
of someone standing in the shadows.
Terrified I had been caught,
I turned and raced back through the forest,
checking over my shoulder
to make sure no one was following.

Sunnydale, Wallace Island, Autumn 1862 ❧

"If Ma wants to leave Sunnydale," I said, "then she can pack the rest of our things. I'm not going back to the house. Not ever."

Pa's hands were firm on my shoulders.

"Sometimes, Hope, we must do things we don't want to do. We must give up things we want to keep."

"And sometimes we must defend what is ours," I said. "Don't you think, Pa?"

"It isn't right that you and I and Alec should be happy, Hope, when Ma and Charlotte and Baby Dot are in despair. Where part of our family goes, we all go. I can't let Ma and Charlotte return to England. Never. We must stay in this country. There's nothing more I can do."

Pa was tired—I could tell from the sound of his voice. That much I could understand. But he had given up, and that was something I couldn't believe. Until that moment, I hadn't thought to be angry with him. Suddenly my blood got hot. I pushed his hands off my shoulders and leapt to my feet.

"You haven't even tried, Pa," I shouted. "How could you let them win? You love Sunnydale. How could you? How could you?"

My face burned and my legs quivered. Pa stood up and wrapped his arms around me. He dipped his head so he spoke directly in my ear. He said, "A man must protect his family and take care of his people."

"But that's not what you are doing," I hollered.

I pulled myself free of his grip and raced along the seashore toward the Indian camp. When I reached the point, I stopped and looked back. Pa had turned and was walking toward Sunnydale.

Charlotte mounted the stairs before I counted to ten. Then how has Pa been persuaded?

I took Ruby out of my pocket.

"If they want to move," I said aloud, "then let them pack our things. Ruby, you and I are not going home until they are finished."

When I said *home*, the word sounded hollow and sad.

I wanted to stay angry, but I was more miserable than mad.

Home. Ruby, we no longer have a home.

My legs felt waterlogged, dragging one step at a time over the pebbles. The tide was low—usually my favourite time on the beach. I loved chasing crabs from under one rock to another, watching the clams spurting, and searching for ivory white skeletons of giant salmon that had been scrubbed clean by the ocean's surge. Pa said we would never be hungry on Wallace Island because when the tide went out, it was the ocean's way of setting the table.

I trudged along toward the Indian camp without looking at the crabs or clams. I could think of only one thing: the Richardsons, my beloved family, were going to leave Wallace Island and Sunnydale...forever.

...nineteen, twenty. If clouds fall from the sky and cover me like ten thousand chicken feathers before I count to twenty-five, then we will stay at Sunnydale. Twenty-one, twenty-two, twenty-three...If thirteen whales swim up on the beach and dance on their tails before I count to one hundred, then we won't move away.

I was now well past the point; soon I would reach the camp.

You are nothing more than a silly child. What does counting have to do with anything? It is perfectly unreliable and amounts to nothing more than a stupid game.

I sat down on the pebbles with my knees up and my chin hooked over my arms. I was determined to ignore Pa's request that I help pack and clean. Why clean the house, just to leave it to the mice and spiders? What difference would it make if the counters were shining?

If I see Letia before I turn for home, then a miracle will happen and we will stay on Wallace.

I closed my eyes and tried to imagine a miracle that could be of some help: Mr. Haws and Old Man Albert would be declared dead in Victoria. A kindly man from Victoria would come to visit and tell Ma that everything the other two men had said was a lie. No settlers would have been murdered. The Indians would not be angry.

But miracles were easier for me to imagine than they were for me to believe. And evil thoughts weighed heavily on my conscience. Such imaginations would not bring good, of that I was sure.

I heard the sound of pebbles scrunching. I opened my eyes. My sight blurred from the sunlight; I shaded my face with my hands.

"Letia," I exclaimed, seeing her shadow in the blinding sunlight. "Letia, what are you doing here?" I asked, knowing fully she would not understand my words.

A miracle? Can this be a miracle?

She crouched beside me and pressed toward me a wooden figure. It was a carved girl. A girl with black painted braids and arms and legs the pale yellow of butter. She pressed it into the palm of my hand. Unsure what she meant by the gesture, I took the doll and held it gingerly. It was the length of my forearm and nearly the same thickness. It fit exactly in my arms, and it smelled of freshly turned cedar. The face had wide-set eyes and lips that curled slightly up in a smile.

"Is this for me?" I said in a futile effort to clarify Letia's intentions.

She lifted my arms until the doll was cradled next to my chest. It was unlike any other doll I had ever held. It was hard like the wood it was made of, but in my embrace it felt soft and supple.

"It is lovely," I said, smiling.

I slid my finger gently over the smooth surface.

She smiled and looked pleased that I had expressed delight at the doll. We kicked stones and sifted pebbles through our fingers in the warm midday sun. It was as if we had been friends forever. Giggling, Letia shovelled gullies and flicked sand with her big toes—her bare feet fascinated me. Never had I taken such an interest in toes. For me, they had been nothing more than something I covered.

Suddenly, the thought of exposing them to my friend, of removing my stockings—the very idea—caused a wave of embarrassment to rush up my legs as if I were baring my underbelly.

Slowly I unlaced my boots and pulled one off and then the other. I bunched my stockings around my ankles and then over my feet. Letia watched as if I were performing a strange ritual.

I buried my toes gloriously in the pebbles. Letia set my boots and stockings on a log and led me barefoot along the shore toward the camp. The pebbles were cold and coarse, and my feet ached as I hobbled along trying to keep up.

In the camp we passed men taking dried fish off a line and others whittling chunks of wood. Each one of them raised an eyebrow, but only long enough to catch a glimpse of me. Their lack of attention made me feel as if I had already become an everyday occurrence.

The women sat on woven mats weaving baskets with grasses and reeds. We squatted beside them. The little girl I had seen with Letia earlier was there, and the old woman who had led me to Pa.

The old woman, a short distance away, hunched herself along the mat until she sat next to me. She was a strange little woman with snow-white hair and thin-slitted eyes that were barely visible under the folds of her coarse, leathery skin. Her fingers were gnarled like the limbs of an old oak tree.

She opened her basket and offered me a piece of dried fish. If I could have thought of a way to refuse her hospitality politely, I would have, but her insistence, the generosity of her expression, left me no choice. I took the portion of fish and, with misgivings, put it in my mouth. It was tough and hard to chew, but in spite of the heavy smoke flavour, it was pleasant enough to taste. She looked pleased.

She stared fixedly at my mouth while I chewed. As soon as I had swallowed, she forced a thin strip of something black and lumpy into my hand. It left a greasy film on my palm. It stank...a thick, rank, inedible stink.

Her scrawny fingers lifted my hand to my mouth.

"Knaw," she said and smiled.

I gagged from the foul smell. How I could say *no, thank you*, and return the putrid little morsel with acceptable manners?

"Knaw." She lifted her chin in a motion that clearly meant I should put the food in my mouth. "Ahhh, knaw."

I held my breath and took a small nibble.

"Ugh!" Unbidden, the food shot out of my mouth and onto the ground. It tasted more fetid than a decomposing fish left to rot in the sun, more foul than rancid butter, more disgusting than cod-liver oil.

The old woman scowled as I wiped the grease off my lips, trying to conceal my repugnance. Then she fell onto her back, shrieking with laughter.

"Tsharr," Letia said, frowning at the old woman. She took the rest of the offending ration out of my hand and gave it to the little girl, who tossed it in her mouth as if she had been given a sweet morsel of candy.

When the old woman stopped laughing, she rolled up onto her haunches and crouched closer to me than before. She stared at my dress. She picked up the hem, with the tips of her fingers at first, as if she were handling hot coals. Then, gaining confidence, she stroked the material between her palms. She lifted it up to her nose and inhaled with a deep, noisy, rattly breath. She leaned her head in my lap and rubbed the cloth over her wrinkled cheek.

She smiled, "Knaw," and placed my dress back down on my legs neatly, smoothing it with her hands. Then she hobbled off to sit down next to the other women, her legs as bowed as bent fishing rods.

Letia picked up two strands of grass and arranged them in an X. She twisted the strands and bent them back and forth. Her fingers were strong and moved with a quick, steady rhythm. Before long, a deep red design that looked like waves emerged in the knots.

The sun was low over the hills to the west and cast a silver glint around heaps of dark grey clouds. The air was thick with moisture; it would rain before long.

I must go.

Letia twisted the grasses, tying in dark brown and yellow strands. Before long the weaving began to curve upward, and a basket was forming.

The boy in The Trapper *stayed with the Indians and wasn't found by his pa until years later, fine as the day he went missing.*

My feet were freezing and goosebumps were crawling along my arms and legs.

Letia gave me two pieces of grass. I formed an X. She held her weaving close to me and twisted and knotted the strands so I could see. I studied her fingers, her movements. I copied her. I twisted the grass. I watched. I made a knot. And another. I fumbled and groped. Another knot and another. Slowly a lumpy mass emerged.

Ma can wait. I am not ready to leave the Indian camp.

It was slack in parts and taut in others, but around and around I went. With each turn my fingers became less confused, the grass more pliable.

If it doesn't rain before Letia puts her weaving down, I will stay with the Indians. Ma and Pa will move to Mayne Island with the other children. I will stay and weave mats. I will teach Letia how to knit.

A V of geese swooped over the Indian camp, flapping their wings, soaring toward Sunnydale, honking. It was getting late. I imagined Pa looking up at the birds, searching for his gun. He would be worried. And Alec would be wondering where I was. I had to go home. But from the way I felt right then, I didn't have a home.

Could I be like the boy in The Trapper? *Could I live happily with the Indians?*

Letia continued to twist the grasses with such speed that her weaving grew as fast as Ma's knitting.

I could see no sign that Letia was about to put her weaving down. But I needed to reassure Pa. Reluctantly, I set my weaving on the mat.

"Home," I said and pointed toward Sunnydale. "I must go home."

Letia looked puzzled at first, but when I continued to point, she understood.

She pointed in the same direction and said, "Home?"

"Yes, home," I said. "I must go home."

Seagulls swarmed like bees overhead as we walked toward the point. There was an unsettling sound to their cries, and the crashing surf sounded wrong. There had been signs of a storm for days. The blustery autumn would soon turn to an early winter.

Along the way I picked up my boots and stockings. My feet were already numb from the cold, so I carried on barefoot until we reached the point. When we stopped, I took the doll that Letia had given me and passed it to her. She held her hands up as if to say *stop*. I cradled the doll against my chest. She smiled, and I knew it was a gift for me to keep.

I said, "Thank you."

She lifted her hands with her palms raised.

"Goodbye," I said.

"Goodbye," she said.

We stood for a few minutes in silence. There were words I wanted to say, but I left them stuck in my head.

I waited until I'd cleared the point and was out of sight. Then I sat on a log and examined the wooden doll. It was firm and hard, but yielding and warm at the same time. Even though the face was carved in wood, its features appeared knowing in a way that even Ruby's didn't.

"Ruby," I said as I pulled her out of my pocket. "Meet your new friend."

What was the doll's name? Surely the doll was an Indian princess.

"Meet Princess," I said.

If the doll is a princess, Ruby might have hurt feelings.

"Her name is not really Princess," I said hurriedly, so as not to offend Ruby. "I just made that up."

I thought hard about what the doll's name should be, but I couldn't think of anything.

Finally I said, "Ruby, meet my wooden doll. She is your new friend."

I put them both in my pocket and rubbed my toes before putting on my stockings and boots.

Lamalcha Camp, Summer Island, Autumn 1862 ≋

The People waited
    for Father to declare his canoe finally completed
    so that we could return to our winter village.
    Mother nagged him, saying,
    "Will you never be satisfied?
    It is already the most beautiful canoe in our territory.
    Now put your knife away.
    Will you still be carving this canoe
    when the first snow falls?"
    But Father would not stop. He would not be content
    until every tiny place on the canoe
    was as smooth as a beach rock.
    The People began to be impatient.
    Not only did they want to return to Winter Island,
    but they had planned a great feast.
    It had been a long time
    since the People had had such a beautiful canoe,
    and there was no better reason
    to have a grand celebration.

    I was fiddling with string,
    tying up the last bundles of dried grass,
    thinking about Hope and the Man
    and what he had said.
    I wondered whether the ancestors had meant

for such an unhappy decision to be made,
or whether things had gotten completely out of hand.
Maybe the ancestors had something else in mind.
I was devising ways to change the terrible course of action
that had been set in place.
I will talk to Acheewan, I thought
and plead with him
to convince the ancestors
to change their minds.
Or
I will persuade Father to talk to the Man.
He will convince Hope's family that they are safe,
that they have no reason to be afraid.
It was an overcast day
with a brisk wind and a light chop on the water.
Shards of light pierced through the clouds
as if the ancestors were present.
I watched without moving.
My eyes flitted back and forth
from one end of the beach to the other,
but I saw nothing unusual.
I settled back and watched the light
burn a silver lining around the clouds.
I listened, hoping the ancestors would speak,
that my heart would hear a message...
something to explain the madness
that had overtaken my People and Hope's.

It seemed to me, as I contemplated
what the ancestors might be saying
about such a turn of events,
that no one had the courage we needed.

Out of the corner of my eye,
I saw a movement near the end of the point.

I stood up and saw,
crouched behind a tangle of logs,
Hope.
This time, I thought, *she will not run away*
before I have a chance to greet her.
Even if she is not brave enough to come to the camp,
she will not be penalized for her lack of courage.
So I decided I would go to her
and welcome her with a gift.

When I reached her,
she sat leaning against a log.
Her elbows hugged her knees
and her head rested on her arms.
I stood directly in front of her.
She stayed perfectly still,
without so much as lifting her head.
I toed the pebbles.
With a start, she glanced up,
squinting into the sun, as if I had awoken her.
"Here," I said
and passed her my doll.
She rubbed her eyes
and made no attempt to take my gift.
Perhaps she did not understand
that I was giving her a gift,
a token of friendship.
I didn't want to feel offended by her rejection,
so I passed the doll to her again.
This time I pressed it into her hand,
and when she took the doll
I was satisfied.
She smiled
and I took that to mean she was thankful.
We played in the sand

and walked to the camp.
Grandmother was pleased that Hope had come to our camp.
She would not leave her alone.
Some of the women disagreed.
"The hwunitum girl should not come here,"
they grumbled.
Tsustea's mother was especially unhappy.

Hope was very quick to learn
when I showed her how to weave.
Grandmother and the other women
watched and were surprised.
"Her hands are pale like old crab shells,"
they said in amazement, "but they are strong."
Her fingers were as thin as the stems of lilies,
but they were nimble and quick.
Even Tsustea's mother was impressed.

Sunnydale, Wallace Island, Autumn 1862 ❧

Pa was in his work shed pulling tools off the shelves when I returned to Sunnydale.

"Look." I took the wooden doll from my pocket and showed it to him. "Look at what Letia gave to me."

If he was surprised, I couldn't tell.

He looked closely and said, "Beautiful," and continued emptying the shelf. "You won't show that to Ma or Charlotte, will you."

"No, of course not," I said.

"Now put the doll away and go inside. There is much to do. We will be leaving tomorrow with everything we have ready. The rest will follow in good time. Mr. Haws and Old Man Albert are coming in the morning with a boat to take most of our things. Ma, Alec, Baby Dot and you will go with them. Charlotte and I will follow in our boat with the rest."

"Please, Pa, let me go with you? Charlotte can go with Ma," I pleaded. I knew his answer already. I was to travel with Ma because she needed my help with Alec and Baby Dot. Charlotte was no help at all when it came to the children.

By the time Pa said, "Ma will need you," I was already out the door and was closing it gently.

There is nothing to be gained by denying what fate has sealed.

Inside the house, three large chests stood half full near the fireplace. Four bundles tightly tied together with leather straps leaned against the chests. The shelves in the kitchen were stripped of all the dishes. The windows were bare. Ma's new lace curtains that had hung so gaily at the windows were neatly folded on top of linen pillowcases and cotton doilies. The only things left undisturbed were Ma and Pa's extra blankets and pillows. They were folded in the basket next to the bench in the sitting room.

My life on Wallace had been reduced to stacks and piles. I was homeless—too hurt and angry to look at Ma face to face. I wandered through the kitchen and ran up the stairs, two at a time. The bedroom window was bare. The bureau drawers were open and empty.

"Where were you?" Charlotte asked. She was folding the contents of the cedar chest. "I have worked all afternoon and have packed everything alone."

I couldn't speak. I knew if I tried, the lump in my throat would explode into a torrent of tears.

"Ma said to leave your belongings for you to pack later, but I've already folded and stored most of them for you," she said expectantly, as if waiting for me to say thank you.

"Who said today was the day we would pack our things?" I blubbered. "Who told me we had not one more day to prepare our belongings?"

"Ma said so, Hope," Charlotte said decisively. "You heard her."

"Sure enough, Ma said so earlier, but she didn't say it in so many words and not to me exactly," I argued. "She was wiping the table when she said, *Shall we finish packing our things?* She didn't say, *Hope, you will pack your things today.*"

Charlotte looked glassy-eyed at me and sighed, "Hope, must you make things so difficult?"

I ignored her and continued, "Ma didn't say, *Each one of us will pack our things.* She only asked the question, *Shall we?* And besides, Charlotte, it was Pa she asked, not me."

This was the very reason I'd chosen to ignore her. And Pa? He did not respond. He did not confirm or reject. "Pa didn't agree that the move should be made until after he visited the Indian camp."

Charlotte slumped onto the bed slack-jawed, as if she had been hit by a horse and knocked off her feet, as if my reasoning had assaulted her.

"Hope, you know it's best for our family that we move to a safe place."

"I know nothing of the sort."

"Ma says—"

"I have heard enough about what Ma says and what Ma thinks. Pa has given way to your complaining—against his will. That's what I know."

She rose to her feet feebly.

"Where's my picture of Grandma?" I asked.

"It's safely wrapped in the chest," Charlotte said helpfully.

"And my knitting? Where is it?" I said, scrambling through the chest.

"I said I put your things away for you. I didn't think you would be cross with me." She sounded hurt.

"I'm not cross," I snapped. I felt panic welling up inside my chest. "But I would have liked to do it myself."

"Then you should have been here earlier. There was a lot of work to do."

"And my comb, Charlotte? Where's my comb?"

Charlotte was the kind of girl to remain hurt only until she could muster enough courage to be angry. And nothing made her angrier than sensing an injustice not in her favour.

"Must you, Hope?" she barked with renewed strength. "After everything I have done for you, must you question me so?"

"Thank you for packing my things." A lie was all I could manage. I wasn't one bit thankful for what she had done. I was defeated, and that was different.

I handed Charlotte a bundle of letters from Grandma that had been left on the bureau. I picked up a porcelain plate that held my collection of shells and brightly coloured rocks. I tipped the plate and slid the rocks and shells onto a doily, then folded it around them.

"Here," I said. "We must not forget these."

It felt as if a large sullied dishcloth had wiped the room of everything that belonged to me. Other than my nightgown that lay folded on the pillow and blankets, nothing was left. I curled up on the bed. The house was cold. I pulled the blanket up to my chin and looked at the painting I had forgotten to take from the wall. It was the first picture I had painted on Wallace Island—the paper was faded and shrunken now, but it was a grand picture of the stately blue camas flower.

I will leave it with the house.

"It's almost suppertime, Hope," Charlotte said. "Why are you getting into bed?"

"I'm not feeling well," I murmured and rolled over to face the wall. "Could you tell Ma I won't be eating supper?"

"Ma will insist you eat."

"I will not be having supper, Charlotte," I said with all the certainty I could manage.

Ma could not make me eat. She could insist that I fold my things and put them in the cedar chest. She could force me to leave Wallace. But she couldn't make me eat. My stomach had no appetite for food, and my heart had no desire to sit at the table for one last supper.

"Tsk, tsk, tsk," Charlotte spat through her teeth and then stomped down the stairs, making sure with each heavy step that I could hear the sound of her exasperation.

Let her be annoyed. I don't care if Charlotte is angry, or Ma is angry. I don't even care if Pa and Alec are angry.

It wasn't long before I heard Ma announce, "Supper's ready."

"Hope says she's not feeling well," Charlotte said. "She doesn't want to eat."

"But she must eat," Ma said.

"Leave her be," Pa said.

I put Ruby on my pillow next to my head and tucked the wooden doll in between us. Rain snapped at the window. The attic groaned as a stiff wind whistled around the roof. Should a miracle not happen between the evening and the morning, this night would be my last at Sunnydale. The house was chilly and soggy. There was no fire, because Ma had made a cold supper, and the blankets didn't block out the uncomfortable dampness in the room.

I slept for a short time and then awoke.

If I can see a star in the night sky before I count to fifty, a miracle will happen. I will wake up and this will all be nothing but a bad dream.

The rain had stopped and the wind was still, but there was no light in the sky. When I awoke the second time, there were still no stars. Pa had given up. There were no deals to be made—no reason to count— no reason to look out into the night sky for stars. Charlotte tossed and turned, wheezed and coughed. The moist air clogged her lungs.

What will become of us?

I was desperate. I did not want to give up all hope for Wallace Island. But there were no stars. If I counted to a million, there would be no stars. We were about to leave Sunnydale, and there was nothing I could do about it.

Near morning, I decided there was one thing I had to do before we left the island. I hugged Ruby and whispered to her every detail of what I was about to do. Then I dozed off and slept briefly.

I awoke before daybreak and reached in the dark for Ruby.

"You understand, don't you?" I whispered. "If there were any other way. Truly, my dearest friend, if there were any other way. But this way we won't really be leaving Wallace Island forever."

First thing after breakfast, we started hauling our belongings out of the house. Alec and I each held one end of the leather strap that tied together a great sausage-shaped bundle. We dragged it over the dewy grass on the knoll and climbed over the rocks to the beach. Mounds of swirling white clouds whisked across the blue sky and over the tips of the mountains on the opposite side of the channel.

"Be careful," Ma called from the seashore. "Oh, darlings, you should have used the path."

"But look, it didn't get dirty," Alec said, pleased with his ingenuity.

I gave the bundle a shove. It rolled down the shore to a safe landing near Old Man Albert's foot. Then I turned and ran like a shot back to the house.

"Hope," Ma called. "Where are you going? We are to depart any time now."

Nothing could stop me.

I dashed past the geraniums and the deserted chicken pen. The best hens and other animals had been picked up by a young man from Mayne Island a few days earlier, and the others had been set free.

Holding tightly to my apron, I whizzed around the shed and onto the path that led into the woods. I scrambled over the windfalls and finally slowed down near where the path turned.

I drew in a deep breath of the moist, fragrant air and cast my sight around me. It would be the last time I entered the forest, my enchanted forest. The billowy green blanket of lush green salal and heaping ferns swathed the forest floor. The mossy trunks of the towering cedars soared into the sky, carrying their dappled canopy. Gnarled roots, like exotic snakes, crawled along the soft, narrow path. Lichen draped like Ma's new lace curtains from low-hanging boughs.

Surely Wallace Island was a blessed place like no other.

I stepped off the path onto the spongy ground and made my way through the undergrowth to the stream. Sparkling water bubbled gently over the rocks near the ledge where Letia had put her cedar skirt and into the shallow, shimmering pool where she had bathed.

I stood and surveyed the scene. I took another breath and wished hard that there was some other way, something else I could do.

Finally, I half-heartedly unbuttoned my coat and pulled Ruby out of my apron pocket. I combed my fingers through her yarn hair and twisted it into a neat knot.

I said, "You are the one, baby doll. It's up to you now."

I hugged her with all my might and prayed, "Dear God, there must be some other way. In your good grace, can you not find it in your heart to save my family from this calamity? And Ruby from this parting?"

I waited for a few moments, though I did not expect God to answer my prayer. I kissed her soft face and said, "I must go, but you will stay on Wallace Island for both of us. Be brave, Ruby. Letia will find you and take you home. You will be her friend forever, and I will be her friend forever too."

I set her down comfortably in a crevice between the rocks. I ripped off branches of salal and built a shelter over her head.

"This will keep you dry," I murmured.

I tried to say, *Goodbye, Ruby, Letia will take good care of you.* But the words got stuck in my throat.

Poor Ruby. Will she think I have replaced her with the wooden doll?

I didn't want to hurt her feelings. In truth, she was the lucky one. Ruby got to stay on Wallace Island with Letia. I was the one to suffer—to be torn from my friend, my doll, my house, my island, my paradise.

"Hope! Hope!"

It was Alec. I buttoned my coat and rushed back to the path, glancing over my shoulder to see Ruby one last time sitting safely on the rock.

"What are you doing?" he asked. "We were all ready to go, and then you disappeared."

"I wanted one last look at the stream..." Tears blurred my sight. "... and the berries."

"Come on, Hope," Alec said. "Ma will be annoyed."

I headed up the path in the opposite direction from Sunnydale.

If Ma was displeased—so be it. Her mood had been altogether too cheerful for such a terrible day.

The sun filtered through the trees, casting a ray of yellow light onto the bushes where Letia and I had picked berries. I imagined what the berry patch would look like in a year, in five years.

Will Letia still come to the same spot? Will she remember me?

I dodged off the path and stood amongst the rock mounds in the clearing.

"Hope," Alec said. "What are you doing?"

"Just one last berry."

"But what about Ma?"

"She can wait."

I searched the shrubs.

"Just one," I said. But every berry I found was either soft and mildewy or red and hard. "I want just one more berry."

"There will be no more berries this season," Alec said impatiently. "You know that."

He was already excited to leave the island behind—ready for the next adventure. I usually loved the way Alec could so easily forget one thing and start something else, but now it made me angry.

Has he not enough love for this place to feel the misery of leaving it? Are we to so quickly forget?

"We must go," he demanded.

"Go, then, if you must," I snapped. "And tell Ma I'll be along shortly."

One, two, three.

I scrambled through the twigs frantically looking for one ripe berry.

Just one berry before I count to ten.

Four, five.

If I can find one ripe berry before I count to ten, then Letia will find Ruby and she will be safe.

I couldn't find an edible berry anywhere.

Six, seven.

"Ouch," I cried. A prickle was hooked onto my hand. Blood spurted into my palm.

"Hope!" Alec said. "Don't be silly. There are no ripe berries left. And the boat is waiting for us."

"You don't understand, Alec." I smeared the blood off my hand onto a clump of damp grass. "I must find one berry. I must."

Suddenly tears burst onto my cheeks like a relentless bubbling stream.

"Don't cry, Hope," Alec said.

Eight, nine.

"Look!" he said. He pointed to a berry hiding behind a wilted leaf. "It's the last berry of the season." He picked the plump purple berry and handed it to me.

Ten.

"Oh, Alec. Thank you. Thank you. You don't know how much I thank you," I sputtered.

The berry looked perfectly scrumptious. It was nearly black, and shiny and plump—as big a berry as I had seen all season. I placed it on my tongue as if I were a seer conducting a ritual to the gods. I slowly sank my teeth into the fruit. Viciously, its juice spurted into my mouth and attacked my tongue like sharp claws: it was so sour I almost spit it out, but I swallowed.

If I can find one ripe berry…

The berry wasn't as it appeared, but it was ripe…ripe enough. It had to be. I winced and swallowed the last drops of the astringent fruit.

Lamalcha Camp, Summer Island, Autumn 1862 ≋

Tsustea's mother was the first to catch sight of the boat
    as it rounded the point.
    "Look," she hollered.
    "It is the whisky traders."
    A crowd gathered at the shore.
    Arm in arm, the People were prepared to send the boat away.
    They had decided that Long Man and Round Man
    were no longer welcome in the camp.
    They wanted nothing more of their troublemaking.
    If Uncle Penu wanted to trade with the men,
    he would have to take his business somewhere else.
    But the boat did not approach the shore.
    It stayed its course, a short distance out in the bay, heading north.
    "Look," Tsustea's mother called.
    "It is not just the whisky traders. The boat is full."
    When it came into view,
    I could see Hope and her mother,
    and the two younger children.
    Pretty soon the People were in an uproar,
    clapping and cheering,
    "The hwunitum are leaving.
    The hwunitum are leaving."
    I looked at the People with dismay.
    How could they be excited?
    What had Hope and the Man done

to deserve such a farewell?
Grandmother saw my resentment,
and so did Father.
"Stop," he said to the People.
"Stop cheering.
Can't you see this is a sad day for Letia?"

By this time everyone knew
that Hope and I had become friends. In fact our friendship
had become the topic of much discussion,
a source of consternation for some of them.
But, it appeared, even the People
who hated the hwunitum the most
could not quibble that I needed a companion
to replace Tsustea.
So after Father spoke, they quieted down
with all their eyes on me.
I walked past the crowd
and waded out to my knees,
to my thighs,
and I waved my hands in the air.
"Hope! Hope!"
I hollered, my throat choking on my words.
She didn't look.
It was as if she had not even heard
the disturbance on the beach.
"Hope! Hope!"
Tears filled my eyes.
Please, Hope, look at me.
The boat sailed directly past where I stood,
all the passengers looking straight ahead.
"Hope! Hope!"
Finally she stood up and turned to face the beach.
Slowly she raised her hands
and began to wave and holler,

"Letia! Letia!"
She didn't sit down
until the boat had disappeared
around the north end of the island.

Later in the afternoon,
when the wind was already getting stiff,
the Man's boat passed the camp.
It carried the Man and the other girl
and was laden with household goods.
Seagulls were crying,
treetops snapping.
I thought the Man should not have set off so late.
      There was such warning of a storm.

Sunnydale, Wallace Island, Autumn 1862 ❧

Everything looked streaked and bleary. I followed Alec down the path, past the house and back to the shore. Pa and Old Man Albert dragged Ma's cedar chest across the sand and lifted it into Pa's skiff. They jiggled it back and forth until it was rightly balanced in the rear of the boat.

"That's everything," Pa said in a voice so faint I could hardly hear him.

"All aboard!" Mr. Haws hollered. "We better set off before the wind catches up with us."

"Yes, mates, it's time to board Old Man Albert's sailing ship," Pa said in a meagre attempt to match the men's excitement.

The boat was hardly a sailing ship. It was no more than a skiff, only a little bigger than Pa's.

"I'll take one last walk through the house and farm to make sure what is left is crated and safe, and then we will follow." Pa lifted Ma first and then Baby Dot into the boat. Alec happily sloshed through the water and crawled over the side, with a leg-up from Mr. Haws.

"You're next." Pa picked me up and turned toward the others.

"Pa," I cried. "Please, please, please. I don't want to leave Sunnydale."

I buried my face in his neck and maintained a firm grip on his shoulders. Instead of putting me directly into the boat, he held me still until I felt the beating of his heart beneath his overcoat. "Neither do I, Hope. Neither do I," he whispered.

After a pause he said, "A man must take care of his family. We'll build another Sunnydale, Hope. I promise we will."

He stepped into the water and lifted me over the side of the boat. I clung furiously to his sleeve.

"Don't send me away, please," I begged.

He broke loose, and I crumpled onto the hard bench seat next to Ma.

"We will be along directly," he said.

Pa and Charlotte stood on the shore and waved when the boat pulled away.

As the distance between us lengthened, I felt as if a weight had been tied around my heart and fastened to Sunnydale—ripping a hole in my chest. I put my hands into my apron pocket and stroked the wooden doll. It was warm and soft.

Ruby, Ruby, Ruby. You'll be fine, baby doll.

Of course Ruby will be fine. Alec found a ripe berry before I counted to ten.

"Goodbye. We'll see you soon," Pa and Charlotte called.

Pa's hair was rumpled. Even from a distance and through the distortion from my watery eyes, I could tell he was sad. Not like Charlotte, whose hair was tied gaily with blue ribbons. She cheered, "We will follow you shortly to our new home. Ma, I will miss you until then."

Lamalcha Camp, Summer Island, Autumn 1862 ≋

Father stood on the beach,
   looking out into the channel.
   Swiltu and I sat on a log,
   watching the Man sail past
   until he was out of sight.
   Father turned toward the camp and said,
   "My canoe is complete.
   We will return to Winter Island."

   Once preparations and packing were done,
   Mother and the other women got busy preparing food for the feast.
   Big Brother shot six ducks.
   Grandmother made soup.
   Uncle Nanute filled the cooking pits with hot stones.
   Father butchered a deer and wrapped it in seaweed.
   He buried it with camas bulbs
   when the pits were steaming.
   Swiltu and I picked onions and late mushrooms.
   Mother roasted them with desert parsley.
   Uncle Penu steamed oysters and clams.
   It was a sumptuous feast.

   After we ate, the men brought the canoe
   and set it down near the fire.
   They formed a circle around it.

They drummed and sang a blessing song.

"Your new canoe, Great Man, will travel faster,
carry more goods and look more beautiful
than any other canoe that sails the waters
of the Lamalcha territory.
It will be the envy of the coast.
Old men will tell stories
about the great canoe of the Lamalcha People.
Young men will fear the eagle
that sails on the bow.
It is a bird from the gods, they will say."
After the men finished singing,
it was the women's turn.
They sang a prayer song:

"May the greedy hands of neighbouring thieves
and the hatchets of envious warriors
be stopped, and may the paddles
of the Lamalcha be swift."

When the singing was over,
Father and Mother climbed into the canoe.
The men picked it up,
set it on their shoulders
and carried it amongst the People
with Mother and Father aboard,
as if it were a wedding procession.
Mother and Father looked grand
sitting in a place of such honour.
We sang and danced
until we were hoarse and tired.

That night in my dream I thought I heard the ancestors speak:
The Lamalcha are a mighty People.

The men carve mighty canoes.
The women weave beautiful blankets.
Once again the island belongs to the People
and the People alone.

Travelling to Mayne Island, Autumn 1862 ❧

As we withdrew, Charlotte and Pa became like puppets, their hands attached to strings, their motions stiff and unearthly. I rubbed my eyes, and when my vision cleared, Charlotte remained gesturing absurdly toward the ocean while Pa, his back to us, walked up the shore toward the house.

"Mates, the weather will be good to us today if we hurry, it will," Old Man Albert announced, as if he were the captain of a large and important ship. "The tides are running in our favour, they are, and with a little luck we should arrive at Mayne Island by noon. So, my mates, settle in and enjoy the scenery."

To sail with the tides, the men sent the boat first in a northerly direction—heading toward the point and the Indian camp. I kept my eyes on Sunnydale, determined to watch my home until all hope of a view was lost.

One day, when I am a grown woman, I will return. I will wipe the dust off the stairs and rafters, and clear away the cobwebs. I will light the fire and put on the kettle. I will fill Pa's workshop with tools and dig the kitchen garden. I will plant tomatoes and geraniums. Sunnydale will be my home again.

When the boat reached the end of the point, it turned, and suddenly before my eyes was the Indian camp. Thin columns of smoke from the sheds curled into the sky. As the boat approached the camp, people began to gather near the women's weaving mats.

One, two, three...If I see Letia before I count to ten, then I will return to Sunnydale one day.

I didn't want to look. I couldn't bear the disappointment if she wasn't there. But I had to look. I couldn't bear to miss seeing Letia one more time. Without turning my head, I strained to see if she was amongst them.

Four, five...

A crowd was gathering. They began hollering and chanting. I could not see her. Ma's eyes remained focused straight ahead, her face stern. Stripped of all her good humour of minutes before, she seemed to be mustering everything in her power to ignore the Indians.

Six, seven...

By the time I counted to nine it was becoming difficult to see the people individually. There were too many. They were milling about together, their backs coming and going.

Where is Letia?

At the very moment that I reluctantly said *ten*, Letia appeared. She walked over the bank to the water's edge in front of the gathering. She stepped into the water until she was waist deep. She waved her hands frantically in the air.

"Hope, Hope," the breeze caught Letia's lone voice.

Letia, my friend. My heart ached. I wanted to rush to be with her. But I was stuck in the boat—forced to be separated from my friend forever. I remained silent, my arms glued to my sides and my hands clutched tightly around my new wooden doll. The others in the boat ignored the sound of my name. But it was ringing across the bay. It was as if a bird were calling out the sound of the morning.

"Hope, Hope, Hope."

When Letia's voice grew louder, Old Man Albert turned the boat and pointed it away from shore.

Mr. Haws, who had been looking ahead, turned to glance at the crowd. "What is that Indian saying?" he asked.

Alec, as if suddenly released from shackles fixing him to the bench, jumped up and shouted enthusiastically, "Hope, Hope, that's the girl. She is calling your name!"

He waved both hands and shouted, "Goodbye, goodbye. Goodbye, Indian camp."

Then he turned around and shouted, "Goodbye, Sunnydale. Goodbye!"

The sound of his farewell made the sad lump in my stomach explode. I stood up and lifted my arms in the air. I swayed from side to side as if I were a giant willow, slowly at first and then frantically as the boat passed the camp.

"Letia, Letia," I hollered. "Goodbye. Goodbye."

At first Ma ignored me, but when I shouted, "Goodbye, my friend," Ma could disregard the ruckus no longer.

"Hope! Alec!" she barked. "That's enough! Sit down—you are rocking the boat."

I paid no attention and continued calling and waving.

"Goodbye, my dear friend."

"Hope, stop, right now!" Ma said, becoming hysterical.

"Goodbye, goodbye. My friend. My friend, goodbye," I called.

What difference does it make if I behave or not? I have lost everything. There is nothing left that I can lose.

Ma tugged on my coat. "Sit down, sit down," she cried.

When Letia was out of sight, I fell down onto the seat, reached into my pocket and held the wooden doll. I touched the indentations of the doll's eyes and nose. I traced my finger along the smile on her lips and over the smooth bumps that formed her long braids. I wanted to pull the wooden doll out of my pocket and cradle it as I would have cradled Ruby, but the doll would have to remain my secret.

Ruby will be fine, and I will return to Sunnydale…for I saw Letia before I finished counting to ten.

For a few seconds, I was satisfied. But upon thinking about counting, I knew it meant nothing at all, especially now that we had left Wallace Island and Sunnydale behind. For all the counting I had done to prove otherwise, I was stuck in a boat, next to Ma, heading toward Mayne Island. All was lost in spite of the deals I had struck.

Yet I counted nevertheless. I couldn't help myself. It was a reassuring habit, even if it wasn't completely reliable.

The boat rounded the northern tip of the island and turned toward the east. The sun disappeared behind the trees. We were in shadow. Although there was blue sky in patches overhead, dark grey rain clouds loomed over the island.

Mr. Haws and Old Man Albert rowed furiously. The boat was heavy and travelled low in the water under the weight of its passengers and their belongings. The channel was choppy, and we rolled in the rough water until I felt I would throw up at any minute. Pa had said many times that in weather such as this we should stay home and wait. But in everyone's hurry to leave Wallace Island, we had taken a risk, and I was afraid.

I pulled a blanket over my head to stay warm.

The wooden doll must have a name. Shall I call her Letia? Shall I call her Ruby Two?

But the doll didn't feel like Letia or Ruby. She was someone else altogether. She felt to me as if she already had a name—one I just did not yet know.

"One day," I said quietly, "when I meet Letia again, she will tell me your name. Until then you will be called my Wooden Doll."

Mayne Island, Autumn 1862 ❧

It was shortly after noon when we arrived at the wharf on Mayne Island. The thick planks on the wharf had been hewn recently and were tethered securely with new ropes. At least at the start, Mayne Island looked like a nice enough place.

"Home sweet home, it is," Old Man Albert hollered as he fastened the boat to the post. He climbed over the side and onto the wharf, followed by Mr. Haws.

"Hurrah!" Alec shouted. He sprang to his feet, grabbed Mr. Haws's hand and scuttled out of the boat.

Ma stood up and stretched her arms. She leaned on my shoulder for balance as the boat bumped against the wharf. Carefully she edged around my knees, with Baby Dot close behind. Mr. Haws lifted them both out. He took Ma by the arm and helped her to the shore.

"Oh, thank you, my dear man," she said in her most elegant, although slightly seasick, voice. "I am so grateful for all your hard work bringing my family to our new home."

"Safe and sound, you are," Old Man Albert said, puffing his chest out as if he were a cat that had just caught a bird. "Safe and sound."

The sound of Ma saying *our new home* made my blood run hot. Having had such a short time to deal with the reality of moving, I was not in any way prepared to accept this place as *our new home*. It was nothing but a compromise, a third choice, one that would satisfy neither Ma's fear nor Pa's love for Wallace Island.

One thing I was sure of was that I was not, and never would be, thankful that Old Man Albert and Mr. Haws had stuck their noses into my family's business. However, when we finally stepped out of the boat, I was thankful that the journey was over. I couldn't have endured another minute cramped up in that uncomfortable tub, rolling and lurching through the choppy water. My stomach was queasy, my head ached and my bottom felt permanently frozen in a sitting position.

I staggered to stand, but I turned my shoulder to Mr. Haws when he offered his arm to help me disembark. I would rather have fallen into the water than taken his arm. Stubbornly I struggled over the side of the boat and onto the wharf. I wobbled to the shore and stepped down off the wharf, trying hard to stay upright as my legs trembled.

"Now, little girl," Old Man Albert said. "Wasn't that a wonderful boat ride?"

I might have been only twelve years old, but right then I felt as though I had lived for a long time. I had the sense climbing off the boat that I had left the paradise and innocence of my childhood behind on Wallace Island and had abruptly become, without my consent, an adult.

"No. It was too windy. And now the weather is worsening. I think you put us at great risk," I said defiantly. Then I became worried. "Do you think Pa will wait?"

"Don't you trouble yourself," he replied, looking down at me over his layers of chin and inflated chest. "Your pa won't have any difficulty with this weather. He's an expert boatman."

I said, "I know he is an expert boatman. But do you think he will wait?"

"He's on his way, little girl, he is. He'll be here directly behind us. That's what he said, he did."

I wasn't sure what to hope for: that Pa had followed, or that he had stayed behind and waited for the weather to change. His boat was small and heavily loaded, but I was confident he could handle almost any travelling conditions.

From the shore, Mayne Island looked like England. To the left of where I stood was a meadow that pushed into the seashore and was lined with groves of maple and oak trees. Directly in front of the wharf was a white shell shoreline. The backs of small painted houses and their gardens overlooked the channel and the hills beyond. I felt as if I were in an

England somewhere close to Sunnydale but still too far away.

I followed the others to a white path of crushed shells that led to a lane. We looked like a throng of poor and bedraggled wanderers as we trudged along. I was appalled that my family had been reduced to such circumstances. We were homeless beggars depending upon others for assistance. How could we?

My life had been turned upside down. Ma and Charlotte were afraid of both life and death. Pa was afraid of Ma's threat, and now I was becoming afraid. But my fear was not of life or death or anything else in particular. I was afraid of something that lay ahead, of what I didn't know. The feeling was one more of dread than fear.

I could see two houses on one side of the lane, and one on the other. The grounds that surrounded the houses were meadows from which some of the stones and bushes had been removed or repositioned to make a simple landscape. Apart from the lack of trimmed flower beds, the lane reminded me of where Grandma lived on Whittington Lane in Bristol.

Mr. Haws walked in long strides ahead of the rest of us. He turned in to the last house on the lane. It was larger than the others and had a porch with posts and turned spindles. A stone pathway led past a small garden to the front door. Foxgloves, delphiniums and chrysanthemums, now mostly withered, filled the garden.

Before we reached the door, it swung open.

A woman appeared and said, "Good day and welcome."

She was a plain but pleasant-looking woman, not more than an inch taller than I was and as thin as a broomstick. Her hair was braided and wrapped around her head like a scarf. She had deep blue eyes that searched from one person to the next.

"My name is Helen Cooper," she said. "You will be staying with us until the men convert the barn into a house."

She spoke as if she was the person in the village who had been put in charge of our family.

When Ma reached the top of the stairs, Mrs. Cooper linked arms with her and led her and Baby Dot inside. Alec and I followed, with the men behind us. It was a bigger house by far than our house on Wallace Island. A stone fireplace divided the kitchen from the sitting room. It was a room full of knick-knacks, with a piano at one end and a sunroom extending off to the side. The kitchen was large enough to have a table that would seat ten people at least, and with extra room.

Mrs. Cooper said, "You must be exhausted." She led Ma to a large stuffed chair. A small group of adults was sitting, looking at us expectantly, as if they had been waiting for our arrival. "I have a pot of tea on the stove."

"Oh, my dear lady. You are so kind. You are all so kind," Ma said, looking from one person to the next and smiling graciously.

"And how tragic that you had to leave your precious home," Mrs. Cooper said.

Ma touched her fingers to her lips. "Oh, but what a relief," she gasped. "What a relief."

Mrs. Cooper looked surprised by Ma's response. She served tea from a large silver tray and then sat down, curiously examining the newcomers.

"You will like it here," she said. "It is a pleasant island."

Alec and I stood like sentinels, one on each side of Ma's chair. I was aware of the stiffness of our appearance, but it seemed strange to be on display: examined, weighed up, as if we were new pieces of furniture. I wondered if Alec felt the same way I did—out of place, a foreigner, as if I had nothing whatsoever to do with the occasion that was passing before me. I would have sat down if I had thought to, but my mind was befuddled. Everything about the situation made me nervous: the muted smiles on the people's faces; the soft, murmuring *ummm*s, *ohh*s and *aha*s; the ticking clock on the bureau; the clinking silver; the sips and slurps. The room and its contents were lurking, watching, ready—as if waiting to trap me.

"Your youngest will sleep with you and John in the parlour," Mrs. Cooper said.

"Yes, forgive me," Ma said. "Please let me introduce my family. I have been so rude."

Mrs. Cooper smiled and nodded at Ma. She looked nice enough, and if I had not been on Mayne Island in strange and unusual circumstances, I would have thought she was a kind and generous woman.

"This is Dorothy and Alec and Hope," Ma said, motioning with her chin to each of us. "Charlotte, the oldest, will be along soon with John, my husband."

The people sat gaping at the introductions, as if they had never seen the likes of us before. All except Mrs. Cooper. "Hope," she said. "You will like it here. And Alec. Lizzie and Joseph are almost the same age as you children. They will be here soon, I am sure. Alec will share Joseph's bed in the lean-to. Hope will sleep with Lizzie and Daisy. Charlotte will stay across the street with William and Lenora. We will be crowded but comfortable. Samuel thinks the barn conversion will only take a few months at the most."

She proceeded to introduce each person in the room. I wanted to appear interested, but as hard as I tried to remember, each name raced through my brain without pausing for more than a fleeting second.

Lamalcha Camp, Summer Island, Autumn 1862 ≋

In the morning the sky was layered,
    red and yellow and orange blankets of light.
    The wind was still.
    At long last we could fill
    Father's new canoe
    with our personal things.
    The time had arrived to paddle back to Winter Island.
    I moved carefully, so I didn't disturb Swiltu,
    and folded my new sleeping mat
    neatly around the red bundle
    containing my carving knife.
    Next to the mat
    I put my comb, jewellery, string,
    shell collection, precious stones and blankets.
    I was ready to go,
    impatient to leave the summer
    and all its disturbances behind.

The People had feasted late into the night
and were still sleeping soundly.
I crouched near the lodges
and listened to the deep rumble of their snoring.
It would be a while before anyone rose.
To pass the time,
I headed to the beach

and walked around the point to the shell beach.
The maple tree leaned over
just above the water's surface.
Its leaves lapped the face
of the high-tide sea.
Beyond the gleaming white of the broken shells
and the grey craggy cliffs,
the shore was scattered with beach wood.
The shell beach looked the same
as it had before the line was drawn
around the Man's settlement.

I walked past the maple
and then past the sign the Man had left
nailed to two posts, near the path
that led to the house.
There were flowers in bloom,
potatoes loosened but not removed in the garden,
and other roots red and orange bulging out of the soil,
lined up in rows as straight as cedar planks.
It was a peculiar sight,
the hwunitum's garden,
with growing things so orderly.
And in what a hurry they must have been to get away,
that they would leave their winter food
in the ground.
I stepped onto the porch and reached for the door.
The house was dark.
The windows stared at me
        with square black eyes.
I yanked my hand away and hurried back to the path.
I passed the sheds and fences
that had once held the Man's animals
and collapsed onto a thick, low stump
near the Man's work shed.

I leaned against the wall.
What a waste it has all been, I thought.
One year the Man laboured
to build all this.
And now food, wire, wood cut into pieces, shelves, crates
and a fine house,
all left behind.
Hope's family was gone,
       and the emptiness stuck to me like an eerie dream.

I wandered into the forest,
past the Man's woodpile
and over decaying cedars.
A storm had snapped the treetops.
Debris and dried leaves
lay strewn on the path.
Birds wheeled around in circles,
squawking and shrieking.
I stepped off the path and tiptoed through the salal
to the stream,
careful not to put my feet in the same place twice,
just as I had done each time I came to bathe.
I was proud that I left no evidence,
no hollowed-out path,
no wear and tear of my weight
on the forest floor.
Then, in the sun,
a brightly coloured piece of cloth
caught my eye. On the stone ledge,
hidden under broken-off branches of salal,
lay the likeness of a girl.
A girl made of soft cloth.

I lifted the leaves to look more closely.
She bent in the middle,

sitting with her legs out straight in front.
She wore a green dress
and had yellow hair and red lips,
very red lips,
and brown cloth shoes, just like Hope.
I didn't touch her,
for Grandmother had taught me
to be cautious with images,
to be careful to know what they represent
        and what powers they might possess.
But she was a gift.
I was certain of it.
Hope had returned my favour.
I poked the doll with my finger.
She was soft.
When I picked her up,
my eyes filled with tears.
I wiped them and my nose, but they streamed,
and I couldn't stop them.
I cried and cried.
And I wasn't the kind of girl
who cried out loud very much,
only once before,
when Tsustea died,
and then I had made a promise
that I would not cry again.

But I held the doll and wept the kind of tears
that come up from the bottom of the belly.

Mayne Island, Autumn 1862 ᵅ

A girl burst into the room. "Hello, my name is Lizzie," she said breathlessly. "I was next door, and I only just heard that you had finally arrived."

"Lizzie, dear," Mrs. Cooper said. "Let me introduce our guests."

The girl glared impatiently at her mother. She looked older than me by a year or two, but she was only slightly taller. At first glance she reminded me of Charlotte: her milky white skin, her thick golden hair, the kind every girl wished for, with ringlets tied back in a red ribbon. She had cold blue eyes and full pink lips. I would have envied her, except that the spoiled look on her face detracted from her beauty.

"Come on. I have been waiting for you for what feels like forever." Lizzie made an exaggerated sigh. She grabbed my hand and dragged me out of the room. "I'm going to show you around."

We went down a narrow hallway and up one step to a room set off to the side of the house.

"My room is hardly more than a closet. It isn't even big enough for me and my sister. How we will have space enough for you to sleep I'll never know," she said, pointing to a featherbed in the corner of the room.

From the tone of her voice, I could not be sure whether Lizzie was pleased that we had come to stay at her house or not.

"Your room is lovely," I said, with as much appreciation as I could muster.

She ignored my remark and said, "Daisy will sleep by the wall; she's my nuisance little sister. I will be in the middle, and you will be on the outside. Mother says there is room enough. I hope you don't snore. I can hardly sleep already, with the incessant sound of Daisy grinding her teeth."

"The arrangements will be fine," I said, trying to please her. It was a big enough bed, although I didn't like the idea of sleeping with two girls I had only just met. "It is kind of you to share your bed with me. I'll only be imposing for a few months."

"I hope so. Come on. It will be wonderful," she said unconvincingly. "You will be my best friend."

"Yes. Yes, of course." I wanted to say, *No, I have a best friend already*.

I could see that for now I didn't have any choice about friends. I'd agree to anything just to preserve Lizzie's good humour.

"You will be moving into the Walsh place over the hill. The house isn't really a house. You can use it for a tool shed, but Father said the *barn* could be converted to a house big enough for your family."

Lizzie swung her hand wildly in a general northerly direction. I looked out the small window but could not see any evidence of a barn or shed.

"Anna Walsh hated it there," Lizzie continued without taking a breath. "Day and night she complained to her husband until he was so broken down from her nagging that he agreed to relocate his family to Victoria."

The way she said *barn*, the thought of living in a *barn* didn't sound very appealing. But if living in a barn meant that my family would be together, it would be an agreeable improvement over living in a stranger's house with a girl who didn't stop talking.

"My ma hated Wallace Island," I said.

"She will adore it here," Lizzie said. "Mrs. Walsh was just an old crab."

We went outside and walked through the garden past the chicken pen, tool shed and outhouse. The place was ordinary enough, but as hard as I tried, I couldn't imagine how Mayne Island would ever become my home.

When we reached the front of the house, Lizzie closed the gate behind us.

"This is it," she announced, spreading out her arms. "This is Miners Bay village."

"Maude lives there." She pointed at a tiny, tattered cabin, no bigger than two rooms, across the lane. "She's supposed to be my friend. She's a halfwit. You know the kind of girl. William and Lenora live over there; she has a baby and is already expecting another. I help out around their place sometimes. Poor woman; William is no help at all." She pointed somewhere. I didn't see. Her voice trailed in and out of my consciousness like the sound of Pa's saw.

I interrupted her. "May I take a rest from our tour? I'd like to go to the wharf and wait for my pa."

"Marvellous," she said. "We'll be the first to greet him when he arrives."

She charged ahead. I trailed reluctantly, wishing I could be alone.

Pa should arrive at any moment. I must see him.

We reached the path. I could see several men from the village and Mr. Haws unloading Old Man Albert's boat. The wind was strong. Waves surged onto the wharf and sent the boat banging against the post.

It was at least two hours since we had arrived. If Pa had left directly, as he'd said he would, he should have reached Mayne Island by now.

"You will put your things in the trunk outside my bedroom door," Lizzie said. "We will be so crowded, but at least I will have a friend besides Maude. Sometimes I don't think her brain has the least bit of sense. She's stupid as a mule."

I watched the cold grey water pound against the shore. Seagulls circled over the bay screeching at each other. Mounds of black clouds loomed over the mountains. A storm was coming. I thought of Pa's little boat.

"I wonder what time it is," I said. I rubbed my ears to clear a buzzing sound that filled my head.

"I don't know," Lizzie said dismissively, then continued her guided tour. "Our village is very small. Five families live on our island, and a few men without wives. Your family will make six."

"From the sound of the gulls and the look of the threatening sky, it appears there is going to be a bad storm," I said, immediately wishing I hadn't used the words *bad storm*. The buzzing sound became louder.

"Come on," Lizzie said. "Let's go home. It's too cold to stay on the beach."

"I want to wait." Spits of rain snapped against my cheeks and dampened my dress.

"Don't be a dummy. He will arrive whether you are waiting or not. We are surely going to freeze if we wait here another minute. And besides, the wind and rain are spoiling my hair."

She held both hands over her head and turned impatiently toward the house. I reached in my apron pocket for my wooden doll.

"Come on, dumdum," Lizzie called over her shoulder. "You'll catch your death of cold."

The smooth wood of the doll warmed my stiff hands and arms.

"Hope!" Lizzie shouted. "I can't wait for you another moment. I am freezing; can't you see?"

"Yes, Lizzie."

Is it raining on Wallace? Are the salal leaves keeping Ruby dry? Has Letia found her yet?

I followed ten steps behind Lizzie.

"What is wrong with you?" Lizzie said crossly. "Didn't you hear me? I said I was cold."

I held my doll tightly.

"You poor girl," she said when I had caught up. "Mother said you were the only family living on Wallace Island. She said that you haven't had anyone to talk to for two years. What a dreadful situation!"

"Yes," I said. I didn't like it when Lizzie talked about Wallace. What did she know? "I mean no…well, yes. Your mother is right, in a way. But no, it has not been dreadful. I loved living on Wallace. We weren't the only family who lived there. During the fishing season the Indians had a camp very close to our house."

"Oh, how dreadful," she exclaimed. Her nose twitched in disgust.

"No," I said, becoming annoyed. "Wallace Island is *not* dreadful. It is wonderful. I loved it there."

"But how unpleasant to have only Indians nearby." She looked frightened.

"What's wrong with that?" I asked.

"They are so dangerous. There are Indians on our island also. They come into our village selling fish and clams. But we're forbidden from going near them."

"I like the Indian camp on Wallace," I said. "The people are nice."

Lizzie stared in disbelief. "Do you mean to say you were actually in the Indian camp?" she gasped.

"Yes, I was," I said. I let go of my doll and walked ahead.

Lizzie was silent. That was good enough.

Travelling to Winter Island, Autumn 1862 ≋

I wrapped my red blanket around my shoulders
    to hide the doll
    out of the sight of the People.
    If they saw it, they would be afraid.
    The doll, they would say,
    has magical powers to bring bad luck from the hwunitum.
    Big Brother would take the doll
    and burn her,
    or he'd tie her to a tree near Hope's house
    as a warning.
    He would not understand.
    The doll was a gift.
    So I hid her under the blanket
    and did not tell Little Brother
    or even Grandmother.
    I had learned by now to keep my mouth closed.

By the time I was safely bound in my blanket,
    everyone was preparing to leave Summer Island.
    Father had already crammed the canoe full of our belongings.
    He had strapped cedar shingles on top
    for our winter house.
    "Where will we sit?" I asked,
    surveying the mound of goods.
    He stood proudly by the side of the bow,

admiring the beautiful eagle.
It stared back at him
with a respectful look in its eye.
"There is more room than enough," he said.
"Our new canoe can carry
the weight and supplies of three ordinary canoes.
He held Mother's arm.
He hoisted her and Swiltu over the side.
I got in next,
and Little Brother got in the middle beside me.
Big Brother sat at the front,
with Mother behind him.
The People shouted wildly in approval.
We wiggled our bottoms comfortably
on the cedar sitting slats
that Father had carved in a gentle curve.
Uncle Nanute and the others
helped Father push the canoe,
which was very heavy,
out into the water.
Once it was afloat, Father jumped in the back.
He tried his paddle first:
the canoe was steady and strong.
Our paddles dipped silently into the water,
and the eagle bow sliced through the whitecaps.
The canoe moved easily.
We circled the bay while we waited for the People.
One by one, they pushed their canoes into the water.
We took our position at the front
and paddled across the channel.

When we approached Winter Island,
we sang a welcome home song.
The People were excited.

There was so much to do.
The men used the cedar
they had brought from Summer Island
to attach new slats
to the walls and roof of the longhouses.
They dug out the hollow for the fire, cut firewood
and cleaned and restocked the food pit.
Swiltu and I
helped Mother and the other women
sweep the floors,
beat the dust out of the wall mats,
wash the sleeping ledges,
roll out blankets and sleeping mats,
gather firewood
and haul water.
That night I slept more comfortably than I had all summer.
My beautiful new sleeping mat
nestled on my freshly scrubbed ledge.
With my new cloth doll tucked safely between my belly and arms,
I thanked the ancestors that they had spoken
and that I was safe.

But it was as if I was waiting,
even when I was asleep.
In my dreams I was waiting
        for something to happen,
                        something dreadful.
My heart was heavy.
My shoulders curled,
as if I were carrying a heavy burden.
I watched over the mountains
for something to descend from the sky.

Mayne Island, Autumn 1862 ❧

"Brr. It's so cold. I'm chilled through to the bone," Lizzie said when we entered the house. "Mother, will you be bringing us hot tea?"

"Yes, of course, dear."

"We'll take it in my room," Lizzie said as she whisked through the kitchen.

"I'll bring it right in," Mrs. Cooper said.

"I'll help," I said, lingering beside the stove.

"Oh, don't bother about it." Lizzie grabbed my sleeve. "Mother will bring it along shortly."

I had never heard of such a thing, a girl demanding to be served by her mother. And what was even more surprising was Mrs. Cooper's response: how quickly she executed her daughter's commands. Even Charlotte, when she was deathly sick, did not demand such service from Ma.

Lizzie flopped backwards onto her bed and kicked her heels in the air.

"Shall we read a book?" she said.

"Yes, I would love to read," I said. If Lizzie was reading, she would at least be quiet. Maybe then I could rid my brain of the terrible sound like a thousand wasps that filled every corner of my head.

Lizzie opened the cedar chest at the end of her bed. She pulled out dolls and books and hair ribbons. I took a book, but I didn't read. The words blurred on the page. There was only one thing on my mind.

Where was Pa?

The supper table was crowded and noisy. Mr. Cooper, a young-looking man with unruly dark hair, soft brown eyes and a bristly black beard, sat at one end. He waited until everyone was quiet. Then he prayed.

"Thank you, God, for blessing us with the fellowship of strangers. Thank you for the gift of new friends. Be with John and Charlotte, who have not yet arrived safely. For you know all things, protect all things and care for all things. Bless the food. Amen."

Lizzie and Mrs. Cooper struck up a lively conversation with Old Man Albert and Mr. Haws. It didn't take long for Ma to join in. I stared at my plate of potatoes and fish, Mr. Cooper's prayer stuck in my head: *Be with John and Charlotte, who have not yet arrived safely.* He was right, surely: only God could protect them, because He was the only one who knew their whereabouts. And only God knew if Letia had found Ruby.

Dear God, I need my pa and sister. I need to know they are well. Can you not send me a sign? A message?

What good was it to me if only God was privy to such important information?

Please, God, let Pa and Charlotte walk into the room—now.

I stabbed a small chunk of fish and put it in my mouth. I chewed and tried to swallow, but my throat refused to cooperate. I tried again, but once more the food remained in the back of my mouth.

If I swallow five bites of fish, then Pa will arrive before everyone leaves the table.

I gulped hard. The fish scraped my throat as it went down and settled like a lump of coal in my belly. *One.* I stabbed another piece and stuffed it in my mouth. I chewed. I swallowed. I took a deep breath and swallowed again. And again. The second chunk of fish finally went down. The third bite was even more difficult than the previous two. I swallowed hard. I coughed and choked, driving the fish back up into my mouth. I snapped my lips closed in time to prevent the chewed food from spewing onto my plate. I gulped and the regurgitated food went down my throat. *Three.* I put down my fork and held onto my stomach.

Two more bites, two more swallows, and I can be sure that Pa will arrive before everyone leaves the table.

I swirled my fork through a mound of potatoes. Just two more bites. The door rattled and I looked up eagerly, but it was only a gust of wind.

Rain snapped at the kitchen window.

The conversation had become quiet. Even Mrs. Cooper's and Lizzie's voices were hushed. Ma was silent, and Mr. Cooper never said a word. Suddenly it was as if everyone at the table was thinking the same thing I was: *What has happened to Pa and Charlotte?*

After a few minutes, Mr. Haws said, "John must have assessed the weather and decided against departing."

"He may have left Wallace Island and then been accosted by the weather. He would pull into a nearby cove for shelter, he would," said Old Man Albert.

"One thing we can be sure of," Mr. Haws said. "He has found himself a safe place for the night."

"We have nothing to worry about," Ma said. She held her chin high and firm and forced a look of confidence. "John would not travel in a storm such as this, not in his little boat." Her voice sounded certain, but her face looked like a window with its shutters closed, as if to say, *This is what I am choosing to believe.* "He has decided to stay one more night on Wallace Island."

"Yes, Eva, I am sure of it," said Mr. Haws, nodding furiously. "Yes. Yes. He will set out tomorrow when the weather clears."

If they are all so sure, why do they look so worried?

I took another bite. But my stomach felt full all the way up my throat and into the back of my mouth. I chewed and chewed. There was no room for the food. I couldn't spit a mouthful of chewed fish back onto the plate. I continued to chew until there was hardly anything left and then gulped.

Four.

I slowly scooped a small piece of fish onto my fork.

If I can only swallow one last bite...

I put it in my mouth. I didn't chew. I swallowed hard, as if it were a spoonful of cod-liver oil. I gagged, but the food went down.

Five.

Surely now Pa will arrive before the supper table is empty.

I sat, my head down, my fork resting beside my plate, and listened to the storm pound the house minute after minute. The main course was cleared; bread pudding with custard and cranberries was served and eaten. Everyone had finished. The last person, Mr. Cooper, pushed his chair back and stood up. Half-heartedly, I did the same.

"Thank you for supper, Mrs. Cooper," I said. "Can I help you with the dishes?"

"Oh, my dear," Mrs. Cooper gasped when she looked at me. "You are ashen white. You must lie down."

Mrs. Cooper wrapped her arm around my waist and guided me into Lizzie's bedroom.

That night I had a dream. Charlotte heard a wolf howling at the moon, and she was afraid. She crawled into my bed beside me and lay so still I could not hear her breathing.

"Charlotte," I said and pushed her shoulder. "Charlotte, why aren't you breathing?"

Without taking a breath, Charlotte smiled and said, "I am well, sister. I am well."

It was early and still dark when I awoke. I slipped silently out of bed so I didn't disturb Lizzie, and dressed quickly. In the kitchen the adults were sitting around the table.

"John will be leaving Wallace Island soon if he stayed on the island. The weather has changed. The wind has died down, and the rain has stopped." Mr. Haws sipped his tea.

"We expect him to arrive well before noon, we do," Old Man Albert added.

Secretly I envied Charlotte. I wished it were me who'd been able to spend one more day at Sunnydale. If only Pa had chosen me to travel with him. If only I could have seen Letia one more time. Mayne Island was a miserable substitute for our real home.

"Maude and her ma will be here shortly," Mrs. Cooper said to me when she saw me by the door. "She is just your age."

If Maude has freckles, if she is shorter than me, if she speaks with a stutter, then Pa and Charlotte will arrive before noon…Stop that, Hope. You can only pick one thing, and you said freckles first.

It wasn't long before Maude and her mother arrived. She was a small, frail girl with short-clipped hair that looked like dried grass. Her skin was the colour of onions. She slunk through the front door, her shoulders stooped and her head facing the floor. She stood behind the sofa in the sitting room and leaned against the wall.

She was much shorter than me. Once I caught a glimpse of her face, it was easy to determine that she had blotches of reddish freckles over her nose and cheeks.

"Maudie," Mrs. Cooper said. "This is the girl from Wallace Island. Her name is Hope, and she is just your age."

"N-n-n-nice t-t-to m-m-meet you," she said without lifting her head.

"And you," I said and then whispered to myself, "Thank you, God."

Maude is everything I expected. Surely Pa will arrive before noon.

Lizzie was called to Lenora and William's house to help with the baby, and I was left alone. Mrs. Cooper directed me to spend the morning with Maude. It turned out that Maude chose to remain inclined against the wall. I went to the seashore and sat squinting, watching for Pa's boat. In the late morning, Mr. Haws and Old Man Albert and a few men from the village gathered at the wharf.

"I had calculated their arrival before now," Mr. Haws said.

He cupped his hand over his brow and looked out into the channel. "The time is a quarter of twelve, and there is still no sign of him."

His usual hearty confidence was being replaced by a clear sound of concern.

I stood not far off and listened.

"Shall we wait the afternoon," Old Man Albert asked, "before we return to Victoria? To be sure."

"To be sure of what?" I asked.

He glowered at me. "To be sure," he said, without finding the right words, "that they don't arrive safely."

"Then what will you do?" I asked. "If they don't arrive safely?"

"Young lady, you ask too many questions," Mr. Haws snapped, and trying again to sound confident, he said, "John will tie his boat to this very wharf this afternoon."

Old Man Albert said, "He will."

I wished I could be so sure.

Lamalcha Village, Winter Island, Late Autumn 1862 ☜

I dreamed of gales and thunder and lightning,
                            of rain that drenched the earth
    until our longhouses flooded.
    Human beings,
    dogs and deer,
    wildcats and bears,
    darted here and there
    to find high ground…
            the terrible noise of their splashing.
I awoke early.
The sky was still dark.
I slipped out of bed quietly, took my cloth doll
and pulled a blanket tightly around my shoulders.
I went outside and along the ridge
that led to the end of the bay.

The tide was low.
I stepped carefully down the bank to the rocks.
I walked over a pathway of smooth, cold stones,
out into the water.
I climbed up the jagged side
to the top of the Rock.
I had never climbed it before.
Although it was not against our laws
to sit on the Rock,

it was a sacred place,
visited only in extreme circumstances.

Grandmother had told me, "In the old days,
long before I was born,
and even before Grandfather was born,
and his father before him,
the Rock was a boy.
When the boy was young,
his father died and he lived alone with his mother.
When the boy was old enough, it was his job to supply food
for their little family.
Go, catch us a seal, his mother said.
But the boy would not learn how to tie ropes
or set the spears. He was afraid
and refused to go out into the deep sea
in the boats of the seal hunters.
Go, catch us a salmon, his mother said.
But the boy was a weakling
and did not like to exert himself.
Throwing a spear was too much effort.
The boy did not like the messy work of cutting and gutting his catch.
So the boy did not learn to catch a fish.
Go, take your father's carving knife, his mother said,
and build a canoe.
She gave the boy a beautiful sharp knife
with the finest stone blade and bone handle.
But the boy could not find wood easily,
and when he did, the tree was too heavy to haul to the village.
The boy did not want to carve the canoe in the forest
as his father had done,
for the boy liked the comforts of home too much for that.

"So it was that the boy denied whatever task his mother asked of him.
Pretty soon the boy became fat,

for all he did was sit around
and eat the food that others gave to his mother
and that she cooked for him.
Soon his mother became angry.
For she had had high hopes for the boy
that he would become an important man
and serve the People.
After a while the boy became sick
and died of a complication of his laziness.
His mother saw what had happened to him and said,
The boy can no longer refuse my requests.
So she turned the boy into a rock.
She waited until the tide was low
and took the Rock and walked out into the channel
on a pathway of smooth stones
and set the Rock in the water.
Satisfied, she said,
Now my son will have the most important job of all:
to protect the People and drive away our enemies."

I sat on the Rock
and thought about Grandmother's story
until the morning sun
broke through the darkness over the eastern mountains.
I talked to the Rock
and told him almost everything that had happened on Summer Island.
I told him about Hope and her family,
and how Hope's little brother ate the berries.
I warned the Rock that something terrible was about to happen,
for I was not sure that the Rock had heard
about the whisky traders or
the trouble Acheewan was in or
the murders of the hwunitum and
the threats from the Queen's men.
I told him everything I had heard,

229

and I apologized because I could not tell him more.
I could not tell him what was about to happen,
only that I had been feeling anxious
and was unable to sleep peacefully.
I asked the Rock to be especially watchful.

I kept my cloth doll hidden under my blanket,
to make sure the Rock could not see her.
She was the only secret I kept from the Rock,
for I wasn't sure he would understand.
I didn't stop talking to the Rock
until the morning sun began to warm my face.
I realized that the People would be getting out of bed.
If I didn't get off the Rock immediately,
someone would surely see me.
I slipped down the rough side
and crept over the smooth stone path,
now slippery and covered in water.
The tide had come in.
I had to wrap my doll in my blanket
and hold her over my head
as I sloshed through water up to my waist.
I stole my way back to the longhouse,
wet and icy cold,
without being noticed.

Mayne Island, Autumn 1862 ❧

I returned to the house in the afternoon. In the sitting room, neighbours sat on chairs and stools and overturned boxes, with their heads hung low. A heavy, worried hush lingered over the group. If they spoke at all, they whispered. "I wonder what has happened to them." "Do you think they have been attacked?"

Ma's pinched lips trembled. Her confidence of the day before had vanished. Appearing cold and nervous, she stroked Baby Dot, who was curled on her lap sucking nervously on her thumb. I looked away. I wanted to scream, *Ma, this is all your fault. If it weren't for you, we wouldn't be here!* But there was no point. Ma was worried sick, as I was, and nothing good would come of my anger.

I had swallowed five mouthfuls of fish at supper. Maude spoke with a stutter. She had freckles, and she was very short for her age. Surely more than three signs should make my wish indisputable. But there were no signs of Pa and Charlotte.

Mr. Haws was the first to speak out loud. "The journey from Wallace Island to Mayne Island takes no more than four hours even in unpleasant weather. It has now been more than eight hours since daybreak. If John set out this morning, he would have arrived by now. There is no doubt."

I yawned to fill my lungs, but my chest felt tight, as if I were suffocating. If I could have run, I would have fled the room, but my legs were as heavy as lead. I forced my lumbering legs to move and slowly inched my way through the room. When I reached the porch, Mr. Cooper put out his hand and said, "Come here, Hope."

"But I would like to go to the seashore," I said, trying to avoid his grasp. "Please let me go."

He held my shoulder and looked at Lizzie, who had appeared on the steps. "Maybe Lizzie should go with you," he said.

He was trying to be kind. But as hard as I tried, I could not be grateful for Lizzie's company, or Mrs. Cooper's hospitality, or even Mr. Cooper's compassion. What I wanted was simple enough: that Pa and Charlotte should safely arrive. After that was accomplished, there would be time enough for me to graciously appreciate my hosts.

"What has happened to your pa, Hope? Where is he?" Lizzie said loudly.

"They are on their way. I am sure of it," I said.

"How can you be sure?" she asked.

"Lizzie, be quiet," Mr. Cooper said and pointed his finger directly at his daughter.

"I am sure because Mr. Haws and Old Man Albert just try to scare everyone," I said. They were much the same words Pa had said, but today I did not believe them.

As if on cue, Old Man Albert's voice reached us from inside. "If we wait any longer to send out a search party, it will be too dark to find anything, it will. We have four hours before darkness sets in, we do."

"But is four hours enough?" Mr. Haws said.

We went back inside and listened as one man after the other stated his opinion. Maude's pa thought it was too late already, and that the men should wait until the morning to send out a search party. William agreed and thought it would serve no purpose to set out when it was already afternoon. They would no sooner reach a neighbouring island than dusk would have them return.

"I am ready to set out on the search immediately," said one young man, holding a paddle. He stood at the threshold. "Why do we wait? The man and his daughter may need our help now."

Searching for Pa? It seemed so strange to hear people talking of him in this way—he was not the sort of man who ever needed the help of strangers. But now I was relieved that this stranger was offering his help so willingly.

Mr. Cooper said, "I agree. I think we must form a search party immediately. There is time if we depart without further ruminations."

I bolted out the door, through the garden, down the path and over the bank to the shore. I turned to the right and sped along in search of a spot with the best view of the channel.

The sun was low over the hills. I scrambled to the highest place on the bank and stood on my toes. It was a clear day. I could see well into the channel. There were no ravens or seagulls out at sea and no eagles flying overhead. The trees were unusually still for the mid-afternoon. Wispy grey clouds looked painted in the sky, and only the current rippled the water.

"Pa," I called. My voice echoed as if I were calling into an empty room. "Pa, where are you? Pa. Pa."

The sound of my voice reverberated through my body until I wailed, "Please, please, please, Pa, come home. Please, please, you must be safe. You must be somewhere."

I sat on a large rock and took my wooden doll from my pocket. "Maybe Maude doesn't even have any freckles," I said out loud. "Maybe she is taller than me."

"What did you say?" Lizzie stumbled over the rocks to where I was sitting. "What did you say about Maude?"

"Nothing," I sobbed. I stuffed my doll back into her hiding place. "Nothing at all. It's all just a silly game."

"A silly game?"

"Yes. Maude probably doesn't even stutter either. Stuttering probably has nothing whatsoever to do with anything."

"Hope." Lizzie looked disdainful and confused. "I truly have no idea what you could be talking about. Why don't you come home with me?"

I stood up and looked again, first to the north and then ahead in the shadows of the mountains.

"I want to be the first person to see Pa and Charlotte."

"It's cold," she said. She shrugged her shoulders. "I'm going home. Father sent me to inquire of you, no more. And I find your physical condition to be fine. Of your state of mind, Hope, I am not certain."

I sat down again to wait, expecting the search party of men to appear at any minute. Only Alec stood near the path. He seemed such a small boy, hugging himself and shivering as if the sea would swallow him up.

"Alec," I called. "Come here."

He tunnelled under my arm, and we sat quietly until he said, "Did you hear what they were saying, Hope? Mr. Haws says if they don't send out a search party today it will be too late. What does he mean, too late?"

I hunted in vain for words.

"They think Pa has been attacked by the Indians," Alec added, his voice quavering.

"Who said that?"

"Old Man Albert. And some of the other men agreed."

"No, Alec. They think Pa's boat was hit by the storm yesterday. By the grace of God, Pa and Charlotte will be stranded on the shore of a nearby island."

"That's not what they were saying in the house."

"Alec, maybe Pa was feeling ill and decided to stay on the island for a few extra nights. Or Charlotte, she may have come down with a fit, and Pa is waiting until she settles down. You know how Charlotte is, Alec. They couldn't possibly embark on a journey with her coughing and wheezing."

"Do you think the Indians would hurt them?"

"Pa and Charlotte will be hungry and cold. We will serve them hot tea and soup when they arrive."

"Do you think they have been attacked?"

He squeezed his body into a tiny, tight ball, as if my answer might make him explode.

"No, Alec, the Indians have not attacked them. There are all sorts of reasons for Pa's delay."

"Do you think the men will find Pa and Charlotte on an island waiting to be rescued, Hope? Do you think that?"

"Yes, Alec. And I am sure that Pa will be impatient by now. I do hope the men hurry," I said. But the words fell flat. Although I had been the one to say them, I didn't really believe any of them.

Pa would have judged the storm and travelled only if it was safe. It had been a full day of good weather—plenty of time for him to make the journey. Pa would not have delayed sailing because of Charlotte—not for an entire day. He would have wrapped her in blankets and made her comfortable in the boat. He would have sung her favourite songs to ease her apprehension along the way. He would have.

After chasing my thoughts for a few minutes and finding no answers, I said, "No, Alec."

"What do you mean, no?"

"I mean I don't know," I whispered. "I don't know anything, except I hope they arrive soon."

"Do you think we should pray and ask God?" he said. "They are praying in the house."

"Of course, praying will help."

He sniffled and said, "You pray."

"I don't know what to say."

"Me neither."

"I suppose we could ask God to speed their arrival," I said.

"Yes, we could do that."

"…and keep them safe."

"Yes, we could do that as well."

I couldn't think of anything else.

Alec said, "And we could ask Him to let the Indians know that Pa is friendly and won't take anything that belongs to them."

"Certainly, Alec, we could ask Him that."

He let go of his legs and slumped limply onto my lap. He felt like a little child no bigger than Baby Dot.

"I don't want to go back to the Coopers' house," he said and then began to weep.

"Neither do I," I said.

I tucked my wooden doll into his arms, and we sat together until he breathed easily. I prayed silently, *God help me*. I knew it was a selfish prayer, but I could not think of another word to say to God who had, it seemed to me, deserted my family.

"Alec," I asked. "Why aren't the men coming to the beach? Is there to be no search party?"

"I think they are afraid of the Indians," he said, wiping his nose with his sleeve.

"We must go back to the house."

"No, Hope."

"Yes. Ma will worry about us. And she doesn't need anything more to worry about."

We stopped on the porch before entering the house. I took a long breath and clutched Alec's hand. We made our way through the throng of people and crouched next to Ma's knees. I covered her clenched, ice-cold fists with my hands.

The men sat around the table. The women huddled in the sitting room, some sitting, some standing and others serving tea and wiping up. Ma, Alec, Baby Dot and I drew together like orphaned kittens in a cluster near the fireplace. Without Pa we were like a carriage without a driver—like a team of horses without a bit and reins.

If Pa were here, I knew he would clap his hands against his thighs and say, *We are the Richardsons. We take care of our own. Why are we sitting around looking like wounded ducks?*

I stood up.

"We still have time, we do," Old Man Albert mumbled. "We could survey the coves nearby."

Mr. Haws wagged his head in disagreement. "If we were going to search today, we should have gone earlier," he said under his breath. Mr. Cooper nodded at Mr. Haws. Maude's father wagged his head, also disagreeing with Old Man Albert. Still no one had made a decision.

Why couldn't they make up their minds and do something? Or not do something? They were as sorry a bunch of people as I could imagine.

"No, it's too late," I said, loudly enough for everyone to hear. "You should have gone earlier. Now the water is dark. Pa will surely not be expecting anyone to search for him at this time of the day."

I crouched down. Ma took my hand and squeezed my fingers as if she might have been thanking me for speaking. Other than with their gaping mouths, their sign of surprise that a girl had been bold enough to speak on such matters, no one responded. One by one the men got up from the table.

"We will meet tomorrow morning, before dawn," Mr. Haws said.

During the day I had thought about Pa mostly—how Ma needed

him, and how without him, our family didn't know what to do. But that night I missed the noisy sound of Charlotte's breathing.

Did Charlotte have enough blankets? Was she cold and damp? Pa would be fine sleeping on the beach—but Charlotte?

If Daisy begins to grind her teeth before I fall asleep, I will be the one to find Pa and Charlotte stranded on a beach. They will be cold and hungry and very happy to see me.

Sure that Daisy would grind her teeth as she had done the night before, I hunched up on my elbows and listened to every breath. But the only thing I could hear was the adults praying in the other room.

Lamalcha Village, Winter Island, Winter 1862 ≋

The winter set in early and cold.
    Swiltu and I sat wrapped in a blanket near the front of the longhouse.
    Uncle Moosma paddled furiously toward the beach.
    The sound of him sucking in the freezing air
    carried all the way to where we were bundled,
    like the crying sound of someone in mourning.
    He pulled his canoe out of the water
    and hurried up the shore.
    "Where is your father?" he asked
    when I met him on the edge of the bank.
    "I will get him," I said, sensing his impatience.
    By the time Father and I entered the longhouse,
    Uncle was gulping down great spoonfuls of stew.
    Mother stood silently next to her brother.
    Father was stiff with apprehension,
    for he could tell from Uncle's appearance
    that it was for a serious reason he had come to the village.
    Uncle Moosma wiped the bowl with his finger
    and then licked off the remains of the stew.
    "The Queen's warrior boats
    are standing by in the harbour in Victoria,
    ready to set sail to your island.
    The only thing that will hold them back is the approaching winter,"
    Uncle said abruptly.
    "They accuse Acheewan of the murder of the hwunitum.

Three more hwulmuhw have also been accused.
One is a woman from a nearby island."

Father listened, stroking his chin.
He said, "We have had enough threats and alarm.
Can we not live in peace?"
He fixed his eyes on Uncle
as if to charge him with instigating the unrest.
"Do you accuse me
of being the menace to your People?"
Uncle said in his defence, his voice becoming shrill.
"Am I the creator of this peril?
Did I invite the hwunitum to this territory as my personal guests?
Are you saying that I am responsible
for the whisky and the madness that has followed?"
Father did not move;
he only deepened his gaze.
Uncle Moosma continued,
"I am the one who is bringing you a warning.
I am the messenger.
Beware, I say;
the Queen's men on the ships are the menace.
Their boats are armed,
their warriors anxiously waiting the season to be sent into action.
They will come for Acheewan
and the others they have accused.
They believe the culprits
reside here on your island.
They will not be gentle with your People.
These men from Victoria
say that they will make an example out of you.
They have made a decree
that whoever harbours a murderer
            will suffer the same fate as the murderer himself."

"Scoundrels," Father muttered.
"They are nothing but scoundrels.
Who would have such a law
that accuses a whole People
without so much as evidence against one soul?"
And so it was that when Uncle Moosma left,
he did not embrace Father and Mother as usual.
He said reluctantly, "Our People will join your People
if you need our support."
He tugged on my braids and whispered,
"My beautiful butterfly."
But his words were cold and brittle,
          not friendly as usual.
He left swiftly,
leading me to believe that he was afraid.
I thought he wanted to depart
before trouble arrived.
And if it did,
Uncle's words gave me no reassurance.
I was unsure whether or not
Uncle's People would come to Father's defence.

Mayne Island, Autumn 1862 ❧

In the morning, Lizzie pushed my shoulder.

"Come on, get up," she said. "People are arriving already."

It was dark outside. I felt as if I had only just gone to sleep.

"They are arranging search parties," Lizzie said with the sort of enthusiasm someone would have for the planning of a country fair or wedding. "Come on, come on."

I dressed, brushed my hair and tied it back neatly with a ribbon. Already, I didn't like how the day had started. I was rushed and had no time to think or plan. When I shook my head to clear its sleepy muddle, one thing became clear—today would be different from yesterday. I had two choices: either I let Mr. Haws and Old Man Albert and the people on Mayne Island remain in charge of my family, or I would take charge of it myself. I would be the one to find Pa and Charlotte. The Richardsons would be a family again.

Ma and Baby Dot were already sitting by the fire.

"Come with me, little sister," I said as I pulled Baby Dot's thumb out of her mouth. "You are too big for that. If you suck too hard on that thumb, it'll get stuck in your throat. And where's Alec?"

Ma hunched her shoulders and stared in my direction.

"Would you like me to go and get him?" I said.

She nodded.

"They'll be here soon, won't they, Hope?" Alec said when I found him sitting on the back stair.

"I don't know, Alec. But the men are going out to search for them, and I am going with them."

"You are?"

"Yes, I am. Surely Pa would not leave strangers the duty of finding us, if we were lost, and I will not leave it to strangers either."

"Can I come?"

"No, Pa would want you to look after Ma and Baby Dot."

"But Hope—"

"Alec, Ma needs you."

We returned to the kitchen. The men surrounded a roughly drawn map, which they had spread out on the table. I edged my way into the circle, between Mr. Cooper and Mr. Haws, and eyed the illustration. It was the first map I had seen of the area, sketched by someone's pencil with crudely drawn shapes labelled Wallace and Mayne and Prevost and Vancouver Island. Miscellaneous unnamed other shapes fitted together neatly like a puzzle. Large Xs marked Sunnydale, Miners Bay village and Victoria. Circles had been drawn and labelled REFUGE and INDIANS.

"Here are the sheltered coves, places John may have camped to weather the storm." With a pencil, Mr. Haws shaded the circles of refuge.

"And these"—he did the same to the places marked INDIANS—"are the Indians' most common travel routes and the locations where we have seen them camp." He put thick black arrows on the tides and strong currents and a fencelike design around the places where settlers lived. He traced a line along the route he thought Pa would have taken if he had encountered dangerous weather.

His voice became grave. "And here and here and here"—he drew three black crosses—"is where murders have taken place..."

The men and I dipped our heads to examine the murder locations. I thought how cruel it was for Mr. Haws to draw the crosses. Determined not to succumb to my feelings, I remained with the men and kept my eyes steady on the diagram.

"We have three boats," Mr. Haws said. "I'll mark an area for each boat to explore. We'll look closely for any evidence of John's presence."

Mrs. Cooper set bowls of porridge around the map, and Maude's ma poured cups of tea.

"May I go with you?" I asked.

The room became quiet, except for the sound of the men shuffling to sit where a bowl had been set.

"Can I go in one of the boats?" I asked—louder this time. "I want to help find my pa and sister."

Old Man Albert tightened his brow and coughed a short laugh. He looked down at the map Mr. Haws was folding and said, "Oh, my dear, this is not work for a little girl, it's not."

"I am not a little girl," I said, sitting myself down on the bench next to Mr. Cooper. "In the present circumstance, I am the oldest in my family next to Ma. I must help find my pa and sister."

"Oh, no, no," Mr. Haws said dismissively, as if my request was of no consequence. Maude's pa nodded his head in agreement with the other men.

"And why not?" I said.

Mr. Cooper cleared his throat and said, "She can come with me."

He looked over the heads of the men and directed his words to Ma. "When we find Charlotte, she will need her sister's help."

"No, Hope," Ma said in a low and unsteady voice.

Her voice surprised everyone. Every head at the table turned to look at her. Until then she hadn't said a word all morning.

"Please, Ma," I begged.

She shook her head without looking up.

Ma didn't understand. I needed to be the one to find Pa and Charlotte, but the most important reason I wanted to join the search was that I couldn't bear another minute of waiting. Time would pass more quickly in the boat. I would have a hope of seeing them sooner if I was with Mr. Cooper—even though I wasn't sure there was any hope.

Daisy hadn't ground her teeth the night before. There had been no good signs. Fear gripped me as if it had claws around my neck.

"Ma, we have to do something. Pa would want us to do something." My cheeks burned, and my eyes filled with hot, salty tears.

Ma won't do anything. Alec is too young. I am the only one left.

"I am sorry, Hope. You must stay with your mother," Mr. Cooper said. "But I promise you, I will search with all my might."

Lamalcha Village, Winter Island, Spring 1863 ≋

The spring came quickly after a dark and cold winter.
    And with the change of season
    came another visit from Uncle Moosma.
    This time his message, the same as before,
    was more urgent.
    "You must protect your village," he said to Father.
    "The gunboats are pointed northward.
    The storms have subsided.
    The snow has melted.
    They will come.
    Send Acheewan away.
    They will find him.
    And us too."

    Father instructed the men to use the logs
    they had cut and stacked the year before.
    "We will use them to bolster our walls," he said, then turned to me.
    "Letia, find Little Brother and come.
    I need you to run a most important errand."
    We arrived breathless.
    "Yes, Father," I said,
    pleased that at a time of such great significance
    he had an errand for me.
    "You will go through the deer trail to the eastern shore.
    You will climb to the ledge of the cliff

to the caves."
He looked at me as if to say,
Do you understand?
"Yes, yes," I said, "I know the place.
I have been there before
with Grandmother and Mother
to collect eagle feathers and eggs."
"Yes, exactly," he said.
He looked relieved that I knew the place.
"When you reach the cliffs,
call for Acheewan
and the others with him. Holler loudly,
for they may be deep within the caves.
Tell them your father wants them to come quickly."
I was proud that Father
would give me such an important task,
that I should be the one to deliver the message to such a great man.
"Now hurry," Father said.
Little Brother and I ran off toward the forest.
"Return quickly," he hollered after us.

It was cold and gloomy in the trees
when we started out.
It would be a long run.
I had never been in the eastern forest alone,
without Mother or Grandmother.
I couldn't help thinking about Forest Man.
When I had asked to play
in the forest behind the village,
Mother had said, "No, and here is why my answer is no."
Then she warned me about Forest Man.
"He is as large or as small as he needs to be.
He lurks in the trees and bushes
        looking for prey.
He is usually satisfied with

small animals, which he can catch
and eat
so that he can run as fast as the sleekest wildcat.
Or birds, which he can catch
and eat
so that he can leap to great heights.
He snatches the winged creatures from the trees
by raising his long arms
and trapping them in his spindly fingers.
Or bats, which he can catch
and eat
so that he can see in the dark."

When Mother got to this part of the story, she scowled.
Her voice sounded deep and growly and whispery.
She looked directly at my face
to make sure I didn't miss a word she said.
"Once in a while,
Forest Man looks for a small child, which he can catch
and eat
so that he can be human."
And then, so that I was sure her story was true, she said:
"At night he rubs himself
with the sleeping embers from our fire
to keep warm.
In the morning,
you can see for yourself the mess he leaves behind."
And I believed her.
I had seen the evidence:
ashes strewn across the beach,
Mother's pots upended
and our logs tossed about.

It was because of Forest Man
that Little Brother and I had never been given permission

to go deep into the forest on Winter Island.
It was not like Summer Island,
for Forest Man did not live there.

I kept the red blanket tightly wrapped around my shoulders,
and we ran, as fast as we could.
I hoped that Forest Man would not be waiting for us
in dark and shadowy places,
not at a time when we had to deliver
a message of such consequence.

When we reached the cliffs that Father had described,
Acheewan was perched on the ledge,
waiting.
With great importance,
I delivered Father's message word for word.
Acheewan gave me a crooked smile
and disappeared into the caves.
He returned a short time later
followed by two men I had never seen before.
Each of them carried a musket and a sling of powder and shot.
Little Brother and I ran a few steps behind the men,
charging through the forest.
We were exhausted by the time
we arrived back at the village,
and excited, and willing to put up with being tired,
given the magnitude of our mission.

That night Acheewan and the two men
ate in our longhouse.
Father had disagreed with Uncle Moosma;
he would not send Acheewan away.
Many of the People crowded around our fire.
They were angry at the news
that Uncle Moosma had delivered.

Father, who had always spoken in favour of
friendship and peace with the hwunitum,
now spoke about war.
"Scoundrels," he said.
"The Queen's men will not come and threaten us
as if we are weaklings.
When they come, we will face them as warriors.
We are a proud People.
They will not treat us like disobedient children in need of discipline.
We will let them know they are mistaken.
We are men."

I went to bed and covered my head.
But I could not block out the sound of the voices.
I hugged the cloth doll that Hope had given me.
"They are wrong, my doll," I said. "The hwunitum's gunboats
will not come to Winter Island.
And if they do,
the Rock will protect us.
Great winds from the north
will drive away their sails.
The hulls of their boats
will crash against the cliffs.
The Queen's men will be thrown into the channel.
They will swim to the village
and beg to be allowed to live.
Our People will decide what should become of the scoundrels.
That's what will happen."
I hoped,
          but I did not sleep.

Mayne Island, Autumn 1862 ❧

I was convinced now that Mayne Island was not a good place, although there was nothing obviously wrong with it. Mr. Cooper was nice enough. In fact, I liked him very much. He was helpful and kind and, without question, a generous host. But with the others, I felt uncomfortable.

When the men got in the boats to depart on the search, I felt as if hot coals were pressed against my skin—it hurt to touch. My face throbbed. I wanted to scream. Inside I was hysterical. I was unable to form words. Around the outside edges of my brain, I heard the villagers call goodbye to the men.

"God be with you."

"Only God can help us now."

"God willing, they will be found."

Please, God, I don't want any of the men to return alive unless Pa and Charlotte are with them—vigorous and in good health.

I sat on a log next to Alec and gazed at the boats disappearing into the distance.

"I am afraid, Alec."

"No, Hope. You can't be afraid. You are never afraid."

"I am now."

"The men will return. They will find Pa and Charlotte."

"I hope I never see the men again if they don't find them."

"Oh, Hope. God would not be pleased to hear you say those words."

"But it's true. I hate this place. I hate everything about it, Alec. I wish that awful Mr. Haws and wretched Old Man Albert had never set foot on Wallace Island."

"They are only trying to help."

"They are nothing but whisky traders."

"No, Hope. They will find Pa."

"What if..."

I stopped.

"They will find them, Hope. They have to."

I took the wooden doll in my hands and thought about the last words Pa had said: *We will be along directly.*

Pa was a man who kept his word. Nothing short of a catastrophe would keep him from his family. Of that much I was absolutely certain. "A man must take care of his family." That's what he'd said.

Nothing short of a catastrophe.

"Come on, Alec. Let's go back to the house."

"I don't want to." He'd put his hands under his legs and rested his chin on his knees. His hands were clenched tightly together to keep from shaking.

"Neither do I, but we can't sit here all day."

Alec and I wandered in and out of the house and to the end of the lane. We walked along a path that led along the seashore. I held his hand with one hand and my wooden doll with the other. After what seemed like hours, we returned to the wharf and sat on a rock watching the water lap the pebbles on the shore. I listened to the gentle push and pull, push and pull, push and pull, until I didn't hurt, or fear, or think of anything at all.

Suddenly Alec roused me from my numbness. "Look," he said. "Hope, there's a boat!"

I peered out into the channel and spotted a tiny black form. "Yes," I said. "I suppose it may be one of the boats."

"It is, Hope," he said excitedly. "Of course it is. It may be Pa."

I held him while he teetered on the rock. He stretched on his tiptoes to get a better look. He could look if he wanted; I couldn't find in me any hopefulness whatsoever. What good had it done me up until now?

"It's not Pa's boat," I said.

"It might be," he said. "I can't be sure. I don't remember what Pa's boat looks like from a distance."

He took a long breath, trying hard to hold back his tears.

"It's Maude's father," I said matter-of-factly when the shape of his wide-brimmed hat came into view. "And one of the young men with him."

"No, Hope, it is Pa," he cried.

"Alec, it is not Pa. And don't say that again," I said sternly, unwilling to bear the disappointment I knew would follow closely. "Come with me. We will greet the men as they arrive."

Alec wrapped his arms around my neck, and I pulled him off the rock.

"What if—," he persisted.

"I told you, Alec. It is Maude's father. And we will greet them."

We stood hand in hand at the water's edge until the men had climbed out of the boat and met us at the end of the wharf.

"Did you find anything?" I asked.

They shook their heads.

"Nothing," Maude's father said. "Not a thing."

The young man said, "We saw whales swimming on either side of the boat. There might have been fifty of them. Beautiful creatures."

By the time they had tied up the boat and headed up the path, another boat was visible in the distance.

"Could that be Pa's boat?" Alec asked, staring out into the channel.

"No," I said. "It's too big and the wrong shape." Pa's boat was long at the front, good for choppy seas, and wide and deep at the back. Stable and seaworthy even with a load, that's how he described it.

The boat that approached was wider. It bobbed about in the water, even though the wind was still.

"But maybe they have Pa and Charlotte with them," Alec said. His face brightened with anticipation.

"I only see two people," I said, sitting back down on the rock. "And the boat is sitting much too high to be carrying our belongings or extra passengers."

It was Old Man Albert. His size made that certain.

"Come on," Alec said. "Let's go see."

"You go," I said.

I pulled my coat around my chest. I couldn't bear to see Old Man

Albert, not now, not ever. I turned my head the other way when he walked past.

The young man who accompanied him said, "I'm sorry."

I was struck by his sincere manner. I felt he wanted to say more, but he passed, only repeating, "I'm sorry."

If one more boat comes in without Pa and Charlotte, I think I will die.

"Mr. Cooper will have them, Hope," Alec said, his hopefulness unchecked. "I am sure he will."

Time was running out. The blue sky was changing to turquoise as the golden glow of the sun descended behind the mountain horizon.

If Mr. Cooper's boat appears before the sky turns grey, then he will bring good news.

No sooner had I thought the words than I began to notice how quickly the autumn afternoon light weakened—from one second to the next the colour faded and light dimmed, each moment unlike the one before. To avoid seeing how quickly dusk was approaching and how little time I had given Mr. Cooper to appear, I closed my eyes, and what seemed like only a few minutes passed.

"There he is!" Alec shouted in a startled voice, jolting me out of the darkness. I was shocked by the complete absence of turquoise in the sky.

"I can see his boat. It's over there." Alec pointed to the north.

"Where?" Lizzie appeared suddenly, running down the shore toward us. "Where is my father?"

"There is a boat!" Alec hollered. "Look."

She squinted. "It's just a tiny speck. How can you tell who it is?"

"It might be my pa," he said.

She leaned forward in the direction of the boat and sheltered her eyes with her hand as if the sun had blocked her view.

"No, it's my father, it's my father," she said. "I can see him from here."

It was Mr. Cooper's boat, and the closer it got, the more certain I was that it carried only two passengers—Mr. Cooper and William.

"Oh, it is, it is!" she screamed. "It's Father. And William."

Alec's head drooped at the sight of the men, and he sank onto the rock beside me.

"Oh, Mother!" Lizzie hollered. Mrs. Cooper stood at the foot of the path. "It's Father. It's Father. I was so worried."

I squeezed my wooden doll until my fingers hurt. If I didn't hold them still, they might, on impulse, pick up stones and throw them at Lizzie and Mrs. Cooper.

If only Mr. Cooper's boat would sink right in front of everyone.

I didn't wish harm on Mr. Cooper. But for Lizzie's sake, I wished he would die.

When there was no doubt that Pa and Charlotte were not in the boat, I grabbed Alec's hand, dragged him off the rock and dashed up the path.

Mayne Island, Autumn 1862 🐾

At supper I concentrated on the chewing sounds in my ears. I tried to drown out the sound of Old Man Albert and the other men talking about the inlets they had searched. They had found nothing—no signs of Pa or Charlotte, no campfires, no boat.

"And you, Samuel?" Mr. Haws asked. "Was your search as futile as ours?"

Mr. Cooper raised his head, sat straight-backed and took a long breath. His lips were dry and quivered nervously. He swallowed, took a gulp of tea and swallowed again.

He spoke softly. I could only just hear him say, "We explored the coves and sandy beaches in the area marked out on the map. We rowed as close as the rocky seashore allowed. We examined everything carefully until late this afternoon, when we passed Prevost Island at quite a distance."

He paused. He had something else to say, but he appeared unsure of what words to use. He gave me a quick look, and just as quickly he looked away. "We sighted something there that might have been a boat or milled lumber. It was difficult to identify, and with dusk coming we were obliged to return home and leave the object behind."

"Could the object have been Pa's boat?" I blurted out.

"I don't know." A deep V creased his forehead. He moved his head slowly side to side. "I don't know."

"What did William think it was?" I asked. I needed to confirm that something of significance had been found.

"William will be here at the break of dawn. We will revisit the location. At that time we will look more closely," he said.

Mr. Haws and Old Man Albert cross-examined Mr. Cooper. How long would it take to reach the location? Where exactly was the inlet in question? Where was the unidentified object? How large was the object? Could it have been driftwood?

"I hesitate to speak on this matter any more. I do not want to create unwarranted hope, nor do I want to generate unnecessary fear," Mr. Cooper said. From the worried look on his face, I knew he was more fearful than hopeful. "I think it is best that we all pray that tomorrow will bring good news. Tomorrow William and I will return to Prevost Island and investigate the object."

"I will come with you," I declared without consideration. "I will recognize Pa's boat and our belongings. You will need me to identify items that may be found."

Ma's face was ashen. She spoke so quietly through her thin blue lips that she could scarcely be heard. "They don't need you to identify our things. They will find John and Charlotte. They will identify themselves."

An icy wave of silence swept over the room; no one moved. My impulsive request had brought into the open what everyone at the supper table was thinking. Pa's boat was wrecked on an island, and Pa and Charlotte would not be found alive. The only people who might have thought differently were Ma, Baby Dot and Alec. Ma, stone-faced, rigid, held Baby Dot and Alec next to her. Alec chewed and swallowed with a look of determined optimism.

The men paid no attention to my appeal or Ma's response. It was as if we were both of no consequence. Mr. Haws and Old Man Albert went about planning the next morning's search without even one word from Mr. Cooper or one glance in his direction. After a few minutes of silence and disregard, he said, "I will instruct you in the morning where the cove is located. You can follow William and me across the channel. I will examine the object."

He got up and left the table, the forcefulness of his words marking the end of the conversation.

At bedtime Lizzie said, "I was so worried, Hope. I know how you feel. I thought my father had drowned. Or worse, that he had been murdered.

It was a dreadful afternoon. And poor Mother."

"Your father is well," I said coldly. "As is your mother."

That wasn't what I wanted to say, but it was all I could manage without spitting harsh words at her. I considered Lizzie the most mean-hearted person I had ever met. I turned my back to her and hugged my wooden doll. When Lizzie spoke again, I pretended to be asleep.

In the night I woke to the sound of Daisy grinding her teeth and Lizzie snoring.

I will tell her she makes a more ungainly noise than all of Daisy's teeth grinding—that her nose snorts like a pig when she breathes in, and her throat rattles when she breathes out.

I devised mean and nasty things I could say to Lizzie, ways to humiliate and disgust her. I needed to put an end to her haughty, vain and demanding behaviour. If I had to have a friend on Mayne Island, it would be Maude, in spite of the fact that she hadn't said more than a few words to me since I arrived.

If Lizzie is trapped in a cave, falling from the cliffs, choking on her food—I will not help her. I will walk past Lizzie as if she were invisible. I will hold Maude's hand. We shall appear like best friends. Lizzie will know she is worse than poison to me.

I lay awake until I heard the sound of movement in the kitchen. I got up and dressed. Mr. Cooper was making the fire. He placed kindling in the stove. He measured each stick methodically with his eyes before stacking it on the fire. I wanted to ask him about what he had seen the day before. Had he seen more than he had described at supper? Why was he so insistent that he be the first to examine the wooden object?

The fire began to crackle; he rubbed his hands together over the flames.

"A blanket?" he asked me. "Do you want a blanket? You must be cold."

"No, thank you," I said, tucking my feet under my body. "The fire will warm up soon enough."

I liked sitting near him; he was solid and strong. He reminded me of Pa.

We weren't alone for long. The kitchen was soon full of people. Ma slumped on a chair near the stove, and Baby Dot sat sucking her thumb on Ma's lap. Alec leaned against the doorpost. His hair sprang out in all directions, his eyes were red and bloodshot, his shirt was untucked and twisted, and one pant leg was stuffed in his sock. We were an unsightly muddle—Pa would surely have disapproved.

I looked at Ma. She was too tired, too pale and drawn to step forward and take charge.

If not I, then who in this pitiful family will take charge? Which one of us will find Pa and Charlotte...no matter what their condition?

But when I thought about searching for my pa and my sister, the gravity of the situation became clear. Perfectly, dreadfully, horridly clear.

In England, I had been the one Pa taught to use his clamps and mallet. After I had completed my school lessons in the morning, he would say, "Come on, Hope. We have work to do."

Charlotte was too sickly and Alec too young to help Pa, so I often spent the afternoon in his work shed making furniture. I held the spindles in place while he set the back of a chair in a perfect arch. I tapped the upright pieces into their holes in the seat and tightened the clamps so he could keep them aligned properly.

He would say, "You will be a fine craftsman one day, my Hope." He paid no heed that I was a young girl, too young to cast a measured eye on the angles of a sideboard or a window frame.

When he finished a bureau or davenport, he loaded it in his cart and packed it with straw bales. I rode with him to make deliveries to the customers, and I watched while they examined Pa's craftsmanship.

"Ahhh," the fine gentlemen would say. "First-rate handiwork, my good man." I marked the payment in the ledger next to the name. Pa said I had a mind for numbers and business the way he did.

"Ma and Charlotte are of a different sort," he said. "They make a good pie, but they don't have the constitution for decisions and dealings in business and commerce."

Now it seemed as though Ma didn't have the constitution to make decisions of any kind.

"With all due respect, Mr. Cooper," I said, trying to sound as mature as I could for my twelve years, "I believe it would be an appropriate measure for you to accept a member of my family as part of the search. As we discussed yesterday—"

"Hope," he interrupted. His face drained of colour. There had been a distinct change in his manner since the day before. His previous willingness to have me accompany the search had all but disappeared. "Yesterday your mother said no."

I looked at Ma. Mr. Cooper looked as well. Her eyes flickered, and for a second I thought she was preparing to speak. I waited. Nothing.

"But Pa would want one of us to be with you," I persisted. "The search will affect my family more than the others."

Mr. Cooper stared at Ma as if appealing for her support. She remained silent.

"Of course," he said and rubbed his hands together over the fire more vigorously than before.

"The Richardsons must take care of their own," I said. I used a voice that sounded as much like Pa's as I could make it. "One of us should accompany the search."

"Eva?" he asked. He looked imploringly at Ma, as if to say, *Put a stop to your daughter's pleading.*

"Ma?" I said. "Please, Ma."

She moved her eyes in my direction. It seemed as if she was gazing at an object far beyond where I was sitting.

"Should not one of us accompany the search?"

She said in a voice that was almost a whisper, "Yes, dear, you do as you please." That was all she said. She had changed her mind, although from the worried look on her face, she wasn't pleased to grant me permission.

I looked at Mr. Cooper and said, "It is settled, then. I will accompany you on your boat today."

His eyes were sharp and piercing. He fixed them on me and said in a low, deliberate voice, "Yes, Hope. I heard your mother." He frowned and turned away.

I helped Mrs. Cooper pour tea and serve porridge. There was scarcely room for the men at the table. They sat elbow to elbow, heads bowed, waiting for Mr. Cooper.

He said, "Hope, you must sit and eat if you are coming with me."

William made an opening for me on the bench. I wriggled into place and didn't look up.

Mr. Cooper bowed his head and said, "Dear God in heaven, we, your most humble servants, plead with you: bless our endeavours this morning. May the fruits of our labour be a blessing to you and to our dear friends. Protect us and keep us safe. Be with Eva and the children."

"Amen," each person said. "Amen, amen," they said again.

Why hadn't Mr. Cooper prayed for Pa and Charlotte to be found alive?

I looked up at William. He scooped porridge into his mouth, his head down. I wiggled a little. I wanted to have his attention, to catch the look in his eye, to get a hint of what he thought about Pa and Charlotte. But he didn't stir. It was as if he were the only person in the room. He ignored the men's conversation about the weather—a storm in the air...rain... heavy rain. He kept his eyes on his spoon, which he swirled nervously around in his porridge.

I began to change my mind. Maybe, I thought, I should not have been so adamant about taking part in the search.

But the order of the day had been declared. Ma had agreed, Mr. Cooper too.

The men finished eating and headed to the porch one by one. They dressed in heavy overcoats, boots and rain hats. I remained at the table while Mrs. Cooper removed the bowls and spoons and put them in the wash bucket.

"Hope," Mr. Cooper said quietly, leaning over with his face near my ear, "I don't think you should come with us today."

"But Mr. Cooper," I protested impulsively, in spite of my own misgivings. "I must."

"I know you want to come. But I do not think it is what your Pa would—"

I interrupted him. "Ma said I could go with you."

Since I was a little girl, Pa had said that the Richardson trait I had in overabundance was stubbornness. *Stubborn enough for two or three children together*, he would say.

Once, when I was no bigger than Baby Dot, I had been tugging defiantly on a piece of kindling. "I am big enough," I said, insisting that I could make the fire on my own. "I do it myself."

"Hope, Hope, Hope," Pa said, patting my head. "You hold on as tight as a barnacle to a rock. Sometimes, my girl, you have to change your mind."

This time changing my mind would be easy; in fact, I had already changed my mind. Admitting it would be the hard part, especially after I had argued so insistently for Ma's concession.

"Alec is too young to go," I said. "That leaves me. There is no one else in our family to take part in the search. And it is my pa and sister you are looking for."

Mr. Cooper put his hand on my shoulder. "I am a father, Hope," he said. "I know that your pa would not want you to accompany us this morning. Please believe me. I know, Hope. I know."

I sat quietly before the awful truth. Mr. Cooper was trying to protect me from what I might see on the search.

"I will remain here with Ma and the children," I said, struggling to keep my voice steady. "She will need me here with her."

I dried the dishes, rinsed out the rags and hung them on a line strung across the front porch. I combed my hair and tied it back with a ribbon Pa had bought me in Victoria. I put on a clean apron and tucked my wooden doll into the pocket. I pulled up my stockings and fastened them snugly to my garter to prevent them from bunching at my knees and ankles. I put on the dark green velvet hat that Grandma had made for me to wear to church. I found Alec's coat and boots and brought them to him.

"Come on," I said. "We are going outside."

"Why?" he asked.

"To wait for the boats." I tucked in his shirt and folded his collar down neatly. I spat on my fingers and arranged his hair before I put his cap on his head. I tightened his suspenders and folded the hem of his trousers up to make a tidy cuff. I helped him with his coat and boots. I fastened the buttons and smoothed the wrinkles out of the sleeves.

"There you are, young man," I said. I looked at Alec and then at myself. "We are fit to meet the Queen."

I took his hand. "Ma," I said, "Alec and I will be outside. We will wait for the boats to return."

We went to the back of the house and sat on the stairs overlooking the water and the mountains beyond.

"Red sky in the morning," Alec said. I wrapped my arm around his shoulder. "What did Pa say about red sky in the morning?"

The grey dawn had lifted toward the east, but in the direction the men had gone, the sky was still streaked with streams of red and orange light.

"Red sky in the morning is the shepherd's warning. Red sky at night is the shepherd's delight."

"What does that mean?" he asked.

"Never mind."

Lamalcha Village, Winter Island, Spring 1863 🖎

The gunboat appeared
    just as Uncle Moosma said it would.
    The water was choppy
    and the tide was running swiftly.
    The giant boat pushed its way through the water
    as if nothing protected the island.
    The boy who had turned into the Rock was lazy,
    as his grandfather had said.
    He must have been asleep.
    The Rock did nothing to protect the island.
    The gunboat pulled so far
    into the mouth of the bay
    that the points to the north and the south
    surrounded it like a huge mouth.
    On the deck of the boat
    —I could see them clearly—
        were the Queen's men
    dressed in bright red uniforms.
    They folded down the sails and set down a tether
    to hold the boat in front of our longhouse.
    The People stood in a huddle
    and murmured about the audacity
    and downright rudeness of the hwunitum.
    The men took their muskets and found cover.
    Three or four went to the north point,

three or four to the south point.
Two or three found hiding spots along the bay.
"This is war," Father said
when he went with a few of the men
to barricade themselves in our longhouse.

I had heard of wars far off,
how the northern People destroyed villages
and took captives and slaves.
But wars were only stories told around the fire.
Until today,
I had not believed Mother's warnings
that the newcomers in the south
would cause wars with the People.
No one had believed her.

I scrambled into the forest
and crouched behind a giant cedar.
I watched in terror.
The vague fears in my dreams
were taking shape and unfolding before me.
The Rock had betrayed us.

                                        Time stopped.

The island paused.
The birds stopped singing.
The wind was still.
The men on the boat scurried back and forth without a sound.
On the deck, enormous black guns,
the size of large bears,
pointed at our village.
Grandmother appeared, dragging Swiltu behind her.
"Hurry along," she said.
I scurried behind her up a grassy hill
to a hollowed-out place behind a shelf of rocks.
Little Brother was there with the other boys,

three or four of them,
huddled together like rabbits.
I couldn't see what the men were doing.
I looked around,
but Grandmother had made sure
we were well enough away from the gunboat.
We couldn't be seen,
nor could we see anything.
I only knew what happened next
by the sounds I heard.

Gunshots exploded,
smashed branches
and thudded against tree trunks.
A heavy blanket of quiet
was cut short by another explosion,
then an ear-splitting crack
as a musket shot hit the boat.
Another moment of deathly silence
was cut short by a dreadful cry
        of a man in agony.
Warriors from the boat shouted coarse words
I didn't understand.
Their voices echoed over the water
        like the calls of wounded animals.
Foreign words penetrated the forest
where I curled around my cloth doll
wrapped in a blanket next to the boys.
I held my breath
until I thought my head would explode.
I squeezed my knees together hard until they ached.
Then another crack of gunshot,
and another and another,
so many I couldn't count them
or tell from which direction they had been fired.

The air was pulsing with thunder.

I pulled my blanket over my ears
to dull the painful sound.
I rolled into the sleeping position of a newborn baby,
for how long I couldn't tell.
I began to breathe lightly again,
in and out.
The crashing in my ears subsided.
I turned onto my hands and knees
to see what had become of our village
and the Queen's boat.
I twisted to sit.
BOOM...
BOOM...
BOOM...
The detonations went off,
so thunderous that the earth shook.
My body was hurled against a rock.

WHACK.

Blood gushed out of my forehead.
Then the terrible shattering sound of wood,
and the dense thuds of logs collapsing.
Men from the north point shouted, "Get clear of the longhouse!
Is everyone out?
They are preparing to fire again!"
My heart raced.
Where was Father?
The last I'd seen, he was headed to the longhouse
with other men,
to fire their muskets from behind the palisade.
A woman screamed, "Where is my son?"

Grandmother grabbed the children
as if her arms could hold us all.
She pulled us together on the ground
and wrapped her arms around us
like a mother goose protecting her goslings.
"Keep your heads down."
Her voice was unsteady.

"Where are the children?" someone hollered a long time later.
"Letia? Swiltu? The boys?"
With a flood of relief, I recognized Mother's voice.
Grandmother raised her head. "They are here," she shouted.
This time her voice was strong.
"With me."
Mother's voice rose into the air,
wailing.
Then I heard a chorus of women weeping.

Mayne Island, Autumn 1862

We sat without speaking—a long time or a short time? Time. It was as if we were waiting for time to change our lives.

If only it was over. If only it had never begun. If only I knew the truth. If only the truth could never be made known.

"Let's go to the wharf," I said when the morning was spent, and I thought that the boats would soon be returning.

I pulled Alec up to a standing position.

"Soon the men will be here." I straightened out his pant legs. "With Pa and Charlotte."

He didn't say anything.

"We must be there to greet them," I said.

I took his hand, and we walked down the path. No matter what time had in store, we would meet Pa and Charlotte with dignity.

"We are the Richardsons," I said to Alec. "We look after each other."

The white shapes of squalling, frantically circling seagulls were an unnerving sight. The men would hurry and return before the storm set in.

I led Alec from log to log until I found a place to sit.

"We will wait for them here," I said, plunking my bottom down. He sat down and shoved over as close to me as he could. A cold breeze skimmed off the water. We hugged each other. His body trembled. Again we waited.

A pleasantly hungry feeling fills my belly. I am warm. The smell of roast duck and onion stuffing filters through the room. "A meal fit for a king," Pa says. "And prepared by a queen." Ma sits at the end of the table facing Pa, with Baby Dot beside her. Charlotte has pink ribbons in her hair and sits across from Alec and me. Ma's face is rosy and plump, her lips full, when she smiles at Pa.

I woke with a start. Seagulls were making a hellish noise, plunging toward the shore as if someone were tossing them fish guts. I pushed Alec's sleeping body off my shoulder and stood up cold and stiff. I rubbed my eyes and looked into the channel. It was choppy and clouds cast dark shadows on the water. And there was a speck on the water.

If I see Mr. Cooper's boat first, he will bring good news.

I squished my eyes tightly shut for a minute. Then, one eye at a time, I opened them. It was Mr. Cooper's boat. It was William's hat for sure. I swallowed a lump in my throat.

This means good news.

I made a feeble attempt to hope. I nudged Alec in the side. He awoke with a jolt.

"What?" he said. "Are they here?"

"Someone is coming."

The boat approached quickly, the wind pushing it from behind. The hull sat lopsided, the stern lower than the bow.

We walked to the water's edge.

"They have found Pa, Hope, haven't they?" he said. "Someone will bring them to us?"

"No, Alec," I said as I examined the listing boat. Something appeared to be sitting between the men.

They hadn't loaded it evenly. Not only was the boat lower at the back, it was leaning dangerously to one side. They carried a heavy and awkward freight. "I don't think they will."

"But look, Mr. Cooper has brought something. I can see it in his boat."

"Yes, Alec. I see."

"What do you suppose it is?"

"I don't know."

"And where is Pa?"

"Please don't ask so many questions."

The tide was high. Instead of pulling the boat up to the dock, Mr. Cooper rowed it to shore almost directly in front of where we stood. The bottom of the boat scuffed along the loose pebbles until it was lodged firmly on the beach. Without moving a step, I peered into the boat. There, lodged between the two men, were a trunk and pieces of splintered wood. It was the trunk Pa had made in England shortly before our departure. I could tell without a question. The latch. I was certain.

"This latch is as strong as the day it was made," Pa had said when he used a lever to pry it loose from an old chest. "But the trunk won't survive the journey to the new country."

He'd fastened the old latch to the new chest and said, "Ma will be pleased. She can fill it with linens for the voyage."

At Sunnydale the chest was placed near the wood stove in the kitchen. I sat on it when I warmed my hands by the fire.

"That's our trunk," Alec shouted, at first excited, then startled as he took in the damage. "Where is the lid?"

The trunk had been torn apart. The lid was ripped from its hinges and broken in pieces. A small pile of rumpled linens lay in the bottom of the demolished box. I stared at the scene as if my body and mind had been separated, the one from the other, until I felt the chill of cold water seeping through my boots.

Maybe this isn't our trunk, and Alec is wrong.

My toes stung from the icy water, but I stepped deeper into the shallow surf and reached for the chest. Mr. Cooper took my hand and lifted me into the boat. I pulled out a pillowcase embroidered with a violet: Grandma's favourite flower. And a lace doily, unravelling and dirty. It was the doily Ma made when she was expecting Baby Dot. Underneath was a pair of baby shoes—the ones Baby Dot used when she first learned to walk. I stuffed the shoes and doily into my pocket.

I will need to be the one to give them to Ma.

Mr. Cooper stepped out of the boat.

"Come, Hope," he said and helped me onto the shore.

"Where's Pa?" Alec asked in a timid voice. He took a few steps away from the boat. "Mr. Cooper, where's Charlotte?"

"Hush, Alec," I said. "We must go to the house."

"But where's Pa?" His voice quavered, and his face was ghostly white.

"I'm sorry, Alec. Mr. Haws and Old Man Albert..." Mr. Cooper began to speak and then stopped.

My knees started to give way, and from the bottom of my stomach I began to vibrate.

"Please, Mr. Cooper," I spoke in a squeaky whisper.

Can he wait for a few more minutes?

I had a terrible feeling that my future, the future of the Richardsons, everything I would do for the rest of my life, rested with the words he was about to say. I stumbled over the pebbles and leaned over a log. My stomach heaved great dry foodless retches. When I lifted my head, Mr. Cooper picked me up and put me on one of his knees, Alec on the other.

"Children, you must listen closely to what I have to say," he said. "We found the trunk, and we found your pa as well."

"Where is he?" Alec asked.

"He is in Mr. Haws's boat," Mr. Cooper said.

"Then we will wait for him," Alec said.

"No," Mr. Cooper said.

My scalp was light and tingled as if it were opening up and filling with air. Black spots blocked my sight.

"I'm so sorry. Your pa is dead."

The next thing I knew, I was lying on Lizzie's bed. Mrs. Cooper was patting my forehead with a cold cloth. Other than the high-pitched ringing in my ears, the room was silent.

Where am I? What sort of dream is this? I can smell the perfume of Lizzie's room. Lavender. How can that be if this is a dream?

"I am sorry," Mrs. Cooper said. She was close to me and spoke directly into my face. Her face looked distorted, long and narrow, as if I were looking into a bent mirror. "This is a terrible thing."

Why is she saying she is sorry?

"Please try to sleep for a while," she said kindly. "You will feel better after you rest."

My head throbbed.

Have I hurt myself?

Suddenly I heard Alec wailing in a way I had never heard before. It wasn't a sound like when he skinned his knee or fell out of the oak tree.

His cry sounded like the screech of a raven trapped by a net. I found myself looking at Mrs. Cooper clearly. Her lips were pinched, and her eyes were red and swollen. Then I remembered. The trunk, Baby Dot's shoes and the words Mr. Cooper had said before I fainted.

I felt overcome with the need to retch again. I pulled my wooden doll out of my pocket and curled into a tight ball. I had no tears, no sobs. It was as if I had been drained of tears, of blood, of life itself.

If Alec comes into the room before I count to ten, this is all a mistake. One, two—

I grabbed the doll with both hands, straightened out and sat up. There would be no more counting.

"Does Ma know?"

"Yes, dear."

"Who told her?"

"Mr. Cooper."

"Where is she?"

"By the fire."

I had intended to be the one to meet Pa upon his arrival. I had already considered this desperate state of affairs. I had planned to be strong in any case. I had meant to help Ma.

In the kitchen, Ma sat on the chair next to the fire. She had been in the same position since breakfast. She had washed her face; the only colour was thin circles of red outlining her eyes. She made no sound or movement when I approached her.

"Where is Alec?" I said. The sound of his cries had disappeared.

No response.

"Where is Alec?" I asked again.

"He ran to the seashore," Mrs. Cooper said. She stood behind me and held onto my arm.

"Where is Pa?" I asked. "And Charlotte?"

Suddenly I realized Mr. Cooper had said nothing about my sister.

I pulled away from Mrs. Cooper's grasp and dashed out the door and down the lane. From the end of the path I saw that a crowd had gathered near the water. Mr. Haws's boat was lodged in the pebbles alongside Mr. Cooper's. Villagers stood in a semicircle at the water's edge. Through the arms and legs of the adults, I saw Alec standing alone. I charged through the people, grabbed his sleeve and dragged him to a log.

"Hope," he said, sobbing. "They have Pa in the boat. They found him on a beach. He's wrapped up."

"We must go to Ma," I said. I had one thing on my mind. The Richardsons must stand together, with dignity.

"But I can't see Pa."

"You aren't going to see him, Alec."

"But I want to."

"No, you don't. Not now."

"They say he's dead."

"Come with me."

"Where's Charlotte?"

"I don't know."

"Will she be dead too?"

We headed up the path. When I looked back, I saw Mr. Haws and Old Man Albert lifting Pa's body out of the boat.

"Where is Charlotte?" I asked Mr. Cooper when I met him outside the house.

"We don't know, Hope," he said nervously. "We didn't find her."

"Will she be dead too when you find her?" Alec asked shakily.

"I don't know," said Mr. Cooper. He lifted Alec into his arms and cradled him like a baby. "Come with me, Hope. I want to give you something."

I followed them into Mr. Cooper's workshop. It smelled like Pa's workshop at Sunnydale. The brace and bit, chisels and an array of planes looked like Pa's tools. A set of chairs was lined up by the door, and one exactly the same but unfinished sat on the bench. I stroked the buttery soft wood that had been heated and bent and formed into a perfect arc. Mr. Cooper was a good carpenter. I bent over and examined the furniture from every angle, as Pa would have. I checked the fine details.

Mr. Cooper closed the door behind me. He put Alec down and reached into his pocket. He pulled out a blue ribbon. The last time I had seen it was the day we left Sunnydale. Two blue ribbons had been tied in bows on the ends of Charlotte's braids.

"This is for you, Hope," he said, passing it to me.

"You wanted to come with me to look for your sister and pa, to find their things. I found this and thought it might belong to Charlotte."

I held the ribbon end to end. "This is Charlotte's ribbon," I said, as if making a necessary act of identification. "One she had in her hair the day we left."

I pulled my wooden doll from my pocket and tied the ribbon around her neck. Mr. Cooper eyed the beautifully carved wooden figure curiously.

"Thank you, Mr. Cooper," I said.

I put the doll back in my pocket.

Lamalcha Village, Winter Island, Spring 1863 🖋

Little Brother wiggled his way
     through the hiding boys and squished in beside me.
     He was cold and rigid.
     I covered him with my blanket
     and wrapped my arms around his shivering little body.
     "Breathe," I whispered to him.
     "You must breathe deeply.
     We will be all right."
     I didn't believe my own words,
     but Little Brother was
     usually such a brave boy,
     and I needed him to be strong.
     He sipped the air with shallow breaths.
     "I have heard Mother's voice," I told him.
     "You and Swiltu and I are here with Grandmother."
     "Where is Father? And Big Brother?" he asked.
     "And what about the others?"
     "Shhh," I said to him.
     But Little Brother feared
     as I did
     that Mother's voice
     was the voice of someone mourning.
                    It was the noise of a burial.

No one was killed in the village that day,

but our longhouses were crushed
and our winter food supply was destroyed.
Father's new canoe
was fractured end to end,
and others were shattered.
Uncle Nanute and the other men
examined each canoe
and set aside the ones that would not float.

Without a word,
we rummaged through the wreckage.
We salvaged ripped and dusty blankets,
and rescued damaged cooking pots
from the pile of splintered wood.
I stood at the edge
of the massive pile of debris
that had once been our longhouse.
Holding Swiltu's trembling body
under one arm,
and Little Brother's under the other,
I watched Grandmother
tiptoe through the devastation.
She pulled out a basket of string,
and drums that had been stacked in a corner
and had miraculously escaped the crush.
"Letia," she called
in a voice of excitement that was rare that day,
"your carving knife!"
She pulled the red bundle out of the ruins.
"Thank you," I called.
She took the knife
and chopped at the new sleeping mat
Mother had made me the previous summer.
A rafter like a spike
had driven the blanket into the ground.

"Demons," Grandmother said
when she gave me the tattered remnant of my gift.
"Those men are the sons of a monster.
The offspring of real human beings
would not do such things to innocent People."

We put what we could find
into the few canoes that were still seaworthy.
One by one, the People gathered on the beach.
We were a miserable-looking lot.
The battle had hammered our bodies
the way a winter storm
pounds the stubborn autumn leaves
that refuse to fall.
Our blankets drooped over our sagging shoulders.
Our faces were smeared with dust and grime.
I could tell from how they looked
that each one of the People
felt the same way I did.
Every joint in my body was slack and wobbly.
Blood thrashed against my ears, making a
shrieking sound like crows that would not stop.
My eyeballs were loose in their sockets.
I needed food,
but there was no room in my wrenching stomach.
My heart was broken.

After a while the voices of the People
broke through the stunned silence
and began to make plans.
"We will leave the island," they said.
"Someday, when it is safe, we will return
to rebuild the village
and once again become a rich People."

For now, each family decided to take care of itself,
to disperse amongst the other People in the territory.
The Lamalcha would become beggars and strays.
"Our family is the most fortunate of all," Father said,
"for Uncle Moosma has promised to help us.
I will bring you to Uncle's village,
and Mother's family will take you in."
But from the look of despair on his face,
I did not believe him.
For although Uncle Moosma was a headman,
Father knew that Uncle's People
were not as generous as their leader.
Father's family was his responsibility.
Grandmother was his mother.
Who would look after her?

Mother didn't look at Father as he spoke.
She was bowed to the ground,
her shoulders slumped forward.
His words did not convince her.
She knew it was not a plan
he was making,
it was surrender.
"Big Brother and I
will go to Victoria to find work,"
Father said. "We will send for you
when we can."
But there was not a glimmer of hope
in his voice
that we would be a family again.

Mayne Island, Autumn 1862 ❧

Mr. Haws and Old Man Albert carried Pa's body, wrapped in heavy canvas, toward the house. The crowd at the shore followed them. I took Alec and entered the house in front of the men.

"They are coming with Pa's body," I said as I took Ma's hand. "We must stand when they bring him in."

She didn't move at first.

"Ma, we must stand."

I pulled harder, until Ma half rose.

"We are the Richardsons. Please, Ma."

I need you, Ma. I need you now.

She remained as stiff as ice.

"Pa would want us to stand together," I insisted.

I lifted Baby Dot to her feet and propped her against my leg. Ma leaned against me on one side, and Alec leaned on the other. I straightened Ma's body so it was upright. I smoothed the wrinkles on her dress, folded her collar and tucked her hair into her bun. I pulled Baby Dot's thumb out of her mouth.

The men walked in front of us and through the sitting room. People moved aside to clear a space for my poor little family to walk behind the body. Every eye was on us as we shuffled across the room holding onto each other and bumping together uncomfortably. They laid Pa on a makeshift bench in the sunroom.

For the first time since we arrived on Mayne Island, we were a family—a family now missing only Charlotte.

From outside the sunroom I could see the outline of his body—the bump of his head, an indentation at his neck, the rising mound of his chest, his feet sticking up like pegs. Even though it was covered, there was no doubt in my mind that the body that lay under the canvas belonged to Pa. And in a way, I was comforted to know that he was close by.

"We are here to see Pa," I said when I met Mr. and Mrs. Cooper standing at the door of the sunroom.

I braced my feet wide apart as the weight of Ma's body slumped on my shoulder. Mrs. Cooper stepped forward and linked her arm with Ma's to steady her.

"Come, Eva," she said. "You must sit down."

"No," I said with certainty. "She is fine. She is here to see Pa."

"Oh, my dear. I don't think that's a good idea," Mrs. Cooper said.

Ma looked at me as if to say, *Speak for us.*

Mr. Haws and Old Man Albert stood at each end of Pa's body, looking stunned as we approached.

"We are here to see Pa," I said a little more loudly than before.

The men didn't move. For an awkward moment, I wasn't sure what I would do next. I couldn't remove the canvas from Pa's body and keep hold of Ma and Alec if the men didn't assist us. Mr. Cooper stepped in front of me and said, "They are here to see John."

"But Samuel," Mr. Haws protested, "it's not appropriate. You know—"

"Let them see," Mr. Cooper said. He reached for a flap of canvas near Pa's feet.

I didn't *want* to see Pa, and I didn't *want* my family to suffer the pain of it all. I *had* to see him. The Richardsons *had* to stand together as a family to face whatever lay ahead. We had no other choice.

Mr. Haws stood his ground, as if he didn't know what else to do, and looked imploringly at Old Man Albert. Old Man Albert frowned, shrugged his shoulders and lifted his chin to show he agreed with Mr. Cooper. Mr. Haws reluctantly tugged on the canvas and rolled Pa slightly from side to side as the material was removed.

I struggled on one side to hold Ma upright, and on the other I balanced Alec, who now had Baby Dot slumped over his shoulder. I turned to Mrs. Cooper, who was looking aghast at what was about to occur.

"Could you take Baby Dot from Alec; she is much too heavy for him and too young to be here."

She eagerly took Dot, who began to cry as she was taken from the room. Alec took his place in front of Ma and me. Ma's arm followed Baby Dot, but she didn't move. Finally she put her arm around one side of Alec, and I hugged the other. He stood stiffly, as if he could, with effort, make himself big and old enough to take part in what was about to happen.

Thin slivers of light streaked across the canvas and illuminated Pa's face as Mr. Haws pulled the material back. I gasped and fell against Ma. Alec spun around and buried his face in my apron. With a welcome show of strength, Ma reached down and wrapped her arms around the two of us.

Gradually, I turned to look again. The light brightened. Sunlight covered Pa's body as if to warm him. His skin was grey like that of a fish without its scales. His eyes were closed. He had a dark streak across his forehead and down his cheek. His skin was wrinkled and shrunken slightly, and I couldn't tell whether he had been beaten or injured; whether he had drowned or died of exposure. He looked cold. What lay before me didn't look like Pa at all. It was his body, but it wasn't Pa.

Men in the sitting room watched, edgy and ill at ease, hands behind their backs, legs apart. Women sniffled and sobbed, heads bowed in handkerchiefs. The light dimmed again, and the mid-afternoon autumn chill fell upon the room.

Nothing made any sense. People looked the same as they did the day before. They stood together and breathed in and out. Ma's lips were pinched the same way they always were when she was nervous. Alec fidgeted with his pant legs the way he always did. My tongue pressed against the back of my teeth, hard, to keep me from screaming.

"It isn't Pa," Alec whispered. He reached his hand out as if a touch would confirm that it was Pa. Mr. Haws leapt forward, and Alec jerked his hand back to his side.

"Pa has an unpleasant look on his face. Has he been injured? Do you think he is cold?" Alec looked at Pa's face.

"Pa's body isn't feeling anything now, Alec. Pa is in heaven," I said and turned to Mr. Cooper. "Will you pray for us?"

I didn't want prayers for myself. Praying hadn't been of much help since right from the start. God hadn't done a thing to keep us at Sunnydale. He hadn't protected Pa. And now, although only God knew what had happened to Charlotte, I didn't believe He had saved her from the same fate.

I wanted prayers for Ma and Alec. They needed help, and if God had anything He could do, I would be grateful.

"God in heaven, protect this family, be with them, give them strength and bring Charlotte home safely."

At the sound of Charlotte's name, Ma collapsed quietly. I held onto her, until gradually, clenching my arm, she pulled herself back to a standing position.

Can God be trusted to protect my family? Can a man be trusted to protect his family?

It was as if Pa had handed me the family and said: *It's all up to you now.*

Chemainus, Spring 1863 ≋

Uncle Moosma greeted us
    when we arrived in Chemainus.
    It wasn't long before many People
    showed up on the beach.
    They stood in a huddle,
    not as they had done other times,
    when my family visited for a wedding
        or a burial.
    In those days, they eagerly received us.
    They welcomed us with songs and a feast.
    That day they greeted us
    as if we were their enemy.
    We stood together in a huddle of our own,
    looking over our shoulders,
    apart.
    It was a strange meeting for two Peoples,
    relatives;
    it was like no other time.
    My family had been cursed with disaster,
    and Uncle Moosma's People were afraid.
    What had happened to our family
        might happen to them.
    We could be carrying calamity in our canoe.

    It was Grandmother who spoke first.

"They have done just as you warned,"
she said to Uncle Moosma.
"They have destroyed our village.
We are now a poor People,
begging for the help you promised.
We will not be a burden.
We will work for what we eat,
but the winter has only just passed,
and we are hungry."
Uncle Moosma scowled, for it was not right
that Grandmother should be the one
to make a request of him.
She was not his relative,
nor did she come from his village.
She came, an old woman,
with nothing to offer his People.

Father saw Uncle's displeasure and said,
"Our men will not stay with you,
for we can take care of ourselves.
We will go to Victoria to find work.
I am praying
only for our women and children.
Give them a home."

I thought about the stories I had heard
about Tsustea's mother,
the bedraggled girl
with nothing but a blanket and a basket,
begging for a new home,
and how Mother refused her.
I looked at Mother's face.
It was as if her eyes could see
but could not make out the images
before them;

as if she had ears
        but could not hear Grandmother or Father speak.
But even in the cold,
on the beach in Chemainus,
I thought she must remember
Tsustea's mother.

Mayne Island, Autumn 1862 ❧

At supper the men spoke as if they were reporting on a political debate: so-and-so said this, and so-and-so that. I tried to listen. There would be an Indian war like the violent battles in Oregon Territory. John's death would be the cause of it. Surely, someone said, John had been murdered. Surely, another said, John had been wrecked in the storm. It was the Indians, someone said, the same Indians that killed the other settlers. You have no proof, said someone. I couldn't tell who said what through the painful ring in my ears.

"They are bloodthirsty, they are," Old Man Albert said, his voice coming clear.

"These are murderous times," Mr. Haws said in a low voice. "Vicious—"

Mr. Cooper interrupted and said, "Sirs, might I remind you that none of us needs to know your gruesome stories, and might I add that they are just that—stories. As far as I can tell, John has had the misfortune of a terrible storm."

I watched the words coming out of the men's mouths. They looked comical in a way, their mouths flapping open and closed making such certain sounds, as if they knew exactly what had happened.

"We will get the family off the island, we will," Old Man Albert said. "And to Victoria. There arrangements can be made for them to return to England."

Had Ma been right? Had I been wrong about Letia? What about Ruby? What would become of her?

I had thought that I was right about the Indians. What if I was wrong? Very wrong.

Hatred swept over me like a blanket. Hatred for Indians. All of them. Letia, her father, even the little boys who'd played with Alec in the sand. But the coarseness and vile taste of hatred disturbed me. I could not hate the Indians. Not now.

If I was wrong about the Indians, then Pa had been wrong about them as well. And now Pa was dead. He had not been murdered. I could not bear to think that he had been that wrong.

Letia's father and the other men in the Indian camp had smiled at Pa. They had patted me on the head and laughed. They were friendly.

Pa would not have died if we had not left the island.

I looked straight at Mr. Haws and asked, "Where will Pa be buried?"

He looked back hard into my eyes and said, "My dear girl, your pa will be buried on this island or in Victoria. We will decide."

I ignored his presumptuousness for the moment. "And where is Charlotte, do you suppose?" I asked.

He lowered his eyes. "We don't know."

"We may never find your sister," Old Man Albert said. His jowls wobbled as he shook his head in a slow, sorry sort of way. "We found her shoe and a torn piece of her dress, we did. The best we can conclude is that she is buried at sea. Or that some more tragic event has befallen her." He sucked in a long stream of air and saliva through his teeth—the sound made my stomach heave.

"We can do no more than our best for you at this terrible time," Mr. Haws said.

"With all due respect, Mr. Haws, you and Old Man Albert have done quite enough to our family already," I said coldly. "We would appreciate it if you both left us alone. From now on, we will decide what will become of our family. We will decide where our dear pa will be laid to rest."

We were homeless, strangers on an unfamiliar island, and bereft of the head of our household. I wasn't exactly in a position to turn down anyone's help. But what else could I do? The last thing we needed was the sort of help we had been getting—from beggars and whisky traders.

Lizzie gasped. What impudence, that I should talk to houseguests in such a manner. Mr. Cooper looked taken aback.

"We will not return to England without every member of our family,"

I said. "Alive or not."

The room was silent.

"We must continue to search for Charlotte," I added. "I want to go with you, Mr. Cooper. If she is buried at sea, there must be more clues."

Mrs. Cooper stood up. "Hope, dear," she said. "This has been a tragic day for you. You must rest." She walked behind me and placed her hands firmly on my shoulders. "Come, dear. Come with me."

I leaned forward to free myself from her grip. "Mr. Cooper, may I go with you tomorrow? Can we look again for Charlotte?"

His look of surprise had slipped away and was replaced by thoughtfulness. Mr. Haws and Old Man Albert kept their eyes on him.

Mrs. Cooper took my arm and said persistently, "Come along, dear."

I looked at Ma. She was watching Mr. Cooper, waiting for him to speak. There was something different about her. She had had enough. She had no more energy to be afraid. She hadn't said anything, but I sensed that she agreed with me. Ma was on my side. The Richardsons— what was left of us—were a family.

"Mr. Cooper?" I pleaded, pulling away from Mrs. Cooper.

"Yes. Yes, yes." He said it three times—the holy number—as if looking for God's assurance. "If the weather permits, I will bring you to the island. And William. I am sure he will be willing to come along. We will examine the beach carefully for clues."

"Hope," Mrs. Cooper said sternly. She glared at Mr. Cooper, obviously not pleased with his decision. "It's time you lay down, child."

"Thank you, Mr. Cooper," I said and got up. "Thank you, Mrs. Cooper. I will lie down, but first let me say goodnight to my ma."

Going to bed used to be a task to be avoided for the merest excuse, a kiss, an inquiry, a promise. *Pa, will you take me with you tomorrow to dig clams? To fish?* No longer.

I leaned down and kissed Ma on the cheek. She took my hand and squeezed my fingers. She pulled me close so she could speak into my ear.

"Good night, Hope," she said.

"Good night, Ma."

It felt good to hear her voice.

Chemainus, Spring 1863 ≋

The next day Father and Big Brother went to Victoria.
    Uncle Moosma left his village
    and didn't return for a few weeks.
    Mother didn't speak,
    not for the whole time her brother was away
    and longer.
    Not one sound came out of her mouth.
    Grandmother said, "Her silence is because she warned the People.
    She spoke to us of these things,
    but no one listened to her."
    Grandmother gave Mother a bowl of warm medicine
    boiled from roots and bark.
    Mother drank the tea.
    She let out low, mournful sounds,
    but still didn't say a word.
    Grandmother blamed herself and said,
    "If only I had heeded your mother's warnings
    and had not been so stubborn."

No one in Uncle's village spoke to our family very much,
    except the boys.
    They played with Little Brother
    and didn't seem to notice
    that he was a beggar.

It was from the boys that I learned
of the dreadful fate of Hope's father and sister.
For during the winter, the terrible storms,
icy cold
and unusually deep snow
foiled the bearers of bad news

and whisky traders.
I begged Little Brother to ask the boys questions.
So each day he brought the story home,
one piece at a time.
From what I could put together,
the Queen's men had been ready
and waiting to head into our territory.
They had already decided
that Acheewan had murdered the settlers,
even though we knew differently.
Then, once the men in Victoria
discovered that Hope's father had died in our territory,
and that her sister could not be found,
        that was all they needed.
They waited for the winter to pass and the spring to arrive
and then made plans to set sail.
The gunboat made its way to our bay
and wreaked havoc on Winter Island.
Amongst all the chaos, no one told us that
the fate of our longhouses, our canoes and all our goods
was caused by the death
of the Man and the disappearance of his daughter.

My heart turned cold at the thought of the Man.
I hated all the hwunitum.
If it hadn't been for them,
my People would not have become so pitiful.
But hard as I tried,

I couldn't hate Hope.
And after a while I couldn't hate the Man, either.
It wasn't their fault.
Surely her family was even more wretched than mine:
strangers in a new land
without a father,
without a home.
    And her sister
        missing.

We got enough to eat at Chemainus.
Kind People left bundles of dried fish and clams
by the door of Uncle's longhouse.
Grandmother collected roots.
We didn't starve,
    but we were often hungry.

I held onto my cloth doll.
I didn't bother to hide it.
No one was concerned
            with a poor orphan girl
                dragging around a doll.
Even Mother paid no attention to it.

Mayne Island, Autumn 1862 ❧

I lay on top of the bed. The room was dark and quiet. I could hear the adults talking in the other room.

"They can stay on here with us," Mr. Cooper said. "We can make a place for them."

"But how will they be supported?" Old Man Albert said. "A woman and small children?"

"The village will bring them in as our own."

"Samuel..." Mrs. Cooper's voice broke sharply into the conversation, disagreeing with her husband.

"If only John had listened to us in the first place," Mr. Haws said. "This tragedy would not have happened."

"I think if you had left well enough alone," Mr. Cooper said, "if John and his family had remained on Wallace Island, he would have been out of harm's way. The Indians would not have attacked him. He was living safely at Sunnydale."

I wanted to believe Mr. Cooper. It was just what Pa would have said. But now it made no difference one way or the other. Wallace Island was gone; only Ruby remained there. Pa was dead. Charlotte was missing, and no one was safe. But as for Letia, I wanted to believe that I had been right about her. She was my friend. She had to be. I needed her to protect and love Ruby.

I took my wooden doll out of my pocket and dressed for bed.

Pa, what am I to do? Pa could not answer. Pa would never answer. *But what am I to do?*

Suddenly like a river, like a river that had no shores, I burst into tears.

Silently at first, and then a noise came from my body that sounded like nothing I had ever heard before. Ma came in and sat beside me, stroking my hair. After what felt like a long time, the noise became a moan, and then my body was silent and exhausted. Ma kissed my forehead and left me alone.

Thoughts flitted through my brain like barn swallows in the spring.

An Indian war like in Oregon Territory. Letia and her pa will care for Charlotte. Ruby is warm. Ruby will be sad that Pa has been murdered. Poor Ruby.

Restless sleep came and went.

"Hope," Lizzie said. She lit the lamp. "Do you think there will be an Indian war?"

I didn't respond.

"I'm so scared," she said. "Wild Indians, Hope...no one can trust them. Your pa learned that lesson. I don't know why Father can't see that."

She clambered over my body.

"Hope?"

I squished my eyes tightly shut.

Lizzie does not exist.

"Are you awake?"

No.

I didn't sleep easily that night. Wind rattled the house. From the bed I could hear the crashing surf. I woke up early. The storm did not subside. It was impossible that day and the following days to search for Charlotte.

Chemainus, Spring 1863 🖎

The first time that Mother spoke
    after our arrival in Chemainus
    was the day Big Brother returned from Victoria.
    When he appeared at the door
    of Uncle Moosma's longhouse,
    she welcomed him with a silent chin gesture.
    She led him to the cold and dark end of the house
    where we slept crowded together,
    a good distance from the fire.
    Big Brother was confused
    by Mother's silence.
    He asked Grandmother, "What is wrong with her?"
    Grandmother said, "She has not said a word
    since her soul was drained out of her body
    and taken away
    in the clouds of black smoke
    that ruined our village on Winter Island."
    Mother held onto Big Brother's arm
    like a fish she knew would get away.
    I sat on the other side,
    while Swiltu and Little Brother
    found a spot on his knees.

Big Brother said in a hollow voice,
    "The Queen's men decided that

Acheewan and Father were among those guilty of murder.
     They captured them
     and killed them
     by hanging.
There was nothing I could do."

I felt dizzy and could not breathe.
Swiltu and Little Brother wailed.
Grandmother and Mother sat, stunned and silent.

Suddenly we heard the sound
of Uncle Moosma's voice
booming through the longhouse.
"Where is he?" he hollered. "There is a man amongst us
who has no invitation."
He stomped through the house
to where we were sitting.
He glowered at Big Brother
when he saw our family clustered together.
I had never seen my uncle with such rage on his face.
"Who invited you to my house?"
Uncle spat out the words.
"I am here to bring word to my mother," Big Brother said,
"of what has become of my father."
Big Brother spoke
as if he were talking to a stranger.
But Uncle fumed, "You must ask permission
if you are to enter my house.
I will protect my People from the risk of danger."
He ordered Big Brother
to leave his longhouse immediately
     and not return.

Mother let go of Big Brother's arm
and said to Uncle Moosma:

"He is all I have left."
Her voice sounded different than before.
It didn't come from deep in her belly.
It was like a thin cord
stretched around her tongue,
ready to snap.
Uncle set his face hard and glared into his sister's eyes.
"You are a guest in my house.
I have risked the safety of my village
by giving you and your family
a roof over your heads.
Do not make demands of me that I cannot fulfill.
My People will not give
such a man as your son
shelter here."

One thing became clear to me that day:
in times of trouble, old allegiances,
even family,
            don't count for much.
When fear is what is driving a man,
he will do what he needs to do
to protect his People,
even if there is no real threat.

Mother got up from where she was sitting.
She walked with Big Brother directly in front of Uncle,
without so much as casting her eyes
in his direction.
She took Big Brother by the hand
and said, "You must send for us soon."
Big Brother hugged her.

He did not stay the night.
That was the last time I saw him.

He went to work cutting timbers,
but he sent us hwunitum money.
Mother did not speak for a very long time,
          and I never saw her look at Uncle Moosma again.

Victoria, 1872 🦅

I unlocked the door and flipped the sign. I was weary from baking since four o'clock in the morning. The sign read: *OPEN Tuesday to Saturday 7 a.m. to 4 p.m.*

Customers began to stream in the door before I had time to get off my feet for a rest.

"Morning to you, my girl."

"Good morning, Mr. Burns," I said, cheery and tired.

"My usual, please and thank you."

The lawyer came in every day at the same time. He took his scone with butter and blackberry jam, his tea without milk and an Eccles cake wrapped in paper, for later.

I scooped the jam into a small bowl and set it on the table.

"Thank you, dear," he said kindly, pulling out his newspaper. "Freshly made, is it?"

"Just yesterday," I said.

"Enough, then?" he said. "For the winter?"

"Not yet," I said. "But the berries are fat and juicy this year. I'll have plenty."

"And that strapping brother of yours?" he said. "I haven't seen him for some time."

"Alec has moved to New Westminster to take a position in the bank," I said proudly, missing him at the same time.

If Ma arrives soon, I will be able to go home and sleep for an hour or so. As long as I wake up before noon, and as long as Dorothy has picked enough berries, I will make more jam.

It was August, and the day was warm. I pushed the *Wooden Doll Bakery* sign aside and opened the window.

Across the street, a young Indian woman flattened a blanket neatly on the ground. She set a crate upside down, and on it she placed several baskets of clams and oysters. She wrapped a rag doll in a shredded piece of handwoven blanket. After setting it next to the crate, she sat cross-legged beside an old lady. I strained my eyes as my heart pounded. The doll had a faded green dress and scruffy yellow hair.

I put my head out the window and listened.

"We will sell these by noon," she said. Her English was broken and mixed with some Indian words, but I pieced together enough to understand. "If Little Brother gets up early, he will bring more."

The old lady nodded her head.

"Mother, there is much demand for clams and oysters, and these people are willing to pay," the young woman said. "Another month or so, and we'll have enough money to hold a memorial for Father and Grandmother. We'll buy more blankets than we have ever had before."

The old lady didn't speak, but she smiled and squeezed her daughter's hand.

I moved away from the window, my heart pounding harder.

If Mother arrives before seven thirty, I will cross the street and talk to the young woman with the clams.

I looked at the clock. A quarter past seven. I sighed and thought of the years it had been since I had made such a deal with myself.

I will bring my wooden doll with me and ask to look at her doll.

Twenty minutes past seven.

I will invite her and her mother into the bakery and give them scones with blackberry jam.

Twenty-nine minutes past seven.

We will have tea together.

Seven thirty-five.

"I'm sorry I'm late, Hope," Ma said, bursting through the door. "I had breakfast with Dorothy and sent her off for berries."

"Thank you," I said.

Ma didn't arrive by seven thirty. But what use is making deals? What good have they ever been? I will visit the young woman—Letia—in any case. I will show her my wooden doll and ask her to tell me the doll's name. And I will tell her Ruby's.

"When I close up the shop," Ma said, "I'll buy some clams and bring them home for supper."

"That would be wonderful."

Historical Note

First, a note on names: Throughout this story I use the term *Indian* when the characters in the story are speaking from the settlers' point of view. Aboriginal people were defined as Indians in the colonial *Indian Act* (and still are), and accordingly, that was the term in popular usage. However, the geographically inaccurate word *Indian* has since become unpopular. In the 1980s, it began being replaced in Canada by *First Nations person*. But in the nineteenth century there was no such term as First Nation, and I have used terminology in the story as it would have been used in the past.

I use the terms *hwulmuhw* ("people of the land") and *hwunitum* ("hungry people" or "white people") when the characters of the story are speaking from the Lamalcha's point of view. These two terms are Hul'qumi'num words from the language spoken by the Lamalcha people, who lived on Kuper Island.

Contrary to what British Columbians often think, the settlement of the province by Europeans was not without conflict. The newcomers wanted the land where the people they called Indians had lived and worked for millennia. When the newcomers arrived, they settled in areas that were best suited to agriculture and industry. These areas were often the important hunting and gathering grounds of the original inhabitants. The newcomers believed they had the right to own the land and to determine where these "Indians" should live.

It seems the original inhabitants were initially not overly resistzant to the newcomers settling nearby, and even helped them, but they always knew they, not the Europeans, were the legitimate keepers of the territories.

Before long, encroachment by European settlers and their ideas about Aboriginal people and their territories resulted in tension. Surveyors tramped through those territories, setting boundaries for the sale of the land. This uninvited activity created discontent and caused skirmishes between the two groups. James Douglas, who would become governor of Vancouver Island in 1851, tried to solve some of the disagreements by creating treaties, but only fourteen groups of Coast Salish Aboriginal people from the west coast signed treaties.

Even with treaties, boundaries were not immediately defined, nor were the land issues resolved. It took decades for treaties to be fully implemented and understood. To this day there are outstanding disputes over treaties.

In the 1850s and 1860s, British officials were particularly interested in Vancouver Island, the site of Fort Victoria. They were worried that unrest between Aboriginal people and the newcomers would discourage other potential settlers from coming to the island. In order to quell the disturbances once and for all, the government decided to flex its military muscle with a show of force by the Royal Navy on the west coast.

Counting on Hope is a fictionalized story that takes place during this time period off the east coast of Vancouver Island, on the Gulf Islands. It is based on a true event, although I have created many of the characters and details of plot.

The Lamalcha were a Coast Salish people who lived on Kuper Island, but there is no evidence that they had a summer camp on Wallace Island. Nor is there any evidence that a settler family built a house and farm on the island in the 1860s. I have made up these particular families and their meeting place. However, it is true that white settlers, including a father and daughter, were presumed murdered by Indians in 1862, helping trigger a gunboat attack on Kuper Island in 1863. Lamalcha people were tried and hanged in Victoria for murdering the settlers. One was Acheewan, a real Lamalcha warrior. The headman, however, was not really among those hanged. The incident, one of the most devastating attacks ever mounted on Aboriginal people in Canada, changed the lives of the Lamalcha people forever.

I researched this story in the late 1990s, using old newspaper articles and other sources, and decided that this history should be written for young people. It's taken more than ten years, but finally I have done just that. While this book is fiction, written with the goal of bringing these events to life, it's in large part history just the same.

Acknowledgements

Sometimes people think writing is a solitary pursuit, but this book has truly been a team event. I am only one of the players. Thank you, thank you, thank you to the rest of the team. Thank you, Diane Morriss, who is the most amazing, supportive, kind, insightful publisher. She stuck with the story even when others would certainly have given up on it. Thank you, Grenfell Featherstone. He took the book when I had all but lost hope. He saw something worthwhile in the story and some potential in the author. He so generously contributed his brilliance. Thank you, Dawn Loewen, for making the book the best possible book it could be. She has the most amazing ability to attend to the details and the big picture at the same time. Thank you, Jim Brennan, for your beautiful design. Sono Nis books are so beautiful because of your fabulous talent. Thank you, Kathryn Bridge, for reading with a historical eye and keeping the story on track. Thank you, Katherine Gordon, for being a constant source of good advice, humour, encouragement and whatever else I need. Thank you, Tom Kerr, for listening and listening and listening to rewrite after rewrite after rewrite. He never gave up on me or the story. And thank you, Karla Decker, for being there right at the end. I am so grateful for the privilege of being part of such a great group of talented and heartfelt people.

About the Author

SYLVIA OLSEN is an award-winning author of several picture books and young adult novels, including *White Girl*, which was shortlisted for the Sheila A. Egoff Children's Literature Prize. When asked about her reasons for writing *Counting on Hope*, Sylvia says, "For thirty-five years or so I lived on the Tsartlip reserve and watched my children grow up in a cross-cultural world. I guess that's the reason I am fascinated by the place where people from different cultures come together and get along—or not. Even before I wrote *White Girl*, which is a modern-day story about the friendship between a First Nations girl and a non–First Nations girl, I wanted to write a historical fiction set in the early days of contact in British Columbia. I thought about the challenges at that time of friendship between young people from different backgrounds, from families that had conflicting interests and beliefs. I knew as soon as I read historical records of the confrontation between the British navy and the Lamalcha on Kuper Island in 1863 that it was the perfect setting for just such a story."

Sylvia lives just north of Victoria, British Columbia. When not writing, she works in the area of First Nations community management, with a focus on reserve housing.